Ghostly and Ghastly

Rattling chains, creaking floorboards, cobwebs and moonlit graveyards – all the traditional elements of a good ghost story feature in this collection, together with ghastly tales of the strange and unknown. Ray Bradbury, M. R. James and Oscar Wilde are among the writers included, and children play a leading role in all the stories.

Barbara Ireson lives in Yorkshire and writes poems and stories for children. Her poetry collection *Rhyme Time* is also published by Beavers.

Ghostly and Ghastly

Edited by Barbara Ireson

Illustrated by William Geldart

Beaver Books

A Beaver Original
Published by Arrow Books Limited
17-21 Conway Street, London W1P 6JD
An imprint of the Hutchinson Publishing Group
London Melbourne Sydney Auckland Johannesburg
and agencies throughout the world

First published in 1977
Sixth impression 1985
Reprinted 1985

Set in Linotype Pilgrim

Printed and bound in Great Britain by
Anchor Brendon Limited, Tiptree, Essex

ISBN 0 600 34065 1

Contents

The Emissary

Ray Bradbury

Martin knew it was autumn again, for Dog ran into the house bringing wind and frost and a smell of apples turned to cider under trees. In dark clock-springs of hair, Dog fetched goldenrod, dust of farewell-summer, acorn-husk, hair of squirrel, feather of departed robin, sawdust from fresh-cut cordwood, and leaves like charcoals shaken from a blaze of maple trees. Dog jumped. Showers of brittle fern, blackberry vine, marsh-grass sprang over the bed where Martin shouted. No doubt, no doubt of it at all, this incredible beast was October!

'Here, boy, here!'

And Dog settled to warm Martin's body with all the bonfires and subtle burnings of the season, to fill the room with soft or heavy, wet or dry odours of far-travelling. In spring, he smelled of lilac, iris, lawn-mowered grass; in summer, ice-cream-moustached, he came pungent with firecracker, Roman candle, pinwheel, baked by the sun. But autumn! Autumn!

'Dog, what's it like outside?'

And lying there, Dog told as he always told. Lying there, Martin found autumn as in the old days before sickness bleached him white on his bed. Here was his contact, his carry-all, the quick-moving part of himself he sent with a yell to run and return, circle and scent, collect and deliver the time and texture of worlds in town, country, by creek, river, lake, down-cellar, up-attic, in closet or coal-bin. Ten dozen times a day he was gifted with sunflower seed, cinderpath, milkweed, horse-chestnut, or full flame-smell of pumpkin. Through the loomings of the universe Dog shuttled; the design was hid in his pelt. Put out your hand, it was there. . . .

'And where did you go this morning?'

But he knew without hearing where Dog had rattled down hills where autumn lay in cereal crispness, where children lay in funeral pyres, in rustling heaps, the leaf-buried but watchful dead, as Dog and the world blew by. Martin trembled his fingers, searched the thick fur, read the long journey. Through stubbled fields, over glitters of ravine creek, down marbled spread of cemetery yard, into woods. In the great season of spices and rare incense, now Martin ran through his emissary, around, about, and home!

The bedroom door opened.

'That dog of yours is in trouble again.'

Mother brought in a tray of fruit salad, cocoa, and toast, her blue eyes snapping.

'Mother . . .'

'Always digging places. Dug a hole in Miss Tarkin's garden this morning. She's spittin' mad. That's the fourth hole he's dug there this week.'

'Maybe he's looking for something.'

'Fiddlesticks, he's too darned curious. If he doesn't behave he'll be locked up.'

Martin looked at this woman as if she were a stranger.

'Oh, you wouldn't do that! How would I learn anything? How would I find things out if Dog didn't tell me?'

Mom's voice was quieter. 'Is that what he does – tell you things?'

'There's nothing I don't know when he goes out and around and back, *nothing* I can't find out from him!'

They both sat looking at Dog and the dry strewings of mould and seed over the quilt.

'Well, if he'll just stop digging where he shouldn't, he can run all he wants,' said Mother.

'Here, boy, here!'

And Martin snapped a tin note to the dog's collar:

The Emissary

MY OWNER IS MARTIN SMITH — TEN YEARS OLD — SICK IN BED — VISITORS WELCOME.

Dog barked. Mother opened the downstairs door and let him out.

Martin sat listening.

Far off and away you could hear Dog in the quiet autumn rain that was falling now. You could hear the barking-jingling fade, rise, fade again as he cut down alley, over lawn, to fetch back Mr Holloway and the oiled metallic smell of the delicate snowflake-interiored watches he repaired in his home shop. Or maybe he would bring Mr Jacobs, the grocer, whose clothes were rich with lettuce, celery, tomatoes, and the secret tinned and hidden smell of the red demons stamped on cans of devilled ham. Mr Jacobs and his unseen pink-meat devils waved often from the yard below. Or Dog brought Mr Jackson, Mrs Gillespie, Mr Smith, Mrs Holmes, *any* friend or near-friend, encountered, cornered, begged, worried, and at last shepherded home for lunch, or tea-and-biscuits.

Now, listening, Martin heard Dog below, with footsteps moving in a light rain behind him. The downstairs bell rang. Mom opened the door, light voices murmured. Martin sat forward, face shining. The stair treads creaked. A young woman's voice laughed quietly. Miss Haight, of course, his teacher from school!

The bedroom door sprang open.

Martin had company.

Morning, afternoon, evening, dawn and dusk, sun and moon circled with Dog, who faithfully reported temperatures of turf and air, colour of earth and tree, consistency of mist or rain, but — most important of all — brought back again and again — Miss Haight.

On Saturday, Sunday and Monday she baked Martin orange-iced cupcakes, brought him library books about dinosaurs and cavemen. On Tuesday, Wednesday and Thursday somehow he beat her at dominoes, somehow she lost at checkers, and soon, she cried, he'd defeat her handsomely at chess. On Friday, Saturday and Sunday they talked and never stopped talking, and she was so young and laughing and handsome and her hair was a soft, shining brown like the season outside the window, and she walked clear, clean and quick, a heartbeat warm in the bitter afternoon when he heard it. Above all, she had the secret of signs, and could read and interpret Dog and the symbols she searched out and plucked forth from his coat with her miraculous fingers. Eyes shut, softly laughing, in a gypsy's voice, she divined the world from the treasures in her hands.

And on Monday afternoon, Miss Haight was dead.

Martin sat up in bed, slowly.

'Dead?' he whispered.

Dead, said his mother, yes, dead, killed in an auto accident a mile out of town. Dead, yes, dead, which meant cold to Martin, which meant silence and whiteness and winter come long before its time. Dead, silent, cold, white. The thoughts circled round, blew down, and settled in whispers.

Martin held Dog, thinking; turned to the wall. The lady with the autumn-coloured hair. The lady with the laughter that was very gentle and never made fun and the eyes that watched your mouth to see everything you ever said. The-other-half-of-autumn-lady, who told what was left untold by Dog, about the world. The heartbeat at the still centre of grey afternoon. The heartbeat fading . . .

'Mom? What do they do in the graveyard, Mom, under the ground? Just lay there?'

'*Lie* there.'

'Lie there? Is that *all* they do? It doesn't sound like much fun.'

'For goodness' sake, it's not made out to be fun.'

'Why don't they jump up and run around once in a while if they get tired lying there? God's pretty silly—'

'Martin!'

'Well, you'd think He'd treat people better than to tell

them to lie still for keeps. That's impossible. Nobody can do it! I tried once. Dog tries. I tell him, "dead Dog!" He plays dead awhile, then gets sick and tired and wags his tail or opens one eye and looks at me, bored. Boy, I bet sometimes those graveyard people do the same, huh, Dog?'

Dog barked.

'Be still with that kind of talk!' said Mother.

Martin looked off into space.

'Bet that's exactly what they do,' he said.

Autumn burnt the trees bare and ran Dog still farther around, fording creek, prowling graveyard as was his custom, and back in the dusk to fire off volleys of barking that shook windows wherever he turned.

In the late last days of October, Dog began to act as if the wind had changed and blew from a strange country. He stood quivering on the porch below. He whined, his eyes fixed at the empty land beyond town. He brought no visitors for Martin. He stood for hours each day, as if leashed, trembling, then shot away straight, as if someone had called. Each night, he returned later, with no one following. Each night, Martin sank deeper and deeper in his pillow.

'Well, people are busy,' said Mother. 'They haven't time to notice the tag Dog carries. Or they mean to come visit, but forget.'

But there was more to it than that. There was the fevered shining in Dog's eyes, and his whimpering tic late at night, in some private dream. His shivering in the dark, under the bed. The way he sometimes stood half the night, looking at Martin as if some great and impossible secret was his and he knew no way to tell it save by savagely thumping his tail, or turning in endless circles, never to lie down, spinning and spinning again.

On October thirtieth, Dog ran out and didn't come back at all, even when after supper Martin heard his parents call and call. The hour grew late, the streets and sidewalks stood empty, the air moved cold about the house and there was nothing, nothing.

Long after midnight, Martin lay watching the world beyond the cool, clear glass windows. Now there was not even autumn, for there was no Dog to fetch it in. There would be no winter, for who could bring the snow to melt in your hands? Father, Mother? No, not the same. They couldn't play the game with its special secrets and rules, its sounds and pantomimes. No more seasons. No more time. The go-between, the emissary, was lost to the wild throngings of civilisation, poisoned, stolen, hit by a car, left somewhere in a culvert. . . .

Sobbing, Martin turned his face to his pillow. The world was a picture under glass, untouchable. The world was dead.

Martin twisted in bed and in three days the last Hallowe'en pumpkins were rotting in trash cans, papier-mâché skulls and witches were burnt on bonfires, and ghosts were stacked on shelves with other linens until next year.

To Martin, Hallowe'en had been nothing more than one evening when tin horns cried off in the cold autumn stars, children blew like goblin leaves along the flinty walks, flinging their heads, or cabbages, at porches, soap-writing names or similar magic symbols on icy windows. All of it as distant, unfathomable, and nightmarish as a puppet show seen from so many miles away that there is no sound or meaning.

For three days in November, Martin watched alternate light and shadow sift across his ceiling. The fire-pageant was over forever; autumn lay in cold ashes. Martin sank deeper, yet deeper in white marble layers of bed, motionless, listening always listening. . . .

Friday evening, his parents kissed him good-night and walked out of the house into the hushed cathedral weather toward a motion-picture show. Miss Tarkin from next door stayed on in the parlour below until Martin called down he was sleepy, then took her knitting off home.

In silence, Martin lay following the great move of stars down a clear and moonlit sky, remembering nights such as this when he'd spanned the town with Dog ahead, behind, around about, tracking the green-plush ravine, lapping slumbrous streams gone milky with the fullness of the moon, leaping cemetery tombstones while whispering the marble names; on, quickly on, through shaved meadows where the only motion was the off-on quivering of stars, to streets where shadows would not stand aside for you but crowded all the sidewalks for mile on mile. Run now run! Chasing, being chased by bitter smoke, fog, mist, wind, ghost of mind, fright of memory; home, safe, sound, snug-warm, asleep. . . .

Nine o'clock.

Chime. The drowsy clock in the deep stairwell below. Chime.

Dog, come home, and run the world with you. Dog, bring a thistle with frost on it, or bring nothing else but the wind. Dog, where *are* you? Oh, listen, now, I'll call.

Martin held his breath.

Way off somewhere – a sound.

Martin rose up, trembling.

There, again – the sound.

So small a sound, like a sharp needle-point brushing the sky long miles and many miles away.

The dreamy echo of a dog – barking.

The sound of a dog crossing fields and farms, dirt roads and rabbit paths, running, running, letting out great barks of steam, cracking the night. The sound of a circling dog which came and went, lifted and faded, opened up, shut in, moved forward, went back, as if the animal were kept by someone on a fantastically long chain. As if the dog were running and someone whistled under the chestnut trees, in mould-shadow, tar-shadow, moon-shadow, walking, and the dog circled back and sprang out again towards home.

Dog! Martin thought, oh Dog, come home, boy!

Listen, oh, listen, where you *been*? Come on, boy, make tracks!

Five, ten, fifteen minutes; near, very near, the bark, the sound. Martin cried out, thrust his feet from the bed, leaned to the window. Dog! Listen, boy! Dog! Dog! He said it over and over. Dog! Dog! Wicked Dog, run off and gone all these days! Bad Dog, good Dog, home, boy, hurry, and bring what you can!

Near now, near, up the street, barking, to knock clapboard housefronts with sound, whirl iron cocks on rooftops in the moon, firing off volleys – Dog! now at the door below. . . .

Martin shivered.

Should he run – let Dog in, or wait for Mom and Dad? Wait? Oh, God, wait? But what if Dog ran off again? No, he'd go down, snatch the door wide, yell, grab Dog in, and run upstairs so fast, laughing, crying, holding tight, that . . .

Dog stopped barking.

Hey! Martin almost broke the window, jerking to it.

Silence. As if someone had told Dog to hush now, hush, hush.

A full minute passed. Martin clenched his fists.

Below, a faint whimpering.

Then, slowly, the downstairs front door opened. Someone was kind enough to have opened the door for Dog. Of course! Dog had brought Mr Jacobs or Mr Gillespie or Miss Tarkin, or . . .

The downstairs door shut.

Dog raced upstairs, whining, flung himself on the bed.

'Dog, Dog, where've you *been*, what've you *done*! Dog, Dog!'

And he crushed Dog hard and long to himself, weeping. Dog, Dog. He laughed and shouted. Dog! But after a moment he stopped laughing and crying, suddenly.

He pulled away. He held the animal and looked at him, eyes widening.

The odour coming from Dog was different.

It was a smell of strange earth. It was a smell of night within night, the smell of digging down deep in shadow through earth that had lain cheek by jowl with things that were long hidden and decayed. A stinking and rancid soil fell away in clods of dissolution from Dog's muzzle and paws. He had dug deep. He had dug very deep indeed. That *was* it, wasn't it? wasn't it? *wasn't* it!

What kind of message was this from Dog? What could such a message mean? The stench – the ripe and awful cemetery earth.

Dog was a bad dog, digging where he shouldn't. Dog was a good dog, always making friends. Dog loved people. Dog brought them home.

And now, moving up the dark hall stairs, at intervals, came the sound of feet, one foot dragged after the other, painfully, slowly, slowly, slowly.

Dog shivered. A rain of strange night earth fell seething on the bed.

Dog turned.

The bedroom door whispered in.

Martin had company.

The Thing in the Cellar

David H. Keller

It was a huge cellar, entirely out of proportion to the size
of the house above it. The owner admitted that it was
probably built for a distinctly different kind of structure
from that which rose above it. Probably the first house
had been burned and poverty had caused a diminution of
the dwelling erected to take its place.

A winding stone stairway connected the cellar with
the kitchen. Round the base of this series of steps successive owners of the house had placed their firewood, winter vegetables and junk. The junk had gradually been
pushed back till it rose, head high, in a barricade of
uselessness. What was behind that barricade no one
knew and no one cared. For some hundreds of years no
one had crossed it to penetrate to the black reaches of
the cellar behind it.

At the top of the steps, separating the kitchen from the
cellar, was a stout oaken door. This door was, in a way,
as peculiar and out of relation to the rest of the house as
the cellar. It was a strange kind of door to find in a
modern house, and certainly a most unusual door to find
in the inside of the house – thick, stoutly built, dex-
trously rabbeted together, with huge wrought iron hinges
and a lock that looked as though it came from Castle
Despair. Separating a house from the outside world, such
a door would be excusable; swinging between kitchen
and cellar it seemed peculiarly inappropriate.

From the earliest months of his life, Tommy Tucker
seemed unhappy in the kitchen. In the front parlour, in
the formal dining-room, and especially on the first floor

of the house, he acted like a normal, healthy child; but carry him to the kitchen and he began at once to cry. His parents, being plain people, ate in the kitchen save when they had company. Being poor, Mrs Tucker did most of her work, though occasionally she had a char-woman in to do the extra Saturday cleaning, and thus much of her time was spent in the kitchen. And Tommy stayed with her, at least as long as he was unable to walk. Much of the time he was decidedly unhappy.

When Tommy learned to crawl, he lost no time in leaving the kitchen. No sooner was his mother's back turned than the little fellow crawled as fast as he could for the doorway opening into the front of the house, the dining-room and the parlour. Once away from the kit-chen he seemed happy; at least he ceased to cry. On being returned to the kitchen, his howls so thoroughly con-vinced the neighbours that he had colic, that more than one bowl of catnip and sage tea was brought to his assis-tance.

It was not until the boy learned to talk that the Tuckers had any idea as to what made him cry so hard when he was in the kitchen. In other words, the baby had to suffer for many months before he obtained at least a little relief, and even when he told his parents what was the matter they were absolutely unable to comprehend. This is not to be wondered at, because they were both hard-working, rather simple-minded persons.

What they finally learned from their little son was this : that if the cellar door was shut and securely fas-tened with the heavy iron lock, Tommy could at least eat a meal in peace; if the door was simply closed but not locked, he shivered with fear but kept quiet; but if the door was open, if even the slightest streak of black showed that it was not tightly shut, then the little three-year-old would scream himself to the point of exhaus-tion, especially if his tired father refused him permission to leave the kitchen.

Playing in the kitchen, the child developed two

interesting habits. Rags, scraps of paper and splinters of wood were continually being pushed under the thick oak door to fill the space between the door and the sill. Whenever Mrs Tucker opened the door there was always some trash there, placed by her son. It annoyed her, and more than once the little fellow was thrashed for this conduct, but punishment acted in no way as a deterrent. The other habit was as singular. Once the door was closed and locked, he would rather boldly walk up to it and caress the old lock. Even when he was so small that he had to stand on tiptoe to touch it with the tips of his fingers he would touch it with slow caressing strokes; later on, as he grew, he used to kiss it.

His father, who only saw the boy at the end of the day, decided that there was no sense in such conduct, and in his masculine way tried to break the lad of his foolishness. There was, of necessity, no effort on the part of the boy's hard-working parent to understand the psychology behind his son's conduct. All that the man knew was that his little son was acting in a way that was decidedly queer.

Tommy loved his mother and was willing to do anything he could to help her in the household tasks, but one thing he would not do, and never did do, and that was to fetch and carry between the house and the cellar. If his mother opened the door, he would run screaming from the room, and he never returned voluntarily till he was assured that the door was closed.

He never explained why he acted as he did. In fact, he refused to talk about it, at least to his parents, and that was just as well, because had he done so, they would simply have been more positive than ever that there was something wrong with their only child. They tried, in their own way, to break the child of his unusual habits; failing to change him at all, they decided to ignore his peculiarities.

That is, they ignored them until he became six years old and the time came for him to go to school. He was a sturdy little chap by that time, and more intelligent than the usual boys beginning in the primer class. Mr Tucker was, at times, proud of him; the child's attitude toward the cellar door was the one thing most disturbing to the father's pride. Finally, nothing would do but that the Tucker family should call on the local physician. It was an important event in the life of the Tuckers; so important that it demanded the wearing of Sunday clothes and all that sort of thing.

'The matter is just this, Dr Hawthorn,' said Mr Tucker in a somewhat embarrassed manner. 'Our little Tommy is old enough to start school but he behaves childish in regard to our cellar, and the missus and I thought you could tell us what to do about it. It must be his nerves.'

'Ever since he was a baby,' continued Mrs Tucker, taking up the thread of the conversation where her husband had paused, 'Tommy has had a great fear of the cellar. Even now, big boy that he is, he does not love me enough to fetch and carry for me through that door and down those steps. It is not natural for a child to act as he does, and what with chinking the cracks with rags and kissing the lock, he drives me to the point where I fear he may become daft-like as he grows older.'

The doctor, eager to satisfy new customers, and dimly remembering some lectures on the nervous system received when he was a medical student, asked some general questions, listened to the boy's heart, examined his lungs and looked at his eyes and finger-nails. At last he commented,

'Looks like a fine healthy boy to me.'

'Yes, all except the cellar door,' said father.

'Has he ever been sick?'

'Naught but fits once or twice when he cried himself blue in the face,' answered the mother.

'Frightened?'

'Perhaps. It was always in the kitchen.'

'Suppose you go out and let me talk to Tommy by myself.'

And there sat the doctor, very much at his ease, and the little six-year-old boy very uneasy.

'Tommy, what is there in the cellar that you're afraid of?'

'I don't know.'

'Have you ever seen it?'

'No, sir.'

'Ever heard it? Smelt it?'

'No, sir.'

'Then how do you know there is something there?'

'Because.'

'Because what?'

'Because there is.'

That was as far as Tommy would go, and at last his seeming obstinacy annoyed the physician even as it had for several years annoyed Mr Tucker. He went to the door and called the parents into the room.

'He thinks there is something down in the cellar,' he stated.

The Tuckers simply looked at each other.

'That's foolish,' commented Mr Tucker.

' 'Tis just a plain cellar with junk and firewood and cider barrels in it,' added Mrs Tucker. 'Since we moved into that house I have not missed a day without going down those stone steps and I know there is nothing there. But the lad has always screamed when the door was open. I recall now that since he was a child in arms he has always screamed when the door was open.'

'He thinks there is something there,' said the doctor.

'That is why we brought him to you,' replied the father. 'It's the child's nerves. Perhaps feetida or something will calm him.'

'I will tell you what to do,' advised the doctor. 'He thinks there is something there. Just as soon as he finds he is wrong and there is nothing there, he will forget about it. He has been humoured too much. What you want to do is to open that cellar door and make him stay by himself in the kitchen. Nail the door open so that he cannot close it. Leave him alone there for an hour, and then go and laugh at him and show him how silly it was for him to be afraid of an empty cellar. I will give you some nerve and blood tonic, and that will help, but the big thing is to show him that there is nothing to be afraid of.'

On the way back to the Tucker home, Tommy broke away from his parents. They caught him after an exciting chase and kept him between them for the rest of the way home. Once in the house he disappeared, and was found in the guest-room under the bed. The afternoon being already spoiled for Mr Tucker, he determined to keep the child under observation for the rest of the day. Tommy ate no supper, in spite of the urgings of the unhappy mother. The dishes were washed, the evening paper read, the evening pipe smoked; and then, and only then, did Mr Tucker take down his tool box and get out a hammer and some long nails.

'And I am going to nail the door open, Tommy, so you cannot close it, as that was what the doctor said, Tommy, and you are to be a man and stay here in the kitchen alone for an hour, and we will leave the lamp a-burning and then, when you find there is naught to be afraid of, you will be well and a real man and not something for a man to be ashamed of being the father of.'

But at the last, Mrs Tucker kissed Tommy and cried and whispered to her husband not to do it, and to wait till the boy was larger; but nothing was to do except to nail the thick door open, so it could not be shut, and leave the boy there alone with the lamp burning and the dark open space of the doorway to look at with eyes that grew as hot and burning as the flame of the lamp.

That same day Dr Hawthorn took supper with a classmate of his, a man who specialised in psychiatry, and who was particularly interested in children. Hawthorn told Johnson about his newest case, the little Tucker boy, and asked him for his opinion. Johnson frowned.

'Children are odd, Hawthorn. Perhaps they are like

dogs. It may be their nervous system is more acute than in the adult. We know that our eyesight is limited, also our hearing and smell. I firmly believe there are forms of life which exist in such a form that we can neither see, hear nor smell them. Fondly we delude ourselves into the fallacy of believing that they do not exist because we cannot prove their existence. This Tucker lad may have a nervous system that is peculiarly acute. He may dimly appreciate the existence of something in the cellar which is unappreciable to his parents. Evidently there is some basis in this fear of his. Now I am not saying that there is anything in the cellar. In fact, I suppose that it is just an ordinary cellar, but this boy, since he was a baby, has thought that there was something there, and that is just as bad as though there actually were. What I would like to know is what makes him think so. Give me the address and I will call tomorrow and have a talk with the little fellow.'

'What do you think of my advice?'

'Sorry, old man, but I think it was perfectly rotten. If I were you, I would step round there on my way home and prevent them from following it. The little fellow may be badly frightened. You see, he evidently thinks there is something there.'

'But there isn't.'

'Perhaps not. No doubt he is wrong, but he thinks so.'

It all worried Dr Hawthorn so much that he decided to take his friend's advice. It was a cold night, a foggy night, and the physician felt cold as he tramped along the streets. At last he came to the Tucker house. He remembered now that he had been there once before, long years ago, when little Tommy Tucker came into the world. There was a light in the front window and in no time at all Mr Tucker came to the door.

'I have come to see Tommy,' said the doctor.

'He is back in the kitchen,' replied the father.

'He gave one cry but since then he has been quiet,' sobbed the wife.

'If I had let her have her way she would have opened the door, but I said to her, "Mother, now is the time to make a man out of our Tommy." And I guess he knows by now that there was naught to be afraid of. Well, the hour is up. Suppose we go and get him and put him to bed?'

'It has been a hard time for the little child,' whispered the wife.

Carrying the candle, the man walked ahead of the woman and the doctor and at last opened the kitchen door. The room was dark.

'Lamp has gone out,' said the man. 'Wait till I light it.'

'Tommy! Tommy!' called Mrs Tucker.

But the doctor ran to where a white form was stretched on the floor. Sharply he called for more light. Trembling, he examined all that was left of little Tommy. Twitching, he looked down the open space into the cellar. At last he turned to Tucker and Tucker's wife.

'Tommy – Tommy's been hurt,' he stammered. 'I guess he's dead.'

The mother threw herself on the floor and picked up the torn, mutilated thing that had been only a little while ago her little Tommy.

The man took his hammer and drew out the nails and closed the door and locked it, and then drove in a long spike to reinforce the lock. Then he took hold of the doctor's shoulders and shook him.

'What killed him, Doctor? What killed him?' he shouted into Hawthorn's ear.

The doctor looked at him bravely in spite of the fear in his throat.

'How do I know, Tucker?' he replied. 'How do I know? Didn't you tell me that there was nothing there? Nothing down there? In the cellar?'

A Pair of Hands

Sir Arthur Quiller-Couch

'Yes,' said Miss Le Petyt, gazing into the deep fireplace and letting her hands and her knitting lie for the moment idle in her lap. 'Oh, yes, I have seen a ghost. In fact I have lived in a house with one for quite a long time.'

'How you *could*—!' began one of my host's daughters; and '*You*, Aunt Emily?' cried the other at the same moment.

Miss Le Petyt, gentle soul, withdrew her eyes from the fireplace and protested with a gay little smile. 'Well, my dears, I am not quite the coward you take me for. And, as it happens, mine was the most harmless ghost in the world. In fact' – and here she looked at the fire again – 'I was quite sorry to lose her.'

'It was a woman, then? Now I think,' said Miss Blanche, 'that female ghosts are the horridest of all. They wear little shoes with high red heels, and go about *tap, tap*, wringing their hands.'

'This one wrung her hands, certainly. But I don't know about the high red heels, for I never saw her feet. Perhaps she was like the Queen of Spain, and hadn't any. And as for the hands, it all depends *how* you wring them. There's an elderly shopwalker at Knightsbridge, for instance—'

'Don't be prosy, dear, when you know that we're just dying to hear the story.'

Miss Le Petyt turned to me with a small deprecating laugh. 'It's such a little one.'

'The story, or the ghost?'

'Both.'

And this was Miss Le Petyt's story:

'It happened when I lived down in Cornwall, at Tresillack on the south coast. Tresillack was the name of the house, which stood quite alone at the head of a coombe, within sound of the sea but without sight of it; for though the coombe led down to a wide open beach, it wound and twisted half a dozen times on its way, and its overlapping sides closed the view from the house, which was advertised as 'secluded'. I was very poor in those days. Your father and all of us were poor then, as I trust, my dears, you will never be; but I was young enough to be romantic and wise enough to like independence, and this word "secluded" took my fancy.

'The misfortune was that it had taken the fancy, or just suited the requirements, of several previous tenants. You know, I dare say, the kind of person who rents a secluded house in the country? Well, yes, there are several kinds; but they seem to agree in being odious. No one knows where they come from, though they soon remove all doubt about where they're "going to", as the children say. "Shady" is the word, is it not? Well, the previous tenants of Tresillack (from first to last a bewildering series) had been shady with a vengeance.

'I knew nothing of this when I first made application to the landlord, a solid yeoman inhabiting a farm at the foot of the coombe, on a cliff overlooking the beach. To him I presented myself fearlessly as a spinster of decent family and small but assured income, intending a rural life of combined seemliness and economy. He met my advances politely enough, but with an air of suspicion which offended me. I began by disliking him for it: afterwards I set it down as an unpleasant feature in the local character. I was doubly mistaken. Farmer Hosking was slow-witted, but as honest a man as ever stood up against hard times; and a more open and hospitable race than the people on that coast I never wish to meet. It was the caution of a child who had burnt his fingers, not once but many times. Had I known what I afterwards learned of Farmer Hosking's tribulations as landlord of a "secluded country residence", I should have approached him with the bashfulness proper to my suit and faltered as I undertook to prove the bright exception in a long line of painful experiences. He had bought the Tresillack estate twenty years before – on mortgage, I fancy – because the land adjoined his own and would pay him for tillage. Both the house was a nuisance, an incubus, and had been so from the beginning.

' "Well, miss," he said, "you're welcome to look over it; a pretty enough place, inside and out. There's no trouble about keys, because I've put in a housekeeper, a widow-woman, and she'll show you round. With your leave I'll step up the coombe so far with you, and put you in your way." As I thanked him he paused and rubbed his chin. "There's one thing I must tell you, though. Whoever takes the house must take Mrs Carkeek along with it."

' "Mrs Carkeek?" I echoed dolefully. "Is that the housekeeper?"

' "Yes: she was wife to my late hind. I'm sorry, miss," he added, my face telling him no doubt what sort of woman I expected Mrs Carkeek to be; "but I had to make it a rule after—after some things that happened. And I dare say you won't find her so bad. Mary Carkeek's a sensible comfortable woman, and knows the place. She was in service there to Squire Kendall when he sold up and went: her first place it was."

' "I may as well see the house, anyhow," said I dejectedly. So we started to walk up the coombe. The path, which ran beside a little chattering stream, was narrow for the most part, and Farmer Hosking, with an apology, strode on ahead to beat aside the brambles. But whenever its width allowed us to walk side by side I caught him from time to time stealing a shy inquisitive glance under his rough eyebrows. Courteously though he bore himself, it was clear that he could not sum me up to his satisfaction or bring me square with his notion of a tenant for his "secluded country residence".

'I don't know what foolish fancy prompted it, but about half-way up the coombe I stopped short and asked :

' "There are no ghosts, I suppose?"

'It struck me, a moment after I had uttered it, as a supremely silly question; but he took it quite seriously. "No; I never heard tell of any *ghosts*." He laid a queer sort of stress on the word. "There's always been trouble with servants, and maids' tongues will be runnin'. But Mary Carkeek lives up there alone, and she seems comfortable enough."

'We walked on. By and by he pointed with his stick. "It don't look like a place for ghosts, now, do it?"

'Certainly it did not. Above an untrimmed orchard rose a terrace of turf scattered with thorn-bushes, and above this a terrace of stone, upon which stood the prettiest cottage I had ever seen. It was long and low and thatched; a deep verandah ran from end to end. Clematis, Banksia roses and honeysuckle climbed the posts of this verandah, and big blooms of the Maréchal Niel were clustered along its roof, beneath the lattices of the bedroom windows. The house was small enough to be called a cottage, and rare enough in features and in situation to confer distinction on any tenant. It suggested what in those days we should have called "elegant" living. And I could have clapped my hands for joy.

'My spirits mounted still higher when Mrs Carkeek opened the door to us. I had looked for a Mrs Gummidge, and I found a healthy middle-aged woman with a thoughtful but contented face, and a smile which, without a trace of obsequiousness, quite bore out the farmer's description of her. She was a comfortable woman; and while we walked through the rooms together (for Mr Hosking waited outside) I "took to" Mrs Carkeek. Her speech was direct and practical; the rooms, in spite of their faded furniture, were bright and exquisitely clean;

and somehow the very atmosphere of the house gave me a sense of well-being, of feeling at home and cared for; yes, *of being loved.* Don't laugh, my dears; for when I've done you may not think this fancy altogether foolish.

'I stepped out into the verandah, and Farmer Hosking pocketed the pruning-knife which he had been using on a bush of jasmine.

' "This is better than anything I had dreamed of," said I.

' "Well, miss, that's not a wise way of beginning a bargain, if you'll excuse me."

'He took no advantage, however, of my admission; and we struck the bargain as we returned down the coombe to his farm, where the hired chaise waited to convey me back to the market-town. I had meant to engage a maid of my own, but now it occurred to me that I might do very well with Mrs Carkeek. This, too, was settled in the course of the next day or two, and within the week I had moved into my new home.

'I can hardly describe to you the happiness of my first month at Tresillack; because (as I now believe) if I take the reasons which I had for being happy, one by one, there remains over something which I cannot account for. I was moderately young, entirely healthy; I felt myself independent and adventurous; the season was high summer, the weather glorious, the garden in all the pomp of June, yet sufficiently unkempt to keep me busy, give me a sharp appetite for meals, and send me to bed in that drowsy stupor which comes of the odours of earth. I spent the most of my time out-of-doors, winding up the day's work as a rule with a walk down the cool valley, along the beach and back.

'I soon found that all housework could be safely left to Mrs Carkeek. She did not talk much; indeed her only fault (a rare one in housekeepers) was that she talked too little, and even when I addressed her seemed at times unable to give me her attention. It was as though her mind strayed off to some small job she had forgotten, and her eyes wore a listening look, as though she waited for the neglected task to speak and remind her. But as a matter of fact she forgot nothing. Indeed, my dears, I was never so well attended to in my life.

'Well, that is what I'm coming to. That, so to say, is just *it*. The woman not only had the rooms swept and dusted, and my meals prepared to the moment. In a hundred odd little ways this orderliness, these preparations, seemed to read my desires. Did I wish the roses renewed in a bowl upon the dining-table, sure enough at the next meal they would be replaced by fresh ones. Mrs Carkeek (I told myself) must have surprised and interpreted a glance of mine. And yet I could not remember having glanced at the bowl in her presence. And how on earth had she guessed the very roses, the very shapes and colours I had lightly wished for? This is only an instance, you understand. Every day, and from morning to night, I happened on others, each slight enough, but all together bearing witness to a ministering intelligence as subtle as it was untiring.

'I am a light sleeper, as you know, with an uncomfortable knack of waking with the sun and roaming early. No matter how early I rose at Tresillack, Mrs Carkeek seemed to have preceded me. Finally I had to conclude that she arose and dusted and tidied as soon as she judged me safely a-bed. For once, finding the drawing-room (where I had been sitting late) "redded up" at four in the morning, and no trace of a plate of raspberries which I had carried thither after dinner and left overnight, I determined to test her, and walked through to the kitchen, calling her by name. I found the kitchen as clean as a pin, and the fire laid, but no trace of Mrs Carkeek. I walked upstairs and knocked at her door. At the second knock a sleepy voice cried out, and presently the good woman stood before me in her nightgown, looking (I thought) very badly scared.

' "No," I said, "it's not a burglar. But I've found out what I wanted, that you do your morning's work overnight. But you mustn't wait for me when I choose to sit up. And now go back to your bed like a good soul, whilst I take a run down to the beach."

'She stood blinking in the dawn. Her face was still white.

' "Oh, miss," she gasped, "I made sure you must have seen something!"

' "And so I have," I answered, "but it was neither burglars nor ghosts."

' "Thank God!" I heard her say as she turned her back to me in her grey bedroom – which faced the north. And I took this for a carelessly pious expression and ran downstairs, thinking no more of it.

'A few days later I began to understand.

'The plan of Tresillack house (I must explain) was simplicity itself. To the left of the hall as you entered was the dining-room; to the right the drawing-room, with a boudoir beyond. The foot of the stairs faced the front door, and beside it, passing a glazed inner door, you found two others right and left, the left opening on the kitchen, the right on a passage which ran by a store-cupboard under the bend of the stairs to a neat pantry with the usual shelves and linen-press, and under the window (which faced north) a porcelain basin and brass tap. On the first morning of my tenancy I had visited this pantry and turned the tap; but no water ran. I supposed this to be accidental. Mrs Carkeek had to wash up glassware and crockery, and no doubt Mrs Carkeek would complain of any failure in the water-supply.

'But the day after my surprise visit (as I called it) I had picked a basketful of roses, and carried them into the pantry as a handy place to arrange them in. I chose a china bowl and went to fill it at the tap. Again the water would not run.

'I called Mrs Carkeek. "What is wrong with this tap?" I asked. "The rest of the house is well enough supplied."

' "I don't know, miss. I never use it."

' "But there must be a reason; and you must find it a

great nuisance washing up the plate and glasses in the kitchen. Come around to the back with me, and we'll have a look at the cisterns."

' "The cisterns'll be all right, miss. I assure you I don't find it a trouble."

'But I was not to be put off. The back of the house stood but ten feet from a wall which was really but a stone face built against the cliff cut away by the architect. Above the cliff rose the kitchen-garden, and from its lower path we looked over the wall's parapet upon the cisterns. There were two – a very large one, supplying the kitchen and the bathroom above the kitchen; and a small one, obviously fed by the other, and as obviously leading, by a pipe which I could trace, to the pantry. Now the big cistern stood almost full, and yet the small one, though on a lower level, was empty.

' "It's as plain as daylight,". said I. "The pipe between the two is choked." And I clambered onto the parapet.

' "I wouldn't, miss. The pantry tap is only cold water, and no use to me. From the kitchen boiler I gets it hot, you see."

' "But I want the pantry water for my flowers." I bent over and groped. "I thought as much!" said I, as I wrenched out a thick plug of cork and immediately the water began to flow. I turned triumphantly on Mrs Carkeek, who had grown suddenly red in the face. Her eyes were fixed on the cork in my hand. To keep it more firmly wedged in its place somebody had wrapped it round with a rag of calico print; and, discoloured though the rag was, I seemed to recall the pattern (a lilac sprig). Then, as our eyes met, it occurred to me that only two mornings before Mrs Carkeek had worn a print gown of that same sprigged pattern.

'I had the presence of mind to hide this very small discovery, sliding over it with some quite trivial remark; and presently Mrs Carkeek regained her composure. But I own I felt disappointed in her. It seemed such a paltry thing to be disingenuous over. She had deliberately acted a fib before me; and why? Merely because she preferred the kitchen to the pantry tap. It was childish. "But servants are all the same," I told myself. "I must take Mrs Carkeek as she is; and, after all, she is a treasure."

'On the second night after this, and between eleven and twelve o'clock, I was lying in bed and reading myself sleepy over a novel of Lord Lytton's, when a small sound disturbed me. I listened. The sound was clearly that of water trickling; and I set it down to rain. A shower (I told myself) had filled the water-pipes which drained the roof. Somehow I could not fix the sound. There was a water-pipe against the wall just outside my window. I rose and drew up the blind.

'To my astonishment no rain was falling; no rain had fallen. I felt the slate window-sill; some dew had gathered there – no more. There was no wind, no cloud : only a still moon high over the eastern slope of the coombe, the distant plash of waves, and the fragrance of many roses. I went back to bed and listened again. Yes, the trickling sound continued, quite distinct in the silence of the house, not to be confused for a moment with the dull murmur of the beach. After a while it began to grate on my nerves. I caught up my candle, flung my dressing-gown about me, and stole softly downstairs.

'Then it was simple. I traced the sound to the pantry. "Mrs Carkeek has left the tap running," said I : and, sure enough, I found it so – a thin trickle steadily running to waste in the porcelain basin. I turned off the tap, went contentedly back to my bed, and slept.

'—for some hours. I opened my eyes in darkness, and at once knew what had awakened me. The tap was running again. Now it had shut easily in my hand, but not so easily that I could believe it had slipped open again of its own accord. "This is Mrs Carkeek's doing," said I; and am afraid I added "Bother Mrs Carkeek !"

'Well, there was no help for it : so I struck a light, looked at my watch, saw that the hour was just three o'clock, and descended the stairs again. At the pantry door I paused. I was not afraid – not one little bit. In fact the notion that anything might be wrong had never crossed my mind. But I remember thinking, with my hand on the door, that if Mrs Carkeek were in the pantry I might happen to give her a severe fright.

'I pushed the door open briskly. Mrs Carkeek was not there. But something *was* there, by the porcelain basin – something which might have sent me scurrying upstairs two steps at a time, but which as a matter of fact held me to the spot. My heart seemed to stand still – so still! And in the stillness I remember setting down the brass candlestick on a tall nest of drawers beside me.

'Over the porcelain basin and beneath the water trickling from the tap I saw two hands.

'That was all – two small hands, a child's hands. I cannot tell you how they ended.

'No: they were not cut off. I saw them quite distinctly: just a pair of small hands and the wrists, and after that – nothing. They were moving briskly – washing themselves clean. I saw the water trickle and splash over them – not *through* them – but just as it would on real hands. They were the hands of a little girl, too. Oh, yes, I was sure of that at once. Boys and girls wash their hands differently. I can't just tell you what the difference is, but it's unmistakable.

'I saw all this before my candle slipped and fell with a crash. I had set it down without looking – for my eyes were fixed on the basin – and had balanced it on the edge of the nest of drawers. After the crash, in the darkness there, with the water running, I suffered some bad moments. Oddly enough, the thought uppermost with me was that I *must* shut off that tap before escaping. I *had* to. And after a while I picked up all my courage, so to say, between my teeth, and with a little sob thrust out my hand and did it. Then I fled.

'The dawn was close upon me: and as soon as the sky reddened I took my bath, dressed and went downstairs. And there at the pantry door I found Mrs Carkeek, also

dressed, with my candlestick in her hand.

' "Ah!" said I, "you picked it up."

'Our eyes met. Clearly Mrs Carkeek wished me to begin, and I determined at once to have it out with her.

' "And you knew all about it. That's what accounts for your plugging up the cistern."

' "You saw . . . ?" she began.

' "Yes, yes. And you must tell me all about it – never mind how bad. Is—is it—murder?"

' "Law bless you, miss, whatever put such horrors in your head?"

' "She was washing her hands."

' "Ah, so she does, poor dear! But – murder! And dear little Miss Margaret, that wouldn't go to hurt a fly!"

' "Miss Margaret?"

' "Eh, she died at seven year. Squire Kendall's only daughter; and that's over twenty year ago. I was her nurse, miss, and I know – diphtheria it was; she took it down in the village."

' "But how do you know it is Margaret?"

' "Those hands – why, how could I mistake, that used to be her nurse?"

' "But why does she wash them?"

' "Well, miss, being always a dainty child – and the housework, you see—"

'I took a long breath. "Do you mean to tell me that all this tidying and dusting—" I broke off. "Is it *she* who has been taking this care of me?"

'Mrs Carkeek met my look steadily.

' "Poor little soul!"

' "Who else, miss?"

' "Well now" – Mrs Carkeek rubbed my candlestick with the edge of her apron – "I'm so glad you take it like this. For there isn't really nothing to be afraid of – is there?" She eyed me wistfully. "It's my belief she loves you, miss. But only to think what a time she must have had with the others!"

' "The others?" I echoed.

' "The other tenants, miss: the ones afore you."

' "Were they bad?"

' "They was awful. Didn't Farmer Hosking tell you? They carried on fearful – one after another, and each one worse than the last."

' "What was the matter with them? Drink?"

' "Drink, miss, with some of 'em. There was the Major – he used to go mad with it, and run about the coombe in his night-shirt. Oh, scandalous! And his wife drank too – that is, if she ever *was* his wife. Just think of that tender child washing up after their nasty doings!"

'I shivered.

' "But that wasn't the worst, miss – not by a long way. There was a pair here – from the colonies, or so they gave out – with two children, a boy and gel, the eldest scarce six. Poor mites!"

' "Why, what happened?"

' "They beat those children, miss – your blood would boil! – *and* starved, *and* tortured 'em, it's my belief. You could hear their screams, I've been told, away back in the high road, and that's the best part of half a mile. Sometimes they was locked up without food for days together. But it's my belief that little Miss Margaret managed to feed them somehow. Oh, I can see her, creeping to the door and comforting!"

' "But perhaps she never showed herself when these awful people were here, but took to flight until they left."

' "You didn't never know her, miss. The brave she was! She'd have stood up to lions. She've been here all the while: and only to think what her innocent eyes and ears must have took in! There was another couple—" Mrs Carkeek sunk her voice.

' "Oh, hush!" said I, "if I'm to have any peace of mind in this house!"

' "But you won't go, miss? She loves you, I know she do. And think what you might be leaving her to – what sort of tenant might come next. For she can't go. She've been here ever since her father sold the place. He died soon after. You mustn't go!"

'Now I had resolved to go, but all of a sudden I felt how mean this resolution was.

' "After all," said I, "there's nothing to be afraid of."

' "That's it, miss; nothing at all. I don't even believe it's so very uncommon. Why, I've heard my mother tell of farmhouses where the rooms were swept every night as regular as clockwork, and the floors sanded, and the pots and pans scoured, and all while the maids slept. They put it down to the piskies; but we know better, miss, and now we've got the secret between us we can lie easy in our beds, and if we hear anything, say 'God bless the child!' and go to sleep."

' "Mrs Carkeek," said I, "there's only one condition I have to make."

' "What's that?"

' "Why, that you let me kiss you."

' "Oh, you dear!" said Mrs Carkeek as we embraced: and this was as close to familiarity as she allowed herself to go in the whole course of my acquaintance with her.

'I spent three years at Tresillack, and all that while Mrs Carkeek lived with me and shared the secret. Few women, I dare to say, were ever so completely wrapped around with love as we were during those three years. It ran through my waking life like a song: it smoothed my pillow, touched and made my table comely, in summer lifted the heads of the flowers as I passed, and in winter watched the fire with me and kept it bright.

'Why did I ever leave Tresillack? Because one day, at the end of five years, Farmer Hosking brought me word that he had sold the house – or was about to sell it; I forget which. There was no avoiding it, at any rate; the purchaser being a Colonel Kendall, a brother of the old Squire.

' "A married man?" I asked.

' "Yes, miss; with a family of eight. As pretty children

as ever you see, and the mother a good lady. It's the old home to Colonel Kendall."

' "I see. And that is why you feel bound to sell."

' "It's a good price, too, that he offers. You mustn't think but I'm sorry enough—"

' "To turn me out? I thank you, Mr Hosking; but you are doing the right thing."

'Since Mrs Carkeek was to stay, the arrangement lacked nothing of absolute perfection – except, perhaps, that it found no room for me.

' "*She* – Margaret – will be happy," I said; "with her cousins, you know."

' "Oh yes, miss, she will be happy, sure enough," Mrs Carkeek agreed.

'So when the time came I packed up my boxes, and tried to be cheerful. But on the last morning, when they stood corded in the hall, I sent Mrs Carkeek upstairs upon some poor excuse, and stepped alone into the pantry.

' "Margaret!" I whispered.

'There was no answer at all. I had scarcely dared to hope for one. Yet I tried again, and, shutting my eyes this time, stretched out both hands and whispered:

' "Margaret!"

'And I will swear to my dying day that two little hands stole and rested – for a moment only – in mine.'

The House of the Nightmare

Edward Lucas White

I first caught sight of the house from the brow of the mountain as I cleared the woods and looked across the broad valley several hundred feet below me, to the low sun sinking toward the far blue hills. From that momentary viewpoint I had an exaggerated sense of looking almost vertically down. I seemed to be hanging over the chequer-board of roads and fields, dotted with farm buildings, and felt the familiar deception that I could almost throw a stone upon the house. I barely glimpsed its slate roof.

What caught my eyes was the bit of road in front of it, between the mass of dark-green shade trees about the house and the orchard opposite. Perfectly straight it was, bordered by an even row of trees, through which I made out a cinder side path and a low stone wall.

Conspicuous on the orchard side between two of the flanking trees was a white object, which I took to be a tall stone, a vertical splinter of one of the tilted limestone reefs with which the fields of the region are scarred.

The road itself I saw plain as a box-wood ruler on a green baize table. It gave me a pleasurable anticipation of a chance for a burst of speed. I had been painfully traversing closely forested, semi-mountainous hills. Not a farmhouse had I passed, only wretched cabins by the road, more than twenty miles of which I had found very bad and hindering. Now, when I was not many miles from my expected stopping-place, I looked forward to better going, and to that straight, level bit in particular.

As I sped cautiously down the sharp beginning of the long descent the trees engulfed me again, and I lost sight of the valley. I dipped into a hollow, rose on the crest of the next hill, and again saw the house, nearer, and not so far below.

The tall stone caught my eye with a shock of surprise. Had I not thought it was opposite the house next the orchard? Clearly it was on the left-hand side of the road toward the house. My self-questioning lasted only the moment as I passed the crest. Then the outlook was cut off again; but I found myself gazing ahead, watching for the next chance at the same view.

At the end of the second hill I only saw the bit of road obliquely and could not be sure, but, as at first, the tall stone seemed on the right of the road.

At the top of the third and last hill I looked down the stretch of road under the overarching trees, almost as one would look through a tube. There was a line of whiteness which I took for the tall stone. It was on the right.

I dipped into the last hollow. As I mounted the farther slope I kept my eyes on the top of the road ahead of me. When my line of sight surmounted the rise I marked the tall stone on my right hand among the serried maples. I leaned over, first on one side, then on the other, to inspect my tyres, then I threw the lever.

As I flew forward I looked ahead. There was the tall stone – on the left of the road! I was really scared and almost dazed. I meant to stop dead, take a good look at the stone, and make up my mind beyond peradventure whether it was on the right or the left – if not, indeed, in the middle of the road.

In my bewilderment I put on the highest speed. The machine leaped forward; everything I touched went wrong; I steered wildly, slewed to the left, and crashed into a big maple.

When I came to my senses I was flat on my back in the dry ditch. The last rays of the sun sent shafts of golden green light through the maple boughs overhead. My first thought was an odd mixture of appreciation of the beauties of nature and disapproval of my own conduct in touring without a companion – a fad I had regretted more than once. Then my mind cleared and I sat up. I felt myself from the head down. I was not bleeding; no bones were broken; and, while much shaken, I had suffered no serious bruises.

Then I saw the boy. He was standing at the edge of the cinder-path, near the ditch. He was stocky and solidly built, barefoot, with his trousers rolled up to his knees; wore a sort of butternut shirt, open at the throat; and was coatless and hatless. He was tow-headed, with a shock of tousled hair; was much freckled, and had a hideous harelip. He shifted from one foot to the other, twiddled his toes, and said nothing whatever, though he stared at me intently.

I scrambled to my feet and proceeded to survey the wreck. It seemed distressingly complete. It had not blown up, nor even caught fire; but otherwise the ruin appeared hopelessly thorough. Everything I examined seemed worse smashed than the rest. My two hampers alone, by one of those cynical jokes of chance, had escaped – both had pitched clear of the wreckage and were unhurt, not even a bottle broken.

During my investigations the boy's faded eyes followed me continuously, but he uttered no word. When I had convinced myself of my helplessness I straightened up and addressed him :

'How far is it to a blacksmith's shop?'

'Eight mile,' he answered. He had a distressing case of cleft palate and was scarcely intelligible.

'Can you drive me there?' I inquired.

'Nary team on the place,' he replied; 'nary horse, nary cow.'

'How far to the next house?' I continued.

'Six mile,' he responded.

I glanced at the sky. The sun had set already. I looked

at my watch : it was going – seven thirty-six.

'May I sleep in your house to-night?' I asked.

'You can come in if you want to,' he said, 'and sleep if you can. House all messy; ma's been dead three year, and dad's away. Nothin' to eat but buckwheat flour and rusty bacon.'

'I've plenty to eat,' I answered, picking up a hamper. 'Just take that hamper, will you?'

'You can come in if you're a mind to,' he said, 'but you got to carry your own stuff.' He did not speak gruffly or rudely, but appeared mildly stating an inoffensive fact.

'All right,' I said, picking up the other hamper; 'lead the way.'

The yard in front of the house was dark under a dozen or more immense ailanthus trees. Below them many smaller trees had grown up, and beneath these a dank underwood of tall, rank suckers out of the deep, shaggy, matted grass. What had once been, apparently, a carriage-drive left a narrow, curved track, disused and grass-grown, leading to the house. Even here were some shoots of the ailanthus, and the air was unpleasant with the vile smell of the roots and suckers and the insistent odour of their flowers.

The house was of grey stone, with green shutters faded almost as grey as the stone. Along its front was a veranda, not much raised from the ground, and with no balustrade or railing. On it were several hickory splint rockers. There were eight shuttered windows toward the porch, and midway of them a wide door, with small violet panes on either side of it and a fanlight above.

'Open the door,' I said to the boy.

'Open it yourself,' he replied, not unpleasantly nor disagreeably, but in such a tone that one could not but take the suggestion as a matter of course.

I put down the two hampers and tried the door. It was latched, but not locked, and opened with a rusty grind of its hinges, on which it sagged crazily, scraping the floor as it turned. The passage smelt mouldy and damp. There were several doors on either side; the boy pointed to the first on the right.

'You can have that room,' he said.

I opened the door. What with the dusk, the interlacing trees outside, the piazza roof, and the closed shutters, I could make out little.

'Better get a lamp,' I said to the boy.

'Nary lamp,' he declared cheerfully. 'Nary candle. Mostly I get abed before dark.'

I returned to the remains of my conveyance. All four of my lamps were merely scrap metal and splintered glass. My lantern was mashed flat. I always, however, carried candles in my valise. This I found split and crushed, but still holding together. I carried it to the porch, opened it, and took out three candles.

Entering the room, where I found the boy standing just where I had left him, I lit the candle. The walls were whitewashed, the floor bare. There was a mildewed, chilly smell, but the bed looked freshly made up and clean, although it felt clammy.

With a few drops of its own grease I stuck the candle on the corner of a mean, rickety little bureau. There was nothing else in the room save two rush-bottomed chairs and a small table. I went out on the porch, brought in my valise, and put it on the bed. I raised the sash of each window and pushed open the shutters. Then I asked the boy, who had not moved or spoken, to show me the way to the kitchen. He led me straight through the hall to the back of the house. The kitchen was large, and had no furniture save some pine chairs, a pine bench, and a pine table.

I stuck two candles on opposite corners of the table. There was no stove or range in the kitchen, only a big hearth, the ashes in which smelt and looked a month old. The wood in the woodshed was dry enough, but even it had a cellary, stale smell. The axe and hatchet were both rusty and dull, but usable, and I quickly made a big fire. To my amazement, for the mid-June evening was hot and still, the boy, a wry smile on his ugly face, almost leaped over the flame, hands and arms spread out, and fairly roasted himself.

'Are you cold?' I inquired.

'I'm allus cold,' he replied, hugging the fire closer than ever, till I thought he must scorch.

I left him toasting himself while I went in search of water. I discovered the pump, which was in working order and not dry on the valves; but I had a furious struggle to fill the two leaky pails I had found. When I had put water to boil I fetched my hampers from the porch.

I brushed the table and set out my meal – cold fowl, cold ham, white and brown bread, olives, jam, and cake. When the can of soup was hot and the coffee made I drew up two chairs to the table and invited the boy to join me.

'I ain't hungry,' he said; 'I've had supper.'

He was a new sort of boy to me; all the boys I knew were hearty eaters and always ready. I had felt hungry myself, but somehow when I came to eat I had little appetite and hardly relished the food. I soon made an end of my meal, covered the fire, blew out the candles, and returned to the porch, where I dropped into one of the hickory rockers to smoke. The boy followed me silently and seated himself on the porch floor, leaning against a pillar, his feet on the grass outside.

'What do you do,' I asked, 'when your father is away?'

'Just loaf 'round,' he said. 'Just fool 'round.'

'How far off are your nearest neighbours?' I asked.

'Don't no neighbours never come here,' he stated. 'Say they're afeared of the ghosts.'

I was not at all startled; the place had all those aspects which lead to a house being called haunted. I was struck by his odd matter-of-fact way of speaking – it was as if he had said they were afraid of a cross dog.

'Do you ever see any ghosts around here?' I continued.

'Never see 'em,' he answered, as if I had mentioned tramps or partridges. 'Never hear 'em. Sort o' feel 'em 'round sometimes.'

'Are you afraid of them?' I asked.

'Nope,' he declared. 'I ain't skeered o' ghosts; I'm skeered o' nightmares. Ever have nightmares?'

'Very seldom,' I replied.

'I do,' he returned. 'Allus have the same nightmare — big sow, big as a steer, trying to eat me up. Wake up so skeered I could run to never. Nowheres to run to. Go to sleep, and have it again. Wake up worse skeered than ever. Dad says it's buckwheat cakes in summer.'

'You must have teased a sow some time,' I said.

'Yep,' he answered. 'Teased a big sow wunst, holding up one of her pigs by the hind leg. Teased her too long. Fell in the pen and got bit up some. Wisht I hadn't 'a' teased her. Have that nightmare three times a week sometimes. Worse'n being burnt out. Worse'n ghosts. Say, I sorter feel ghosts around now.'

He was not trying to frighten me. He was as simply stating an opinion as if he had spoken of bats or mosquitoes. I made no reply, and found myself listening involuntarily. My pipe went out. I did not really want another, but felt disinclined for bed as yet, and was comfortable where I was, while the smell of the ailanthus blossoms was very disagreeable. I filled my pipe again, lit it, and then, as I puffed, somehow dozed off for a moment.

I awoke with a sensation of some light fabric trailed across my face. The boy's position was unchanged.

'Did you do that?' I asked sharply.

'Ain't done nary thing,' he rejoined. 'What was it?'

'It was like a piece of mosquito-netting brushed over my face.'

'That ain't netting,' he asserted; 'that's a veil. That's one of the ghosts. Some blow on you; some touch you with their long, cold fingers. That one with the veil she drags acrosst your face — well, mostly I think it's ma.'

He spoke with the unassailable conviction of the child in 'We Are Seven'. I found no words to reply, and rose to go to bed.

'Good night,' I said.

'Good night,' he echoed. 'I'll set out here a spell yet.'

I lit a match, found the candle I had stuck on the corner of the shabby little bureau, and undressed. The bed had a comfortable husk mattress, and I was soon asleep.

I had the sensation of having slept some time when I had a nightmare – the very nightmare the boy had described. A huge sow, big as a dray horse, was reared up with her forelegs over the foot-board of the bed, trying to scramble over to me. She grunted and puffed, and I felt I was the food she craved. I knew in the dream that it was only a dream, and strove to wake up.

Then the gigantic dream-beast floundered over the foot-board, fell across my shins, and I awoke.

I was in darkness as absolute as if I were sealed in a jet vault, yet the shudder of the nightmare instantly subsided, my nerves quieted; I realised where I was, and felt not the least panic. I turned over and was asleep again almost at once. Then I had a real nightmare, not recognisable as a dream, but appallingly real – an unutterable agony of reasonless horror.

There was a Thing in the room; not a sow, nor any other nameable creature, but a Thing. It was as big as an elephant, filled the room to the ceiling, was shaped like a wild boar, seated on its haunches, with its forelegs braced stiffly in front of it. It had a hot, slobbering, red mouth, full of big tusks, and its jaws worked hungrily. It shuffled and hunched itself forward, inch by inch, till its vast forelegs straddled the bed.

The bed crushed up like wet blotting-paper, and I felt the weight of the Thing on my feet, on my legs, on my body, on my chest. It was hungry, and I was what it was hungry for, and it meant to begin on my face. Its dripping mouth was nearer and nearer.

Then the dream-helplessness that made me unable to call or move suddenly gave way, and I yelled and awoke. This time my terror was positive and not to be shaken off.

It was near dawn : I could descry dimly the cracked, dirty window-panes. I got up, lit the stump of my candle and two fresh ones, dressed hastily, strapped my ruined valise, and put it on the porch against the wall near the door. Then I called the boy. I realised quite suddenly that I had not told him my name or asked his.

I shouted 'Hello!' a few times, but won no answer. I had had enough of that house. I was still permeated with the panic of the nightmare. I desisted from shouting, made no search, but with two candles went out to the kitchen. I took a swallow of cold coffee and munched a biscuit as I hustled my belongings into my hampers. Then, leaving a silver dollar on the table, I carried the hampers out on the porch and dumped them by my valise.

It was now light enough to see to walk, and I went out to the road. Already the night-dew had rusted much of the wreck, making it look more hopeless than before. It was, however, entirely undisturbed. There was not so much as a wheel-track or a hoof-print on the road. The tall, white stone, uncertainty about which had caused my disaster, stood like a sentinel opposite where I had upset.

I set out to find that blacksmith shop. Before I had gone far the sun rose clear from the horizon, and almost at once scorching. As I footed it along I grew very much heated, and it seemed more like ten miles than six before I reached the first house. It was a new frame house, neatly painted and close to the road, with a whitewashed fence along its garden front.

I was about to open the gate when a big black dog with a curly tail bounded out of the bushes. He did not bark, but stood inside the gate wagging his tail and regarding me with a friendly eye; yet I hesitated with my hand on the latch, and considered. The dog might not be as friendly as he looked, and the sight of him made me realise that except for the boy I had seen no creature about the house where I had spent the night; no dog or cat; not even a toad or bird. While I was ruminating upon this a man came from behind the house.

'Will your dog bite?' I asked.

'Naw,' he answered; 'he don't bite. Come in.'

I told him I had had an accident to my automobile, and asked if he could drive me to the blacksmith shop and back to my wreckage.

'Cert,' he said. 'Happy to help you. I'll hitch up fore-shortly. Wher'd you smash?'

'In front of the grey house about six miles back,' I answered.

'That big stone-built house?' he queried.

'The same,' I assented.

'Did you go a-past here?' he inquired astonished. 'I didn't hear ye.'

'No,' I said; 'I came from the other direction.'

'Why,' he meditated, 'you must 'a' smashed about sunup. Did you come over them mountains in the dark?'

'No,' I replied; 'I came over them yesterday evening. I smashed up about sunset.'

'Sundown!' he exclaimed. 'Where in thunder've ye been all night?'

'I slept in the house where I broke down.'

'In that there big stone-built house in the trees?' he demanded.

'Yes,' I agreed.

'Why,' he quavered excitedly, 'that there house is haunted! They say if you have to drive past it after dark, you can't tell which side of the road the big white stone is on.'

'I couldn't tell even before sunset,' I said.

'There!' he exclaimed. 'Look at that, now! And you slep' in that house! Did you sleep, honest?'

'I slept pretty well,' I said. 'Except for a nightmare, I slept all night.'

'Well,' he commented, 'I wouldn't go in that there house for a farm, nor sleep in it for my salvation. And you slep'! How in thunder did you get in?'

'The boy took me in,' I said.

'What sort of a boy?' he queried, his eyes fixed on me with a queer, countrified look of absorbed interest.

'A thick-set, freckle-faced boy with a harelip,' I said.

'Talk like his mouth was full of mush?' he demanded.

'Yes,' I said; 'bad case of cleft palate.'

'Well,' he exclaimed. 'I never did believe in ghosts, and I never did half believe that house was haunted, but I know it now. And you slep'!'

'I didn't see any ghosts,' I retorted irritably.

'You seen a ghost for sure,' he rejoined solemnly. 'That there harelip boy's been dead six months.'

Miss Jemima

Walter de la Mare

It was a hot, still evening; the trees stood motionless; and
not a bird was singing under the sky when a little old
lady and a child appeared together over the crest of the
hill. They paused side by side on the long, green, mound-
ed ridge, behind which the sun was now descending. And
spread out flat beneath them were the fields and farms
and the wandering stream of the wide countryside. It
was quite flat, and a faint thin mist was over it all,
stretching out as if to the rim of the world. The stooping
old lady and the child presently ventured a few further
paces down the hillside, then again came to a standstill,
and gazed once more, from under the umbrella that
shaded them against the hot sun, on the scene spread
out beneath them.

'Is *that* the house, Grannie,' said the child, 'that one
near the meadow with the horses in it, and the trees?
And is that *queer* little grey building right in the middle
of that green square field the church?'

The old lady pressed her lips together, and continued
to gaze through her thick glasses at the great solitary
country scene. Then she drew her umbrella down with
a click, placed it on the turf beside her, and sat down on
it.

'I don't suppose the grass *is* damp, my dear, after this
long hot day; but you never know,' she said.

'It's perfectly dry, Grannie dear, and *very* beautiful,'
said the child, as if she could hardly spare the breath for
the words. Then she too sat down. She had rather long
fair hair, and a straight small nose under her round hat

with its wreath of buttercups. Her name was Susan.

'And *is* that the house, Grannie?' she whispered once more, 'And *is* that the church where you did really and truly see it?'

The old lady never turned her eyes, but continued to overlook the scene as if she had not heard the small voice questioning; as if she were alone with her thoughts. And at that moment, one after another, a troop of gentle-stepping, half-wild horses appeared on a path round the bluff of the hill. Shyly eyeing these two strange human figures in their haunts, one and another of them lifted a narrow lovely head to snort; and a slim young bay, his mane like rough silk in the light, paused to whinny. Then one by one they trotted along the path, and presently were gone. Susan watched them out of sight, then sighed.

'This is a lovely place to be in, Grannie,' she said, and sighed again. 'I wish I had been here too when I was little. Please do tell me again about the – *you* know.'

Her voice trailed off faintly in the still golden air up there on the hill, as if she were now a little timid of repeating the question. She drew in closer beside her grannie, and pushing her small fingers between those of the bent-up, black-gloved hand in the old lady's lap, she stooped forward after yet another pause, looked up into the still grey face with its spectacles, and said very softly, '*How* many years ago did you say?'

There was a mild far-away expression in the slate-grey eyes into which Susan was looking, as if memory were retracing one by one the years that had gone. Never had Susan sat like this upon a green hill above so immense a world, or in so hushed an evening quiet. Her busy eyes turned once more to look first in the direction in which the trotting comely horses had vanished, then down again to the farmhouse with its barns and byres and orchard. They then rested once more on the grey stone church – which from this height looked almost as small as an old cottage – in the midst of its green field.

'*How* many years ago, Grannie?' repeated Susan.

'More than I scarcely dare think of,' said the old woman at last, gently pressing her fingers. 'Seventy-five, my dear.'

'Seventy-five!' breathed Susan. 'But that's not so very many, Grannie dear,' she added quickly, pushing her head against her grannie's black-caped shoulder. 'And now, before it is too late, please will you tell me the story. You see, Grannie, soon we shall have to be going back to the cab, or the man will suppose we are not coming back at all. *Please.*'

'But you know most of it already.'

'Only in pieces, Grannie; and besides, to think that here we are – here, in the very place!'

'Well,' began the old voice at last, 'I will tell it you all again, if you persist, my dear; but it's a little *more* than seventy-five years ago, for – though you would not believe it of such an old person – I was born in May. My mother, your great-grandmother, was young then, and in very delicate health after my father's death. Her doctor had said she must go on a long sea voyage. And since she was not able to take me with her, I was sent to that little farm-house down there – Green's Farm, as it was called – to spend the months of her absence with my Uncle James and his housekeeper, who was called Miss Jemima.'

'Miss Jemima!' cried the little girl, stooping over suddenly with a burst of laughter. 'It *is* a queer name, you know, Grannie.'

'It is,' said the old lady. 'And it belonged to one to whom it was my duty to show affection, but who never cared much for the little girl she had in her charge. And when people don't care for you, it is sometimes a little difficult, Susan, to care for them. At least *I* found it so. I don't mean that Miss Jemima was unkind to me, only that when she was kind, she seemed to be kind on purpose. And when I had a slice of plum cake, her face always seemed to tell me it was *plum* cake, and that I deserved only plain. My Uncle James knew that his

housekeeper did not think me a pleasant little girl. I was a
shrimp in size, with straight black hair, which she made
me tie tightly back with a piece of velvet ribbon. I had
small dark eyes and very skimpy legs. And though he
himself was kind, and fond of me, he showed his affection only when we were alone together, and not when
she was present. He was ill, too, then, though I did not
know *how* ill. And he lay all day in a long chair with a
check rug over his legs, and Miss Jemima had charge not
only of me, but of the farm.

'*All* the milking, and the ploughing, and the chickens,
and the pigs, Grannie?' asked Susan.

The old lady shut her eyes an instant, pressed her lips
together and said, 'All.'

'The consequence was,' she went on, 'I was rather a
solitary child. Whenever I could, I used to hide myself
away in some corner of the house – and a beautiful house
it is. It's a pity, my dear, I am so old and you so young
and this hill so steep. Otherwise we could go down and –
well, never mind. That row of small lattice windows
which you can see belongs to a narrow corridor; and the
rooms out of it, rambling one into the other, were walled
in just as the builders fancied, when they made the
house three hundred years or more ago. And that was in
the reign of Edward VI.'

'Like the Bluecoat boys,' said Susan, 'though I can't
say I like the yellow stockings, Grannie, not that *mustard*
yellow, you know.'

'Like the Bluecoat boys,' repeated her grandmother.
'Well, as I say, the house was a nest of hiding-places; and
as a child I was small – smaller even than you, Susan. I
would sit with my book; or kneel up on a chair and
watch from a window, lean *out* too sometimes – as if by
so doing I might be able to see my mother in India. And
whenever the weather was fine, and sometimes when it
was not, I would creep out of the house and run away
down that shaggy lane to the little wood down there.
There is a brook in it (though you can't see that) which

brawls continuously all day long and all the night too. And sometimes I would climb up this very hill. And sometimes I would creep across the field to that little church.

'It was there I most easily forgot myself and even my little scrapes and troubles – with the leaves and the birds, and the blue sky and the clouds overhead; or watching a snail, or picking kingcups and cowslips, or staring into the stream at the fish. You see I was rather a doleful little creature: first because I was usually alone; next because my Uncle James was ill and so could not be happy; and last because I was made to feel more homesick than ever by the cold glances and cold tongue of Miss Jemima.'

'Miss Jemima!' echoed Susan, burying her face in her amusement an instant in her hands.

'Miss Jemima,' repeated the old voice solemnly. 'But I was not only dismal and doleful. Far worse: I made little attempt to be anything else, and began to be fretful too. There was no company of my own age, for, as you see, the village is a mile or two off – over there where the sun is lighting the trees up. And I was not allowed to play with the village children. The only company I had was a fat little boy of two, belonging to one of the farm-hands. And he was so backward a baby that even at that age he could scarcely say as many words.'

'I began to talk at one,' said Susan.

'Yes, my dear,' said her grannie, 'and you are likely, it seems, to go on talking the clock round.'

'Grannie, dear,' said Susan, 'I simply *love* this story – until – *you* know.'

'Well, of all the places strictly forbidden me to play in,' continued the old lady, 'that peaceful little churchyard came first. My "aunt", as I say, thought me a fantastic silly-notioned little girl, and she didn't approve of my picking flowers that grow among tombstones. Indeed, I am not now quite sure myself if such flowers belong to the living at all. Still, once or twice in the summer the old sexton – Mr Fletcher he was called, and a very

57

grumpy old man he was – used to come with his scythe and mow the lush grasses down. And you could scarcely breathe for the sweet smell of them. It seemed a waste to see them lying in swathes, butterflies hovering above them, fading in the sun. There never were such butter-cups and dandelion-clocks and meadow-sweet as grew beneath those old grey walls. I was happy there; and coming and going, I would say a prayer for my mother. But you will please understand, Susan, that I was being disobedient; that I had no business to be there at all at any time. And perhaps if I had never gone, I should never have known that there was somebody else in the church-yard.'

'Ah! somebody else,' sighed Susan, sitting straight up, her eyes far away.

'It was one evening, rather like this one, but with a mackerel sky. The day before I had been stood in the corner for wearing an orange ribbon in my hair; and then sent to bed for talking to the grandfather's clock. I did it on purpose. And now – *this* evening, I was being scolded because I would not eat blackberry jam with my bread for tea. I was told it was because I had been spoilt, and was a little town child who did not know that God had made the wild fruits for human use, and who thought that the only things fit to eat grew in gardens.

'Really and truly I disliked the blackberry jam because of the pips, and I had a hollow tooth. But I told my "aunt" that my mother didn't like blackberry jam either, which made her still more angry.

' "Do you really think, James," she said to my uncle, "we should allow the child to grow up a dainty little minx like that? Now, see here, Miss, you will just stay there until you have eaten up the whole of that slice on your plate."

' "Well, then, Miss Jemima," I said pertly, "I shall stay here till I am eighty."

' "Hold your tongue," she cried out at me, her eyes blazing.

' "I can't bear the horrid—" I began again, and at that she gave me such a slap on my cheek that I overbalanced, and fell out of my chair. She lifted me up from the floor with a shake, set me in my chair again, and pushed it against the table till the edge was cutting into my legs. "And now," she said, "sit there till you are eighty!"

'A look I had never seen before came into my uncle's face; his hands were trembling. Without another word to me, Miss Jemima helped him rise from his chair, and I was left alone.

'Never before had I been beaten like that. And I was at least as much frightened as I was hurt. I listened to the tall clock ticking "Wick-ed child, stubborn child", and my tears splashed slowly down on the odious slice of bread-and-jam on my plate. Then all of a sudden I clenched and shook my ridiculous little fist at the door by which she had gone out, wriggled back my chair, jumped out of it, rushed out of the house, and never stopped to breathe or to look back, until I found myself sitting huddled up under the biggest tomb in the churchyard; crying there, if not my heart out, at least a good deal of my sour little temper.'

'Poor Grannie!' said Susan, squeezing her hand.

'There was not much "poor" about that,' was the reply. 'A pretty sight I must have looked, with my smeared face, green-stained frock and hair dangling. At last my silly sobbing ceased. The sky was flaming with the sunset. It was in June, and the air was cool and mild and sweet. But instead of being penitent and realising what a bad and foolish child I was, I began to be coldly rebellious. I stared at the rosy clouds and vowed to myself I'd give Miss Jemima a fright. I'd rather die than go back to the house that night. And when the thought of my mother came into my mind, I shut it out, saying to myself that she could not have cared how much I loved her, to leave me like this. And yet only a fortnight before a long letter had come to me from India!

'Well, there I sat. A snail came out of his day's hiding-place; little moths were flitting among the grasses; the afternoon's butterflies had all gone to rest. Far away I heard a hooting – and then a step. Cautiously peering up above my tombstone, I saw Maggie, one of the girls that helped on the farm. Her face was burning hot, and she was staring about her round the corner of the little church tower with her saucer-blue eyes. She called to me, but couldn't see me, and at that my mouth opened and I let out, as they say, a shrill yelping squeal. It alarmed even me a little to hear it. She screeched; her steel-tipped boot slipped on the flagstones; in an instant she was gone. And once more I was alone.'

'Ah, but you weren't *really* alone, Grannie,' whispered Susan, '*were* you?'

'That is just what I was going to tell you, my dear. Immediately in front of my face stood a few late dandelion stalks, with their beautiful clocks, grey in the still evening light. And there were a few other gently nodding flowers. As I stared across them, on the other side of the flat gravestone a face appeared. I mean it didn't rise up. It simply came into the air. A very small face, more oval than round, its gold-coloured hair over its wild greenish eyes falling on either side its head in a curious zigzag way – like this, I mean.' The old lady took the hem of her skirt, and three or four times folded it together, then loosened it out.

'You mean, Grannie, as if it had been pleated,' said Susan.

'Yes,' said her grannie. 'And strange and lovely it looked in the reddish light. The face was not smiling, and she did not appear to see me. And yet I knew *she* knew that I was there. And though I did not think she minded my being there, I felt more frightened than I had ever been in my life. My mouth opened; I was clutching tight the grass on either side. And I saw nothing else as I stared into that face.'

'That was the Fairy, Grannie,' said Susan, stooping forward again as if to make her words more impressive.

The old lady glanced fixedly at the two blue eyes bent on her from under the brim of the round straw hat.

'At that moment, my dear, I did not know *what* it was. I was far too frightened to think. Time must have been passing, too, very quickly, for as I stared on, it was already beginning to be gloaming between us, and silent. Yes, much more silent even than this. Then, suddenly, behind me a low, sweet, yet sorrowful voice began to sing from out of the may-bushes, the notes falling like dewdrops in the air. I knew it was a nightingale. And at the very moment that the thought came to me – "That is a nightingale" – the face on the other side of the rough grey stone vanished.

'For a few minutes I sat without moving – not daring to move. And then I ran, straight out of the churchyard by the way I had come as fast as my legs could carry me. I hardly know what I thought, but as soon as I saw the lights in the upper windows of the farm, I ran even faster. Up under the ilexes and round through the farmyard to the back door. It was unlatched. I slipped through, quiet as a mouse, into the kitchen, climbed into the chair, and at once devoured every scrap of that horrid bread-and-jam!

'And still, my dear, I don't believe I was really thinking, only dreadfully afraid, and yet with a kind of triumph in my heart that Miss Jemima should never know anything at all about the face in the churchyard. It was all but dark in the kitchen now, but I still sat on in my chair, even at last lifted the plate, and insolently licked up with my tongue every jammy crumb that was left.

'And then the door opened, and Miss Jemima stood there in the entry with a lighted brass candlestick in her hand. She looked at me, and I at her. "Ah, I see you have thought better of it," she said. "And high time too. You are to go straight to bed."

'If you can imagine, Susan, a cake made almost entirely of plums, and every plum a black thought of hatred, I was like that. But I said never a word. I got down from my chair, marched past her down the flagstone passage, and she followed after. When I came to my uncle's door, I lifted my hand towards the handle. "Straight on, Miss," said the voice behind me. "You have made him too ill and too unhappy to wish you goodnight." Straight on I went, got into bed with all my clothes on, even my dew-wet shoes, and stared at the ceiling till I fell asleep.'

'You know, Grannie,' said Susan, 'it was very curious of you not even to undress at all. Why do you think you did that?'

'My dear,' said her grannie, 'at that moment I had such a hard, hot heart in me, that there was not any room for a why. But you see that little jutting attic window above the trees – it was in the room beyond that and on the other side of the house that I lay. And it's now seventy-five years ago. It may be there was even then a far-away notion in my mind of getting up in the middle of the night and running away. But whether or not, I was awakened by the sun streaming through my lattice window, for my bedroom lay full in the light of the morning.

'I could think of but one thing – my disgrace of the night before, and what I had seen in the churchyard. It was a dream, I thought to myself, shutting my eyes, yet knowing all the time that I did not believe what I was saying. Even when I was told at breakfast that my uncle was not better, I thought little of him, and gobbled down my porridge, with the one wish to be out of the house before I could be forbidden to go. But the only sign of Miss Jemima was my dirty jam-stained plate of the night before, upon which she had put my hunch of breakfast bread. Yet although I was so anxious to get out, for some reason I chose very carefully what I should wear, and changed the piece of ribbon in my hat from blue to green. A rare minx I was.'

'You were, Grannie,' said Susan, clasping her knees. 'And then you went out to the churchyard again?'

'Yes. But all seemed as usual there; except only that a tiny bunch of coral-coloured berries lay on a flat leaf, on the very tombstone where I had hid. Now though I was a minx, my dear, I was also fairly sharp for my age, and after the first gulp of surprise, as I stood there among the nodding buttercups, the sun already having stolen over the grey roof and shining upon the hot tombstones, I noticed a beady dewdrop resting on the leaf, and the leaf of as fresh a green as lettuce in a salad. Looking at this dewdrop I realised at once that the leaf could not have been there very long. Indeed, in a few minutes the sun had drunk up that one round drop of water, for it was some little time before I ventured to touch the berries.

'Then I knew in my heart I was not alone there, and that the green dish had been put there on purpose, just before I had come. The berries were strange yet beautiful to look at, too; of a coral colour edging into rose; I could not guess from what tree they had come. And I don't think it was because I had long ago been warned not to taste any wild fruit – except blackberries! – but because I was uneasy in conscience already, that I did not nibble one then and there.

'It was very quiet in that green place, and on and on I watched, as still as a cat over a mouse's hole, though I myself really and truly was the mouse. And then, all of a sudden, flinging back my green dangling hat-ribbon, I remember, over my shoulder, I said half aloud, in an affected little voice, "Well, it's very kind of you, I am sure," stretched my hand across, plucked one of the berries, and put it into my mouth.

'Hardly had its juice tartened my tongue when a strange thing happened. It was as if a grasshopper was actually sitting in my hair, the noise of that laughter was so close. Besides this, a kind of heat began to creep into my cheek, and it seemed all the colours around me grew so bright that they dazzled my eyes. I closed them. I must have sat there for a while quite unconscious of time, for when I opened them again, the shadow had gone perceptibly back from the stone, and it was getting towards the middle of the morning.

'But there was still that dazzle in my eyes, and everything I looked at – the flowers and the birds, even the moss and lichen on the old stones – seemed as if they were showing me secrets about themselves that I had not known before. It seemed that I could share the very being of the butterfly that was hovering near; and could almost hear not only what the birds were singing but what they were saying.'

'Just like the fairy-tales, Grannie.'

'Yes,' said the little old woman, 'but the difference is that I was not happy about it. The flush was still in my cheek, and I could hear my heart beating under my frock, and I was all of an excitement. But I knew in my inmost self that I ought not to feel like that at all; that I had crept into danger through my wicked temper; that these little unknown coral fruits on the tombstone had been put there for a trap. It was a bait, Susan; and I was the silly fish.'

'Oh, Grannie, a "silly fish"!' said Susan. 'I can see you *might* feel wicked,' she added, with a sage little nod, 'but I don't *exactly* see why.'

'That is just when it's most dangerous, my child,' said her grandmother, sharply closing her mouth, very much indeed like a fish. 'But I must get on with my story, or we shall never get home.

'I sat on, keeping my eyes as far as I could fixed on the invisible place in the air where I had seen the face appear, but nothing came, and gradually the scene lost its radiance, and the birds were chirping as usual again, and the buttercups were the same as ever. No, not the same as ever, because, although it was a burning, sunny day, it seemed now that everything was darker and gloomier than usual on so bright a morning, and I skulked away home, feeling not only a little cold, but dejected and ashamed.

'As I went in through the gate between those two

stone pillars you can just see by the round green tree down there, I looked up at the windows. And a dreadful pang seized me to see that their curtains were all drawn over the glass. And though I didn't know then what that meant, I knew it meant something sorrowful and tragic. Besides, they seemed like shut eyes, refusing to look at me. And when I went in, Miss Jemima told me that my uncle was dead. She told me, too, that he had asked to see me an hour or two before he died. "He said, 'Where is my little Susan?' And where you have been," added Miss Jemima, "is known only to your wicked wilful self." I stared at her, and seemed to shrink until she appeared to be twice as large as usual. I could not speak, because my tongue would not move. And then I rushed past her and up the stairs into a corner between two cupboards, where I used sometimes to hide, and I don't know what I did or thought there; I simply sat on and on, with my hands clenched in my lap, everything I looked at all blurred, and my lips trying to say a prayer that would not come.

'From that day on I became a more and more wretched and miserable little girl, and, as I think now, a wickeder one. It all came of three things. First, because I hated Miss Jemima, and that is just like leaving a steel knife in vinegar, it so frets and wastes the heart. Next because of the thought of my poor uncle speaking of me so gently and kindly when he was at death's door; and my remorse that I could never now ask him to forgive me. And last, because I longed to see again that magical face in the churchyard, and yet knew that it was forbidden.'

'But, Grannie dear, you know,' said Susan, 'I never can see why you should have thought that then.'

'No,' replied the old lady. 'But the point was, you see, that I *did* think it, and I knew in my heart that it would lead to no good. Miss Jemima made me go next day into the room where my uncle lay in his coffin. But try as she might to persuade and compel me, she could not make me open my eyes and look at him. For that disobedience she sent me to my bedroom for the rest of the day.

'When all was still, I crept out across the corridor into another room, and looked out over the trees towards the little church. And I said to myself, as if I were speaking to someone who would hear, "I am coming to you soon, and nobody, *nobody* here shall ever see me again."

'Think of it; a little girl not yet nine, angry with the whole world, and hardly giving a thought to the mother who was longing to see her, and – though I didn't know it then – was very soon to be in England again.

'Well, then came the funeral. I was dressed – I can see myself now, as I stood looking into the looking-glass – in a black frock, trimmed with crape, with a tucker of white frilling round the neck, and an edging of it at the sleeves; my peaked white face and coal-black eyes.

'It was, as you see, but a very little distance to my poor uncle's last resting-place, and in those days they used a long hand-cart on wheels, which the men pushed in front of us, with its flowers. And Miss Jemima and I followed after it across the field. I listened to the prayers as closely as I could. But at last my attention began to wander, and, kneeling there beside Miss Jemima in the church, my hands pressed close to my eyes, for an instant I glanced out and up between my fingers.

'The great eastern window, though you cannot see it from here, is of centuries-old stained glass, crimson, blue, green. But in one corner, just above the narrow ledge of masonry outside, it had been broken many, many years ago by the falling of a branch of a tree, and had been mended with clear *white* glass. And there, looking steadily in and straight across and down at me, was the face and form of the being I had seen beside the tombstone.

'I cannot tell you, Susan, how beautiful that face looked then. Those rich colours of the saints and martyrs surrounding that gold hair – living gold – and the face as pale and beautiful – far more beautiful than anything else I had ever seen in my life before. But even then I saw, too, that into the morning church a cold and shadowy darkness had come, and the stone faces on either side the window, with their set stare, looked actually to be alive. I peeped out between my fingers, hearing not a single word of what the old clergyman was saying, wondering when anyone else would see what I saw, and knowing that the coldly smiling lips were breathing across at me, "Come away, come away!"

'My bones were all cramped, and at last I managed to twist my head a little and glance up at Miss Jemima. The broad face beneath her veil had its eyes shut, and the lips were muttering. She had noticed nothing amiss. And when I looked again, the face at the window had vanished.

'It was a burning hot day – so hot that the flowers beside the grave were already withering before Miss Jemima took me home. We reached the stone porch together, and in its cold shadow she paused, staring down on me through her veil. "You will be staying on here for a while, because I don't know what else to do with you," she said to me. "But you will understand that this is my house now. I am telling your mother how bad a child you are making yourself and perhaps she will ask me to send you away to a school where they will know how to deal with stubborn and ungrateful beings like yourself. But she will be sorry, I think, to hear that it was your wickedness that brought that poor kind body to its grave over there. And now, miss, as the best part of the day is over, you shall have your bread-and-butter and milk in your bedroom, and think over what I have said."'

'I think, Grannie,' cried Susan, suddenly bending herself over her knees, 'that that Miss Jemima was the most dreadful person I have ever heard of.'

'Well, my dear,' said her grandmother, 'I have lived a good many years, and believe it is wiser to try and explain to oneself people as well as things. Do you suppose she would have been as harsh to me if I hadn't hated her? And now she lies there too, and I never had her forgiveness either.'

Susan turned her head away and looked out over the countryside to the north, to where the roving horses had vanished, and where evening was already beginning gradually to settle itself towards night.

'And *did* you think over what Miss Jemima had said, Grannie?' she asked in a low voice.

'The first thing I did was to throw the bread-and-butter out of the window, and while I watched the birds wrangling over it and gobbling it up, I thought of nothing at all. It was cooler in the shade on that side of the house. My head ached after the hot sorrowful walk to the church and back. I came away from the window, took off my black frock, and sat there on the edge of my bed, I remember, in my petticoat, not knowing what to do next. And then, Susan, I made up my mind that I could not bear to be in Miss Jemima's house for a day longer than I needed.

'I was just clever enough to realise that if I wanted to run away I must take care not to be brought back. I grew hot all over, remembering what she had said to me, never thinking how weak and silly I was not to be able to endure patiently what could only be a few more days or weeks before another letter came from my mother. Then I tore a leaf from a book that was in my room – a Prayer Book – and scrawled a few words to my mother, saying how miserable *and* wicked I had been, and how I longed to see her again. It's a curious thing, Susan, but I was pitying myself while I wrote those words, and thinking how grieved my mother would be when she read them, and how well Miss Jemima would deserve whatever my mother said to her. But I didn't utter a word in the letter about where I was going.'

'You didn't really *know* where you were going, Grannie,' whispered Susan, edging a little nearer. 'Did you? Not *then*, I mean?'

'No, but I had a faint notion whom I was going *to*; for somehow, from old fairy tales I had got to believe that human children could be taken away to quite a different

world from this – a country of enchantment. And I remembered having read, too, about two children that had
come back from there, and had forgotten their own
English.'

'I know two poems about it,' said Susan. 'One about
"True Thomas" – "Thomas the Rhymer", you know,
Grannie, who stayed with the Queen of Elfland for seven
whole years, and another about . . . I do wonder— But
please, *please*, go on.'

'Well, I hid my little letter in a cranny in the wainscot,
after sewing a piece of cotton to it so that I might pull it
out again when I wanted it. The next morning, I got up
early, and slipping on my clothes, tiptoed out of the
house before breakfast, and made my way to the church.
I thought deceitfully that Miss Jemima would be sure to
find out that I had gone, and that if for a morning or two
she discovered me quietly sitting in the churchyard she
would not suppose at another time, perhaps, that I was
not safely there again. Plots, Susan, are tangled things,
and are likely to entangle the maker of them too.

'The old man who took care of the church, Mr Fletcher,
to save himself the trouble of carrying the key of the
door, used to hide it under a large stone beneath the
belfry tower. I had watched him put it there. It was a
fresh sparkling day, I remember, with one or two thin
silver clouds high in the sky – angels, I used to call them –
and I forgot for the moment in the brightness of it all my
troubles, as I frisked along past the dewy hedges.

'My first thought was to make quite, quite sure about
the strange being in the churchyard, my next to plan a
way of escape. I gathered a bunch of daisies, and having
come to the belfry door, I somehow managed to open it
with the key which I fetched out from beneath its stone,
and crept into the still, empty coolness. I had come to
the conclusion too, Susan, young though I was, that if
the elf or fairy or whatever she might be actually came
into the church to me, it would be a proof there was no

harm in her company, though I knew in my heart that I was in some mysterious danger.

'There are a few old oak pews in the little church, with heads carved upon them, and one or two have side seats that draw out from beneath into the aisle. On one of these I sat down, so that while I could be intent on my daisy-chain – just to show I had something to do there – I could see out of the corner of my eye the open door by which I had come in. And I hadn't very long to wait.

'In the midst of the faint singing of the wild birds, out of the light that lay beyond the stone church wall I spied her come stealing. My heart almost stopped beating, nor did I turn my head one inch, so that my eyes soon ached because they were almost asquint with watching. If you can imagine a figure – even now I cannot tell you how tall she was – that seems to be made of the light of rainbows, and yet with every feature in its flaxen-framed face as clearly marked as a cherub's cut in stone; and if you can imagine a voice coming to you, close into your ear, without your being able to say exactly where it is coming *from* – *that* was what I saw and heard beneath that grey roof down there on that distant morning, seventy-five years ago. The longer I watched her out of the corner of my eye, the more certain I became that she was using every device she knew to attract my attention, even that she was impatient at my stupidity, and yet that she could not or that she dared not cross the threshold. And so I sat and watched her, fumbling on the while with my limpening daisy-stalks. Many strange minutes must have passed like this.

'At last, however, having fancied I heard a footfall, I was surprised out of myself, and suddenly twisted my head. She too had heard, and was standing stiller than a shadow on snow, gazing in at me. I suppose thoughts reveal themselves in the face more swiftly than one imagines. I was partly afraid, partly longing to approach closer. I wished her to realise that I longed for her company, but that danger was near, for I was well aware whose step it was I had heard. And, as I looked at her, there came a sharpness into her face, a cold inhuman look – not of fear, but almost of hatred – and she was gone. More intent than ever, I stooped over my daisies. And in the hush there was a faint sound as of an intensely distant whistle.

'Then a shadow fell across the porch, and there was Miss Jemima. It's a strange thing. Susan, but Miss Jemima also did not enter the church. She called to me from where she stood, in almost a honeyed voice: "Breakfast is ready, Susan."'

'I can imagine *exactly* how she said that, Grannie,' said the little girl, 'because my name's Susan, too.'

'Yes, my dear,' said the old lady, squeezing her hand. 'It was passed on to you from me by your dear mother just because it was mine. And I hope you will always be the Susan I have *now*.' . . . From near at hand upon the hill a skylark suddenly took its flight into the evening blue. The old lady listened a moment before going on with her story.

'Well,' she began again, 'I gathered up my apron and walked towards Miss Jemima down the aisle. Suddenly there came a slight rumbling noise, which I could not understand. Then instantly there followed a crash. And at Miss Jemima's very feet, in the sunlight, I saw lying a piece of stone about the size of a small plum pudding. Miss Jemima gave a faint scream. Her cheek, already pale, went white; and she stared from me to the stone and back again, as I approached her.

'"You were talking in there to someone – in God's church," she whispered harshly, stooping towards me. "To whom?"

'I shook my head, and stood trembling and gazing at the stone.

'"Look into my face, you wicked child," she whispered. "Who were you talking to in there?"

'I looked up at last. "It's empty," I said.

'"There's a lying look in your eyes!" cried Miss

Jemima. "And *you* are the child that goes into a sacred place to weave daisy-chains! Turn your face away from me. Do you hear me, miss? Miserable little *sorceress* that you are!"

'The word seemed to flame up in my mind as if it had been written in fire on smoke; and still I stared at the stone. I felt but did not see Miss Jemima steadily turn her head and look around her.

' "A few inches," she added in a low voice, "and you would have killed me."

' "Me!" I cried angrily. "What has it to do with *me*, Miss Jemima?"

' "Ah!" said she. "We shall know a little more about that when you have told me what company you find here where your poor uncle might hope to be at rest."

'It's a dreadful thing to confess, Susan, but up to that moment, though I had again and again cried by myself at memory of him, though tears were always in my heart for him, I hadn't thought of my uncle that morning.

' "And perhaps," added Miss Jemima, "bread and water and solitude for a day or two will help to loosen your tongue."

'I followed her without another word across the fields, and in a few minutes was alone once more in my bedroom with a stale crust and a glass of water to keep me company.

'I should think that if my angry tears had run into the water that morning they would have actually made it taste salt. But I cried so that not even a mouse could have heard me. Every other thought was now out of my mind – for I dared not even talk to myself about the stone – but that of getting away from the house for ever. One thing I could not forget, however. And that was the word "sorceress". It terrified me far more than I can tell you. I knew in my young mind that Miss Jemima was treating me wickedly, however wicked *I* had been, and I knew too, in fear and horror, that the stone might not have fallen by accident. I had seen the look on the Fairy's face and . . .' The old lady suddenly broke off her story at this point, and looked about her in alarm. 'My dear, we must go at once; the dew is beginning to fall, and the air is already colder.'

'Oh, Grannie,' said the child, 'how I wish we might stay – a little, *little* longer!'

'Well, my dear, so do I. For I am old, and I shall never see this place again. It brings many memories back. Who knows what might have happened if—'

'But, Grannie,' interrupted the child hastily, picking up the umbrella from the grass. 'Please tell me the rest of the story straight, straight, straight on as we go back.' It seemed to Susan, so rapt was her grandmother's face at that moment, and so absent her eyes – that she could not have heard her. Those small aged eyes were once more looking carefully down on the scene below. For an instant they shut as if the old lady had thought so to remember it more completely. And then the two of them began slowly to climb the hill, and the story proceeded.

'No one disturbed me during that long morning,' continued the quiet voice, 'but in the afternoon the door was unlocked, and Miss Jemima opened it to show in a clergyman, Mr Wilmot, who conducted the service in the church every other Sunday. I won't tell you all he said to me. He was a kind and gentle old man, but he didn't so much as think it possible there was any being or thing in the churchyard but its birds, its tombstones, and now and then a straying animal. He only smiled about all that, nor did he ask me Miss Jemima's question.

'He took my hand in his great bony one and begged me to be a good little girl. And I see his smiling face as he asked it. "Not only for your mother's sake," he said, "but for *goodness*' sake."'

'"I am sure, my dear," he went on, "Miss Jemima *means* to be kind, and all that *we* have to do is to mean to be good."

'I gulped down the lump in my throat and said, "But don't you think *sorceress* is a very wicked word?"

'He stood up, holding both my hands in his. "But my poor little lamb," he cried, "Miss Jemima is no more a sorceress than I am a Double Dutchman!" And with that he stooped, kissed the top of my head, and went out of the room.

'In a minute or two his footsteps returned. He opened the door an inch and peeped in. "Why, we are better already!" He smiled at me over his spectacles. Then he came in, carrying a plate with a slice of bread-and-jam upon it, and a mug of milk. "There," he said, "there's no sorcery in that, is there? And now you will be an obedient and gentle child, and think how happy your mother will be to see you?"'

'I think,' said Susan stoutly, 'that that Mr Wilmot is one of the kindest men I ever knew.'

Her grandmother looked down on her with a peculiar smile on her face. 'He was so kind, Susan, that I never mentioned to him that the blackberry-jam on the bread was not a great favourite of mine! A moment after the sound of his footsteps had died away I heard the key once more in the lock. And what did I say to myself when he was gone? I looked forlornly at the plate, then out of the window, and I believe, Susan, that I did what they sometimes describe in the story-books – I wrung my hands a little, repeating to myself, "*He doesn't understand. No! No! he doesn't understand.*"

'In an hour or two, Miss Jemima herself opened the door and looked in. She surveyed me where I sat, and then her glance fell on the untouched slice of bread-and-jam.

' "Ah," said she, "a good man like Mr Wilmot cannot realise the hardness of a stubborn heart. I don't want to be unkind to you, Susan, but I have a duty to perform to your mother and to your poor dead uncle. You shall not leave this room until you apologise to me for your insolence of this morning, and until you tell me whom you were speaking to in the church."

'The lie that came into my mind – "But I was not

speaking to anyone, Miss Jemima" – faded away on my tongue. And I simply looked at her in silence.

'"You have a brazen face, Susan," said she, "and if you grow up as you are now, you will be a very wicked woman."'

'I think,' said Susan, 'that was a perfectly *dreadful* thing to say, Grannie.'

'Times change, my dear,' said the old lady. 'And now – well, it is fortunate there is very little more to tell. For this hill has taken nearly all the breath out of my body!'

The two of them stood now on the crest of the hill. The light was beginning to die away in the sky, and the mists to grow milkier in the hollows of the flat country that lay around and beneath them. Far, far away, facing them across the world, a reddish-coloured moon was rising. From far beneath them a dog barked – it might be from dead Miss Jemima's farmyard. The little church surrounded by its low wall seemed to have gathered in closer to its scattered stones.

'Yes, Grannie, dear?' breathed Susan, slipping her hand into the cotton-gloved one that hung near. 'What then?'

'Then,' replied her grandmother, 'the door was locked again. Anger and hatred filled that silly little body sitting in the bedroom, and towards evening I fell asleep. And I must have dreamed a terrifying dream, though when I awoke I could not remember my dream – only its horror. I was terrified at it in that solitude, and I knew by the darkening at the window that it must be at least nine or ten o'clock. Night was coming, then. I could scarcely breathe at the thought. Another mug of milk had been put beside the plate; but I could not even persuade myself to drink any of it.

'Then in a while I heard Miss Jemima's footsteps pass my room. She made no pause there, and presently after I knew that she had gone to bed, having not even troubled to look in on her wretched little prisoner. The hardness of that decided me.

'I waited until it seemed certain she was asleep. Then

I tiptoed over to the door, and with both hands softly twisted the handle. It was still locked. Then I went to the window and discovered, as if the fairy creature herself had magicked it there, that a large hay-wain half full of hay, its shafts high in the air, had been left drawn up within a few feet of my window. It looked dangerous, but it was not actually a very difficult jump even for a child of my age; and I believe I should have attempted it if there had been no cart at all. My one wild thought was to run away. Anywhere – so long as there was no chance of Miss Jemima's ever finding me again. Could you ever have dreamed of such a little silly, Susan?

'But even in that excited foolish moment I had sense enough left – before I jumped out of the window – to take a warm woollen jacket out of my chest-of-drawers, and to wrap my money-box up in a scarf so that it should not jangle too much. I pulled my letter up from its cranny in the wainscot by its thread, and put it on the pink dressing-table. And at that moment, in the half dark I saw my face in the looking-glass. I should hardly have recognised it. It looked nearly as old, Susan, as I do now.'

'Yes, dear Grannie,' said Susan.

'Then I jumped – without the slightest harm to myself. I scrambled down into the yard and, keeping close to the house, crept past the kennel, the old sheep-dog merely shaking his chain with his thumping tail a little as I passed. And then, as soon as I was beyond the tall stone gate-posts, I ran off through the farm-yard, past the barns, and along the cart-track as fast as I could.'

'But *not*,' cried Susan almost with a shout in the still air, '*not* to the churchyard, Grannie. I think that was the most wonderful thing of all.'

'Not so very wonderful, my dear, if you remember that I was now intensely afraid of the fairy, after seeing that look of evil and hatred in her face when Miss Jemima was approaching the church. Something in me, as you know, had never ceased to counsel me, *Don't be deceived by her. She means you no good.* I cannot explain that;

but so it was. Yet all the time I had been longing to follow wherever she might lead. Why she should wish to carry off a human child I don't know, but that she really wanted me I soon discovered for certain.

'If you follow the tip of my umbrella, you will now just be able to see, Susan, that great meadow sloping upwards beyond the farm. But I don't think even your sharp eyes will detect the circle of old grey stones there. They are called the Dancers, and though I was dreadfully frightened of passing them in the darkness, this was the only way to take. Gradually I approached them, my heart beating beneath my ribs like a drum, until I had come near.

'And there, lovelier than ever, shining in that dark as if with a light of her own, and sitting beneath the largest of the Dancers directly in my path, was She. But this time I knew she was not alone. I cannot describe what passed in my heart. I longed to go on, and yet was in anguish at the thought of it. I didn't dare to look at her, and all I could think to do was to pretend not to have seen her at all. How I found the courage I cannot think. Perhaps it was the courage that comes when fear and terror are almost beyond bearing.

'I put my money-box on to the grass; the scarf was already wet with dew. Then, very slowly, I put my black jacket on and buttoned it up. And then, with my eyes turned away, I walked slowly on down the path, between the Dancers, towards the one that is called the Fiddler, in their midst. The night air here was cold and still. But as I approached the stone, it seemed as if the air was full of voices and patterings and sounds of wings and instruments. It terrified and bewildered me; I could think of nothing.

'I just kept saying, "Oh, please, God; oh, please, God!" and walked on. And when at last I came to the stone, the whole world suddenly seemed to turn dark and cold and dead. And then! Apart from the ancient stone, jutting up out of the green turf as it had done for centuries, there was not a sign, not a vestige, Susan, of anything or anybody there!'

'I think I can *just* see the stone, Grannie, but I don't think I could dare to be alone there in the dark, not for anything – anything in the world. . . . I expect it was what you *said* made the Fairy go. And then, Grannie?'

'Then, Susan, my heart seemed to go out of me. I ran on, stumbling blindly for a little way, then lost my balance completely over a tussock of grass or a mole-heap and fell flat on my face. Nettles too! Without any words that I can remember, I lay praying in the grass.

'But even that did not turn me back. I got up at last and ran on more slowly, and without looking behind me, across the field. Its gate leads into a by-road. It was padlocked, and as I mounted to the top my eyes could see just above a slight rise in the ground, for the lane lies beneath a little hill there.

'And coming along the road towards me there were shining the lamps of a carriage. I clambered down and crouched in the hedge-side, and in a few moments the lamps reappeared at the top of the incline and the horse came plod-plodding along down the hill. It was a wonderful summer night, the sky all faint with stars. What would have happened if it had been cold or pouring with rain, I cannot think. But because it was so warm, the air almost like milk, the hood of the carriage was down.

'And as it came wheeling round by the hedge-side, I saw in the filmy starlight who it was who was sitting there. Neither horse nor coachman had seen me. I jumped to my feet and ran after the carriage as fast as my legs could carry me, screaming at the top of my voice, "Mother, Mother!"

'Perhaps the grinding of the wheels in the flinty dust and the thump of the hoofs drowned my calling. But I still held tight to my money-box, and though it was muffled by the scarf in which it was wrapped, at each step it made a dull noise like a birdscare, and this must at last have attracted my mother's attention. She turned

her head, opened her mouth wide at sight of me – I see her now – then instantly jumped up and tugged at the coachman's buttoned coat tails. The carriage came to a standstill. . . .

'And that,' said the old lady, turning away her head for one last glance of the countryside around her, 'that is all, Susan.'

Susan gave a last great sigh. 'I can't think what you must have felt, Grannie,' she said, 'when you were safe in the carriage. And I can't—' But at this point she began to laugh very softly to herself, and suddenly stood still. 'And I can't think either,' she went on, 'what Miss Jemima must have thought when you and *Great*-Grannie knocked at the door. You did tell me once that she opened her bedroom window at the sound of the knocking, and looked out in her nightdress. I expect she was almost as frightened as you had been, amongst those Dancers.'

The two of them were now descending the hill on the side away from the farm and the church. And they could see not only their carriage standing beneath them, but the evening star had also come into view. There could not be a more peaceful scene – the silver birches around them standing motionless under the deep, pale sky, clothed with their little leaves, and the rabbits at play among the gorse and juniper.

'Bless me, Mum,' said the old cabman as he opened the carriage door, 'I was just beginning to think them *fairises* must have runned away with you and the young lady.'

Susan burst completely out laughing. 'Now don't you think, Grannie,' she said, 'that is a very, very, very curious quincidence?'

The Haunted Doll's House

M. R. James

'I suppose you get stuff of that kind through your hands pretty often?' said Mr Dillet, as he pointed with his stick to an object which shall be described when the time comes: and when he said it, he lied in his throat, and knew that he lied. Not once in twenty years – perhaps not once in a lifetime – could Mr Chittenden, skilled as he was in ferreting out the forgotten treasures of half a dozen counties, expect to handle such a specimen. It was collectors' palaver, and Mr Chittenden recognised it as such.

'Stuff of that kind, Mr Dillet! It's a museum piece, that is.'

'Well, I suppose there are museums that'll take anything.'

'I've seen one, not as good as that, years back,' said Mr Chittenden thoughtfully. 'But that's not likely to come into the market: and I'm told they 'ave some fine ones of the period over the water. No, I'm only telling you the truth, Mr Dillet, when I say that if you was to place an unlimited order with me for the very best that could be got – and you know I 'ave facilities for getting to know of such things, and a reputation to maintain – well, all I can say is, I should lead you straight up to that one and say, "I can't do no better for you than that, sir".'

'Hear, hear!' said Mr Dillet, applauding ironically with the end of his stick on the floor of the shop. 'How much are you sticking the innocent American buyer for it, eh?'

'Oh, I shan't be over hard on the buyer, American or

otherwise. You see it stands this way, Mr Dillet – if I knew just a bit more about the pedigree ...'

'Or just a bit less,' Mr Dillet put in.

'Ha, ha! you will have your joke, sir. No, but as I was saying, if I knew just a little more than what I do about the piece – though anyone can see for themselves it's a genuine thing, every last corner of it, and there's not been one of my men allowed to so much as touch it since it came into the shop – there'd be another figure in the price I'm asking.'

'And what's that: five and twenty?'

'Multiply that by three and you've got it, sir. Seventy-five's my price.'

'And fifty's mine,' said Mr Dillet.

The point of agreement was, of course, somewhere between the two, it does not matter exactly where – I think sixty guineas. But half an hour later the object was being packed, and within an hour Mr Dillet had called for it in his car and driven away. Mr Chittenden, holding the cheque in his hand, saw him off from the door with smiles, and returned, still smiling, into the parlour where his wife was making the tea. He stopped at the door.

'It's gone,' he said.

'Thank God for that!' said Mrs Chittenden, putting down the teapot. 'Mr Dillet, was it?'

'Yes it was.'

'Well, I'd sooner it was him than another.'

'Oh, I don't know; he ain't a bad feller, my dear.'

'Maybe not, but in my opinion he'd be none the worse for a bit of a shake up.'

'Well, if that's your opinion, it's my opinion he's putting himself into the way of getting one. Anyhow *we* shan't have no more of it, and that's something to be thankful for.'

And so Mr and Mrs Chittenden sat down to tea.

And what of Mr Dillet and of his new acquisition? What it was, the title of this story will have told you. What it was like, I shall have to indicate as well as I can.

There was only just room enough for it in the car, and Mr Dillet had to sit with the driver: he had also to go slow, for though the rooms of the Doll's House had all been stuffed carefully with soft cotton-wool, jolting was to be avoided, in view of the immense number of small objects which thronged them; and the ten-mile drive was an anxious time for him, in spite of all the precautions he insisted upon. At last his front door was reached, and Collins, the butler, came out.

'Look here, Collins, you must help me with this thing – it's a delicate job. We must get it out upright, see? It's full of little things that mustn't be displaced more than we can help. Let's see, where shall we have it?' (After a pause for consideration.) 'Really, I think I shall have to put it in my own room, to begin with at any rate. On the big table – that's it.'

It was conveyed – with much talking – to Mr Dillet's spacious room on the first floor, looking out on the drive. The sheeting was unwound from it, and the front thrown open, and for the next hour or two Mr Dillet was fully occupied in extracting the padding and setting in order the contents of the rooms.

When this thoroughly congenial task was finished, I must say that it would have been difficult to find a more perfect and attractive specimen of a Doll's House in Strawberry Hill Gothic than that which now stood on Mr Dillet's large kneehole table, lighted up by the evening sun which came slanting through three tall sash-windows.

It was quite six feet long, including the Chapel or Oratory which flanked the front on the left as you faced it, and the stable on the right. The main block of the house was, as I have said, in the Gothic manner: that is to say, the windows had pointed arches and were surmounted by what are called ogival hoods, with crockets and finials such as we see on the canopies of tombs built into church walls. At the angles were absurd turrets covered with arched panels. The Chapel had pinnacles and buttresses, and a bell in the turret and coloured glass in the windows. When the front of the house was open you saw four large rooms, bedroom, dining-room, drawing-room and kitchen, each with its appropriate furniture in a very complete state.

The stable on the right was in two storeys, with its proper complement of horses, coaches and grooms, and with its clock and Gothic cupola for the clock bell.

Pages, of course, might be written on the outfit of the mansion – how many frying-pans, how many gilt chairs, what pictures, carpets, chandeliers, four-posters, table linen, glass, crockery and plate it possessed; but all this must be left to the imagination. I will only say that the base or plinth on which the house stood (for it was fitted with one of some depth which allowed of a flight of steps to the front door and a terrace, partly balustraded) contained a shallow drawer or drawers in which were neatly stored sets of embroidered curtains, changes of raiment for the inmates, and, in short, all the materials for an infinite series of variations and refittings of the most absorbing and delightful kind.

'Quintessence of Horace Walpole, that's what it is: he must have had something to do with the making of it.' Such was Mr Dillet's murmured reflection as he knelt before it in a reverent ecstasy. Simply wonderful! this is my day and no mistake. Five hundred pound coming in this morning for that cabinet which I never cared about, and now this tumbling into my hands for a tenth, at the very most, of what it would fetch in town. Well, well! It almost makes one afraid something'll happen to counter it. Let's have a look at the population, anyhow.'

Accordingly, he set them before him in a row. Again, here is an opportunity, which some would snatch at, of making an inventory of costume: I am incapable of it.

There were a gentleman and lady, in blue satin and brocade respectively. There were two children, a boy and a girl. There was a cook, a nurse, a footman, and there were the stable servants, two postilions, a coachman, two grooms.

'Anyone else? Yes, possibly.'

The curtains of the four-poster in the bedroom were closely drawn round all four sides of it, and he put his finger in between them and felt in the bed. He drew the finger back hastily, for it almost seemed to him as if something had – not stirred, perhaps, but yielded – in an odd live way as he pressed it. Then he put back the curtains, which ran on rods in the proper manner, and extracted from the bed a white-haired old gentleman in a long linen night-dress and cap, and laid him down by the rest. The tale was complete.

Dinner-time was now near, so Mr Dillet spent but five minutes in putting the lady and the children into the drawing-room, the gentleman into the dining-room, the servants into the kitchen and stables, and the old man back into his bed. He retired into his dressing-room next door, and we see and hear no more of him until something like eleven o'clock at night.

His whim was to sleep surrounded by some of the gems of his collection. The big room in which we have seen him contained his bed: bath, wardrobe, and all the appliances of dressing were in a commodious room adjoining: but his four-poster, which itself was a valued treasure, stood in the large room where he sometimes wrote, and often sat, and even received visitors.

Tonight he repaired to it in a highly complacent frame of mind.

There was no striking clock within earshot – none on the staircase, none in the stable, none in the distant church tower. Yet it is indubitable that Mr Dillet was startled out of a very pleasant slumber by a bell tolling one.

He was so much startled that he did not merely lie breathless with wide-open eyes, but actually sat up in his bed.

He never asked himself, till the morning hours how it was that, though there was no light at all in the room, the

Doll's House on the kneehole table stood out with complete clearness. But it was so. The effect was that of a bright harvest moon shining full on the front of a big white stone mansion – a quarter of a mile away it might be, and yet every detail was photographically sharp. There were trees about it, too – trees rising behind the chapel and the house. He seemed to be conscious of the scent of a cool still September night. He thought he could hear an occasional stamp and clink from the stables, as of horses stirring. And with another shock he realised that, above the house, he was looking, not at the wall of his room with its pictures, but into the profound blue of a night sky.

There were lights, more than one, in the windows, and he quickly saw that this was no four-roomed house with a movable front, but one of many rooms, and staircases – a real house, but seen as if through the wrong end of a telescope. 'You mean to show me something,' he muttered to himself and he gazed earnestly on the lighted windows. They would in real life have been shuttered or curtained, no doubt, he thought; but, as it was, there was nothing to intercept his view of what was being transacted inside the rooms.

Two rooms were lighted – one on the ground floor to the right of the door, one upstairs, on the left – the first brightly enough, the other rather dimly. The lower room was the dining-room : a table was laid, but the meal was over, and only wine and glasses were left on the table. The man of the blue satin and the woman of the brocade were alone in the room, and they were talking very earnestly, seated close together at the table, their elbows on it : every now and again stopping to listen, as it seemed. Once *he* rose, came to the window and opened it and put his head out and his hand to his ear. There was a lighted taper in a silver candlestick on a sideboard. When the man left the window he seemed to leave the room also; and the lady, taper in hand, remained standing and listening. The expression on her face was that of one striving her utmost to keep down a fear that threatened to master her – and succeeding. It was a hateful face, too; broad, flat and sly. Now the man came back and she took some small thing from him and hurried out of the room. He, too, disappeared, but only for a moment or two. The front door slowly opened and he stepped out and stood on the top of the perron, looking this way and that; then turned towards the upper window that was lighted, and shook his fist.

It was time to look at that upper window. Through it was seen a four-post bed: a nurse or other servant in an arm-chair, evidently sound asleep; in the bed an old man lying: awake, and, one would say, anxious, from the way in which he shifted about and moved his fingers, beating tunes on the coverlet. Beyond the bed a door opened. Light was seen on the ceiling, and the lady came in: she set down her candle on a table, came to the fireside and roused the nurse. In her hand she had an old-fashioned wine bottle, ready uncorked. The nurse took it, poured some of the contents into a little silver saucepan, added some spice and sugar from casters on the table, and set it to warm on the fire. Meanwhile the old man in the bed beckoned feebly to the lady, who came to him, smiling, took his wrist as if to feel his pulse, and bit her lip as if in consternation. He looked at her anxiously, and then pointed to the window, and spoke. She nodded, and did as the man below had done; opened the casement and listened – perhaps rather ostentatiously: then drew in her head and shook it, looking at the old man, who seemed to sigh.

By this time the posset on the fire was steaming, and the nurse poured it into a small two-handled silver bowl and brought it to the bedside. The old man seemed disinclined for it, and was waving it away, but the lady and the nurse together bent over him and evidently pressed it upon him. He must have yielded, for they supported him into a sitting position, and put it to his lips. He drank most of it, in several draughts, and they laid him down.

The lady left the room, smiling good night to him, and took the bowl, the bottle and the silver saucepan with her. The nurse returned to the chair, and there was an interval of complete quiet.

Suddenly the old man started up in his bed – and he must have uttered some cry, for the nurse started out of her chair and made but one step of it to the bedside. He was a sad and terrible sight – flushed in the face, almost to blackness, the eyes glaring whitely, both hands clutching at his heart, foam at his lips.

For a moment the nurse left him, ran to the door, flung it wide open, and, one supposes, screamed aloud for help, then darted back to the bed and seemed to try feverishly to soothe him – to lay him down – anything. But as the lady, her husband, and several servants, rushed into the room with horrified faces, the old man collapsed under the nurse's hands and lay back, and the features, contorted with agony and rage, relaxed slowly into calm.

A few moments later, lights showed out to the left of the house, and a coach with flambeaux drove up to the door. A white-wigged man in black got nimbly out and ran up the steps, carrying a small leather trunk-shaped box. He was met in the doorway by the man and his wife, she with her handkerchief clutched between her hands, he with a tragic face, but retaining his self-control. They led the newcomer into the dining-room, where he set his box of papers on the table, and, turning to them, listened with a face of consternation at what they had to tell. He nodded his head again and again, threw out his hands slightly, declined, it seemed, offers of refreshment and lodging for the night, and within a few minutes came slowly down the steps, entering the coach and driving off the way he had come. As the man in blue watched him from the top of the steps, a smile not pleasant to see stole slowly over his fat white face. Darkness fell over the whole scene as the lights of the coach disappeared.

But Mr Dillet remained sitting up in the bed : he had rightly guessed that there would be a sequel. The house front glimmered out again before long. But now there was a difference. The lights were in other windows, one at the top of the house, the other illuminating the range of coloured windows of the chapel. How he saw through these is not quite obvious, but he did. The interior was as carefully furnished as the rest of the establishment, with its minute red cushions on the desks, its Gothic stall-canopies, and its western gallery and pinnacled organ with gold pipes. On the centre of the black and white pavement was a bier: four tall candles burned at the corners. On the bier was a coffin covered with a pall of black velvet.

As he looked the folds of the pall stirred. It seemed to rise at one end: it slid downwards: it fell away, exposing the black coffin with its silver handles and name-plate. One of the tall candlesticks swayed and toppled over. Ask no more, but turn, as Mr Dillet hastily did, and look in at the lighted window at the top of the house, where a boy and girl lay in two truckle-beds, and a four-poster for the nurse rose above them. The nurse was not visible for the moment; but the father and mother were there, dressed now in mourning, but with very little sign of mourning in their demeanour. Indeed, they were laughing and talking with a good deal of animation, sometimes to each other, and sometimes throwing a re-mark to one or other of the children, and again laughing at the answers. Then the father was seen to go on tiptoe out of the room, taking with him as he went a white garment that hung on a peg near the door. He shut the door after him. A minute or two later it was slowly opened again, and a muffled head poked round it. A bent form of sinister shape stepped across to the truckle-beds, and suddenly stopped, threw up its arms and revealed, of course, the father, laughing. The children were in agonies of terror, the boy with the bedclothes over his head, the girl throwing herself out of bed into her mother's arms. Attempts at consolation followed – the parents took the children on their laps, patted them, picked up the white gown and showed there was no harm in it, and so forth; and at last putting the children back into bed, left the room with encouraging waves of the hand. As they left it, the nurse came in, and soon the light died down.

Still Mr Dillet watched immovable.

A new sort of light – not of lamp or candle – a pale ugly light, began to dawn around the door-case at the back of the room. The door was opening again. The seer does not like to dwell upon what he saw entering the room : he says it might be described as a frog – the size of a man – but it had scanty white hair about its head. It was busy about the truckle-beds, but not for long. The sound of cries – faint, as if coming out of a vast distance – but, even so, infinitely appalling, reached the ear.

There were signs of a hideous commotion all over the house : lights moved along and up, and doors opened and shut, and running figures passed within the windows. The clock in the stable turret tolled one, and darkness fell again.

It was only dispelled once more, to show the house front. At the bottom of the steps dark figures were drawn up in two lines, holding flaming torches. More dark figures came down the steps, bearing first one, then another small coffin. And the lines of torch-bearers with the coffins between them moved silently onward to the left.

The hours of night passed on – never so slowly, Mr Dillet thought. Gradually he sank down from sitting to lying in his bed – but he did not close an eye : and early next morning he sent for the doctor.

The doctor found him in a disquieting state of nerves, and recommended sea-air. To a quiet place on the East Coast he accordingly repaired by easy stages in his car.

One of the first people he met on the sea front was Mr Chittenden, who, it appeared, had likewise been advised to take his wife away for a bit of a change.

Mr Chittenden looked somewhat askance upon him when they met : and not without cause.

'Well, I don't wonder at you being a bit upset, Mr Dillet. What? yes, well, I might say 'orrible upset, to be sure, seeing what me and my poor wife went through ourselves. But I put it to you, Mr Dillet, one of two things: was I going to scrap a lovely piece like that on the one 'and, or was I going to tell customers: "I'm selling you a regular picture-palace-dramar in reel life of the olden time, billed to perform regular at one o'clock a.m."? Why, what would you 'ave said yourself? And next thing you know, two Justices of the Peace in the back parlour, and pore Mr and Mrs Chittenden off in a spring cart to the County Asylum and everyone in the street saying, "Ah, I thought it 'ud come to that. Look at the way the man drank!" – and me next door, or next door but one, to a total abstainer, as you know. Well, there was my position. What? Me 'ave it back in the shop? Well, what do *you* think? No, but I'll tell you what I will do. You shall have your money back, bar the ten pound I paid for it, and you make what you can.'

Later in the day, in what is offensively called the 'smoke-room' of the hotel, a murmured conversation between the two went on for some time.

'How much do you really know about that thing, and where it came from?'

'Honest, Mr Dillet, I don't know the 'ouse. Of course it came out of the lumber room of a country 'ouse – that anyone could guess. But I'll go as far as say this, that I believe it's not a hundred miles from this place. Which direction and how far I've no notion. I'm only judging by guess-work. The man as I actually paid the cheque to ain't one of my regular men, and I've lost sight of him; but I 'ave the idea that this part of the country was his beat, and that's every word I can tell you. But now, Mr Dillet, there's one thing that rather physicks me. That old chap – I suppose you saw him drive up to the door – I thought so: now, would he have been the medical man, do you take it? My wife would have it so, but I stuck to it that he was the lawyer, because he had papers with him, and one he took out was folded up.'

'I agree,' said Mr Dillet. 'Thinking it over, I came to the conclusion that was the old man's will, ready to be signed.'

'Just what I thought,' said Mr Chittenden, 'and I took it that will would have cut out the young people, eh? Well, well! It's been a lesson to me, I know that. I shan't buy no more doll's houses, nor waste more money on the pictures – and as to this business of poisonin' grandpa, well, if I know myself I never 'ad much of a turn for that. Live and let live: that's bin my motto throughout life, and I ain't found it a bad one.'

Filled with these elevated sentiments, Mr Chittenden retired to his lodgings. Mr Dillet next day repaired to the Local Institute, where he hoped to find some clue to the riddle that absorbed him. He gazed in despair at a long file of the Canterbury and York Society's publications of the Parish Registers of the district. No print resembling the house of his nightmare was among those that hung on the staircase and in the passages. Disconsolate, he found himself at last in a derelict room, staring at a dusty model of a church in a dusty glass case: Model of St Stephen's Church, Coxham. Presented by J. Mere-wether, Esq. of Ilbridge House, 1877. The work of his ancestor James Merewether, d. 1786. There was something in the fashion of it that reminded him dimly of his horror. He retraced his steps to a wall map he had noticed, and made out that Ilbridge House was in Cox-ham parish. Coxham was, as it happened, one of the parishes of which he had retained the name when he glanced over a file of printed registers, and it was not long before he found in them the record of the burial of Roger Milford, aged 76 on the 11th of September, 1757, and of Roger and Elizabeth Merewether, aged 9 and 7, on the 19th of the same month. It seemed worth while to follow up this clue, frail as it was; and in the afternoon he drove out to Coxham. The east end of the north aisle of the church is a Milford chapel, and on its north wall are tablets to the same persons; Roger, the elder, it seems, was distinguished by all the qualities which adorn 'the Father, the Magistrate and the Man'; the memorial was erected by his attached daughter Elizabeth, 'who did not long survive the loss of a parent ever solicitous for her wefare, and of two amiable children.' The last sentence was plainly an addition to the original inscription.

A yet later slab told of James Merewether, husband of Elizabeth, 'who in the dawn of life practised, not without success, those arts which, had he continued their exercise, might in the opinion of the most competent judges have earned for him the name of the British Vitruvius : but who, overwhelmed by the visitation which deprived him of an affectionate partner and a blooming offspring, passed his Prime and Age in a secluded yet elegant Retirement : his grateful Nephew and Heir indulges a pious sorrow by this too brief recital of his excellences.'

The children were more simply commemorated. Both died on the night of the 12th September.

Mr Dillet felt sure that in Ilbridge House he had found the scene of his drama. In some old sketch-book, possibly in some old print, he may yet find convincing evidence that he is right. But the Ilbridge House of today is not that which he sought; it is an Elizabethan erection of the forties, in red brick with stone quoins and dressings. A quarter of a mile from it, in a low part of the park, backed by ancient, staghorned, ivy-strangled trees and thick undergrowth, are marks of a terraced platform overgrown with rough grass. A few stone balusters lie here and there, and a heap or two, covered with nettles and ivy, of wrought stones with badly-carved crockets. This, someone told Mr Dillet, was the site of an older house.

As he drove out of the village, the hall clock struck four, and Mr Dillet started up and clapped his hands to his ears. It was not the first time he had heard that bell.

Awaiting an offer from the other side of the Atlantic, the Doll's House still reposes, carefully sheeted, in a loft

over Mr Dillet's stables, whither Collins conveyed it on the day when Mr Dillet started for the sea coast.

The Devil's Cure

Barbara Softly

'If God cannot help us, then the Devil must.'

'What are you saying, Kit?' I asked, turning in horror to my brother.

He was leaning on the gate which led from our farm-yard into the hay-field – the hay-field whose crop this summer had promised to be the best for years – which was now lying trampled by a small troop of Parliamen-tary horsemen who, losing the lane in the dark the previous evening, had chosen our meadow as the shortest route to the village.

'Because the grass is past man's power of saving, and God's too, you think the Devil can make it stand up again and be cut as usual?' 'You're wicked, Kit,' I protested. 'What do you expect of Roundhead soldiers?'

'It hardly matters whose men they are,' he went on bitterly. 'In the spring it was Royalists over at Westridge Farm taking Mistress Cray's eggs and butter for nothing and then riding through her cabbage patch to avoid going over the hill. What had she to live on after that? If men want to disagree up in London, let them settle their affairs there – ruin their own lives, without bringing us into their petty quarrels.'

'It's war, Kit, civil war. As for eggs and butter, soldiers must eat—'

'Then they can pay for what they eat!' he exclaimed. 'And there's no need to destroy. We all have to eat whether we want to fight or live in peace, and if both Parliament and the King are bent on destroying the crops of every farm that happens to be in the way of their armies, then we'll all starve; and if we all starve, there'll be nothing left to fight about,' he ended petulantly with childish logic scarcely fitted to his seventeen years.

I glanced from his bowed head across our fields and woods now shadowed in the late evening light, the cattle in the water-meadows, the corn growing tall and, lastly, the hay crop lying so still within its hedges of sweet briar and honeysuckle.

It was not surprising that Kit was dejected. Since our father's death – our mother had died at my birth sixteen years ago and we had then been cared for by Hannah, our father's old housekeeper – the full responsibility of the farm had fallen upon the two of us. Rather than sell it, Kit had given up University; I, my music and embroidery and, as the war between King and Parliament dragged on and labourers became scarce, so every aspect of the farm became more and more a part of our being. Our bitterness grew with that of our neighbours as reckless armies destroyed the produce of the countryside.

There was a hard look on Kit's face when he raised his head.

'They must go, Anne. Somehow or other those men must be driven away. It's only a handful at the moment but others will come to strengthen them, and sooner or later the Royalists will realise they are here and there'll be a pitched battle all over our fields.' He swung to face me. 'Every day I have prayed that we would be able to keep this land as our parents loved it – we have both sacrificed enough and I am not sacrificing this –' his arm swept the hillsides, 'to man's greed and carelessness.' His eyes roved the hay-field. 'A year's work – our fodder for the winter – gone; and what has God done?'

I touched his hand. 'Come in to supper, Kit,' I pleaded.

'Food!' he scoffed. 'A woman's cure for all ills.'

'It's better than threatening to use the Devil's cures!'

'Is it? I wonder?' His eyes narrowed and although he followed quietly enough, throughout the meal I knew his mind was elsewhere.

While Hannah, now stiff with rheumatism, cut the pasties, and I buttered the fresh crusts from loaves and served my rhubarb pie, Kit brooded in silence.

At length, pushing away his plate, he tipped our father's great oak chair, in which he was sitting, on to its back legs and spoke abruptly.

'Is it Alice, the dairymaid, who wants young Jem from Westridge for her husband?' he asked.

He startled us for we had both expected some remark about the hay-field.

'Ay,' Hannah nodded to me over his head as if to tell me she thought it wise to humour him and speak of trivial affairs. 'She's done her best to win him and bought new ribbons off the pedlar last time he was up – but Jem's no eyes for her.'

'Can't she try anything else – a love charm, perhaps?'

Hannah chuckled. 'Hempseed I saw,

Hempseed I mow,

And he that is my sweetheart

Come follow me, I trow—

If she sings that early one Friday morning, sowing her nine rows of seed, she should see the lad she is to marry come reaping after.'

'Is it true?' I asked.

'Ay, it is.' Hannah picked up her hot mug of milk to take with her to bed and turned towards the stairs. 'Many a time I tried it as a girl and never a lad came reaping after, and never a lad has ever asked me for my hand – so it's true enough. But young Alice wants something to fetch the lad to her side and so I helped the lass and gave her beeswax to make an image.'

'An image?' Kit's chair dropped sharply to the stone flags of the kitchen floor.

Hannah nodded. 'To shape herself and Jem. She must baptise them both and bind them tight together in wedlock – and he'll come soon enough, but it's work of the Devil. That's for sure.'

As the door closed softly behind her, Kit's eyes met mine across the table.

'An image,' he breathed. 'Of course!'

He rose quickly, reaching for the candle in the darkening room.

'What are you going to do?' I asked fearfully.

'Fetch wax and other things I may need to help me. You may go to bed, but clear the dishes first.'

'Wax? You mean to make an image? But why?'

'Why not?' he smiled. 'The Devil's cure, which is no more black magic than that spell hempen, hampen of old Hannah.'

'But witchcraft, Kit – to save the farm?'

'Does it matter, as long as the farm is protected? Go to bed, Anne,' he whispered, patting my cheek as he left the room.

I did not go to bed. I washed and stacked the dishes, set the one candle on the bare table and sat waiting like a little ghost in my father's chair.

'Woman's curiosity,' Kit commented on his return, and slipped the bolt on the kitchen door. 'But since you are here, you shall help. I've no doubt your fingers are nimbler than mine.'

On the table in front of me he placed one of Hannah's honey-scented cakes of beeswax.

'Mould it,' he said, 'into the form of a Parliamentary officer – that man, Richard Moreton, who led his men through the hay-field. And when it is made we can decide what to do with it.'

Obediently I crossed to the hearth, tipped hot water from the cauldron into a pan, set an earthenware jar in the water and the lump of wax in the jar. Slowly the jar filled with golden liquid; slowly it cooled, away from the heat – Kit keeping the substance soft with the warmth of his hands while I worked, little by little, piece by piece, until under my fingers, tacky with the hardening wax, the figure of a man began to form.

Anxiously I pressed the stumpy legs to shape the

jackboots, enjoying the pleasure of creation that the modelling gave me.

'Must it be exactly like?' I asked.

'As near as possible. There must be something about him that's recognisable, but it's the naming that counts. Baptise him and then—'

Leaning confidently over my shoulder, he drew from his pocket a crumpled rag which he opened. Out fell a tiny heap of moist soil.

'What's that?' I queried.

'Soil from his footprint to be pressed into the waxen feet, so that there is something of his own. We've no hairs from his head or nail-parings, so this must serve instead.'

A hair from his head, a paring from his nail? I stared in disgust from the heap of soil to the figure in my hand.

'Oh, Kit,' I murmured. 'What are we doing?'

'Getting rid of the Roundheads,' he snapped. 'There are Royalists only a few miles away and this officer will make his handful of men fight them if they attack. Get rid of the leader, the men will disperse, the Royalists will have no one to attack and will leave; then our crops will be safe. It's worth it, isn't it?'

Half convinced, I pressed the crumbs of soil into the waxen feet, shaped the square-toed boots, curved the little figure's arms to his sides and began rounding his hair to his head with my thumbnail. Finally, holding the image at arm's length, I viewed it in the candlelight with the satisfaction of a craftsman.

'It's good, Kit,' I laughed. 'I never thought I could do it so well.'

Kit set the figure upright before us.

'Now, little man,' he said, moistening his finger with his tongue. 'I call thee Richard Moreton, in the name of—'

'No!' I exclaimed. 'Not in God's name, nor the Devil's. Just name it, if you must, and be done.' My voice rose sharply with fear. 'And when he's named, what then?'

'We decide how to get rid of him.'

Get rid of – three words where one would have been sufficient to cover our deed.

'If we put him in front of the fire,' Kit went on casually, 'he'll slowly melt and Richard Moreton will waste away – but that will take too long. We need something quick and sharp – a nail through his head, a knife through his heart . . .' His hand went to his pocket.

'Not that – yet – please,' I protested. 'I've only just made him and it's pity to spoil him so soon.'

'A pin in his arm, then,' said Kit softly. 'A foretaste of what is to come.'

With knuckles pressing my burning cheeks, I waited, not knowing whether my reluctance was a desire to keep the toy intact or to save the man – but I was frightened and dared not think deeply on the black arts in which we were dabbling.

I felt the pin driven through that waxen arm as if it had been my own, and my shudder rocked the table; the pool of candle-flame flowed out like water, the shadows swam across our faces and we were distorted in that light.

'Done,' said Kit. 'I'll put him in a drawer for safety, among the farm accounts where Hannah never pries, for if it were found anyone would know its meaning. Now, to clear the table of our evil practices,' he explained to my wan face, 'and then to bed, 'tis almost fairy time!'

I turned away, sick at heart that he could quote Will Shakespeare at such a moment, for the fairies for whom Hannah still put out a bowl of bread and milk each night seemed harmless beings compared with the ones we had just invoked. For me, they were restless hours until the morning. Lying fitfully awake, I heard the wind rising, the summer rain lashing the panes of my windows – an evil answer to an evil prayer, ensuring that the hay was past all saving. And, in the distance, sounds of intermittent firing as the Royalists drew nearer to the enemy's lightly held stronghold.

At dawn reports came to us from the daily labourers that horsemen had been seen in the valley below us, swift-moving figures in the mist, fighting an almost silent battle for the narrow bridge across the river. Kit scoffed at their ignorance that there was a ford only a few yards lower down and, anxious for his heifers who were grazing in the water-meadows, set off to bring them nearer to the farm.

He appeared in the kitchen, breathless and dripping, barely an hour later.

'Two of the beasts are across the ford on the other bank,' he announced. 'I'm going back.'

There was excitement in his voice and, glancing up from my pastry-making to protest at the mud dripping on his boots, I saw the tense expression on his face.

'He's hurt, Anne,' he whispered, and I needed no explanation. 'He's hurt – a ball through his arm, I think. Isn't that what we wanted? And I can hardly believe it's true.' His wet hands gripped my shoulders. 'He's down there now. I've seen him – his arm in a sling and there's blood all over the stones by the river – but they kept the bridge, whoever else was wounded. It works, Anne, it works!' He flung back his head and laughed. 'Now for the end. Where is the little fellow? A nail through his heart and next time it will all be over.'

He strode to the drawer, but I reached it first.

'No, Kit, you mustn't, you mustn't,' I whispered fiercely. 'And if you dare touch me—' I hissed, eyeing his wary approach, 'I'll bite and scratch your face to shreds.'

'Little firecat!' he said, dangerously calm. 'Isn't this what you wanted? You had no need to wait in the kitchen for me last night, no need to mould such a neat figure, nor be so pleased with it, eh? You enjoyed the task, didn't you? And you're no longer a child, not knowing what you are doing. You knew well enough, and whose aid you were employing!'

'And it's because I'm not a child that I know now what I've done,' I cried. 'And what we will both be doing if we go any further with this thing. It's murder, Kit.'

The word was out, the word that had kept me awake all night.

'Murder at its most foul,' I repeated. 'We're not killing a man in fair fight – challenging him to a duel or joining the Royalists to kill him in battle. It's as bad as stabbing him in the back, only worse. We're creeping in the dark with wax and pins and nail-parings to take the coward's way of removing an enemy; we're sitting safely at home because we haven't the courage to do anything else. You're a coward, Kit, and so am I.'

Kit shrugged his shoulders.

'Let him take his men from the bridge, leave the village, stop spoiling our crops or—'

'If that's all you want of him, why don't you ask him?' I snapped, fear making me angry.

He laughed. 'Why don't you?'

For a moment we glowered at each other.

'Very well, I will,' I replied.

Surprise glimmered in Kit's eyes.

'Come, Anne, be reasonable,' he went on. 'You cannot mean to risk your life by going to the bridge in this weather, among a horde of soldiers, in order to—'

'I'd sooner risk my life than my soul,' I broke in, snatching the apron from my waist. 'I'll be damned to everlasting torment if I go on with last night's plan – that's the Church's teaching, and we both know it.' My hands fumbled in the dresser drawer. 'I don't trust you, Kit, and I'm taking the image with me.'

Swiftly I wrapped the little waxen figure in a clean napkin and tucked it in the folds of the shawl I flung over my head to protect me from the rain. Dodging Kit's out-stretched arm, I darted for the door where, in the yard, I could see his black mare near the mounting-block, awaiting his return. Swiftly I leapt astride her bare, wet back, tugging my skirts almost to my knees, then caught the rope Kit used for a bridle and swung her out into the lane which led to the bridge.

Kit's shout was drowned in the rush of wind and blinding rain, and the thick mist which swirled from the hills on either side. Headlong down the slope we lurched, the ground giving way under the mare's strong hoofs until a cry below us made her slacken speed.

'Horsemen up the hill there!' came the cry again, and to my terror a musket shot rang out.

I ducked, trying to urge the mare from the open track into the cover of the woods; she twisted from my grasp, her glistening sides sliding under me and then, with a whinny of alarm, she tossed me to the ground and crashed down towards the river.

Too frightened to be conscious of any pain I scrambled to my feet.

' 'Tis a woman,' a man shouted, glimpsed momentarily through the wavering mist. 'And a great black horse.'

Catching up my dress I fled, tearing at the undergrowth for shelter.

'A girl! No more'n a child,' a voice exclaimed, drawing nearer. 'Here's her doll.'

My fingers groped helplessly at the empty shawl where I lay hidden, fearful of moving, and now fully aware that anyone would recognise the significance of the waxen figure.

'Doll?' There was a long pause. ' 'Tis no doll. 'Tis an image – and a soldier! See the pin in its arm. Witchcraft!'

'A witch!' The terrible accusation rang in my ear.

'Ay, riding that great black creature. No doubt the Devil himself. Find her!'

'Hunt her out!'

Footsteps pounded across the hillside; panic stricken I sprang up, fleeing between the trees, careless of the noise, only knowing I had to run – tripping – stumbling – on – on – faster – faster—

My shawl caught the brambles, fingers tore at the shawl, clawing into my hair . . .

'Kit – Kit!' I screamed.

My head was dragged back until I felt my neck was breaking, a filthy hand slammed over my mouth, another pinned my arms to my sides.

'Witch!' a man spat.

A knee in my spine urged me forward down the slope to the river bank.

Someone thrust the waxen image before my eyes.

'So that's your way, is it?' a voice snarled, and there was no humanity in the eyes that met mine. 'What's this but witches' weather and what's this but killing a man by witchcraft and the aid of the Devil. No wonder the bridge was nearly lost last night – fire and water's our way with a witch and as we've no fire but plenty of water—'

From the distance came a shout – a command. Iron fingers gripped my kicking feet, forced my arms above my head and slung me screaming into the swollen river.

'Kit – Kit!' I sobbed, fighting the waves that swept over me and other hands that grasped for my throat and hair.

A man swore – grey waters – grey sky – dripping trees – all quivered into semi-darkness and a wild choking dream...

There was a fire flickering, the reflection of the flames washing like water on the polished oak of the four-poster bed. I sat up, feeling the dampness of my hair, the bruised wrists. Hannah moved from the hearth and patted my hand.

'The river – I've been in the river,' I said as I focused my gaze on her.

Recollection and fear flooded my mind.

'Where's Kit?' I asked.

He appeared at my side to sit on the edge of the bed and, obedient to his nod, Hannah left the room.

'You've not harmed the image?' I asked.

'Anne, Anne,' he laughed softly. 'Isn't it more important that you are safe here? Are you still worrying about your soul? You do not think I would harm the man who saved your life, do you?'

'I thought you'd saved me.'

He shook his head. 'I helped drag the pair of you out of the water, and sent off those fools of soldiers. It wasn't easy for a man with an injured arm to rescue a little fire-cat who preferred to drown. He nearly knocked you unconscious before he could do anything with you.' He pushed the hair from the swelling on my temple. 'We carried you home, Hannah put you to bed – it's best she shouldn't know the truth – and Captain Moreton is at this moment clad in my old shirt and breeches, eating a hearty meal in the kitchen. The mare found her own way home, but the Royalists have stolen the two heifers.'

Everything accounted for – 'And the image?' I persisted.

'Floating in the river where I threw it, together with its broken spell and my own evil, cowardly self.' Kit turned away. 'You've more courage in your little finger than I have in my whole body. I've made another vow,' he went on gravely. 'Only with myself this time. I'll not kill except in self-defence or in defence of my property. From now on, this farm is on neutral ground, neither King nor Parliament will be supported; if they cross my boundaries they'll be staved off with pitchforks and clubs and I've no doubt other farmers will gladly follow my lead to teach both armies that unless they discipline their troops they're no more welcome than a frost in May.'

'And what of the officer, Richard Moreton?' I asked slyly. 'The enemy being so kindly entertained in the kitchen?'

Kit smiled, 'God be thanked he came after you into the river, Anne. As for me, he will always be welcome here and I've a strong belief he'll want to come again, and not only in the guise of a Parliamentary officer. In destroying one spell you've unwittingly cast another as surely as if you had whispered Hannah's words –

'Hempseed I sow,
Hempseed I mow,
And he that is my sweetheart
Come follow me, I trow—'

he chanted softly, patting my hand with a knowledge-
able, brotherly air.

The Earlier Service

Margaret Irwin

Mrs Lacey and her eldest daugher Alice hurried through the diminutive gate that led from the Rectory garden into the churchyard. Alice paused to call: 'Jane, father's gone on,' under the window of her young sister's room. To her mother she added with a cluck of annoyance, 'What a time she takes to dress!'

But Jane was sitting, ready dressed for church, in the window-seat of her room. Close up to her window and a little to the right, stood the square church tower with gargoyles at each corner. She could see them every morning as she lay in her bed at the left of the window, their monstrous necks stretched out as though they were trying to get into her room.

The church bell stopped. Jane could hear the shuffle of feet as the congregation rose at the entrance of her father; then came silence, and then the drone of the General Confession. She jumped up, ran downstairs and into the churchyard. Right above her now hung the gargoyles, peering down at her. Behind them the sun was setting in clouds, soft and humid as winter sunsets can only be in Somerset. She was standing in front of a tiny door studded with nails. The doorway was the oldest part of the church of Cloud Martin. It dated back to Saxon days; and the shrivelled bits of blackened, leather-like stuff, still clinging to some of the nails, were said to be the skins of heathens flayed alive.

Jane paused a moment, her hands held outwards and a little behind her. Her face was paler than it had been in her room, her eyes were half shut, and her breath came a little quickly, but then she had been running. With the same sudden movement that she had jumped from the window seat, she now jerked her hands forward, turned the great iron ring that served as a door-handle, and stole into the church.

The door opened into the corner just behind the Rectory pew. She was late. Mrs Lacey and Alice were standing up and chanting the monotone that had become a habitual and almost an unconscious part of their lives. Jane stole in past her mother, and knelt for an instant, her red pigtail, bright symbol of an old-fashioned upbringing, flopping sideways on to the dark wood. 'Please God, don't let me be afraid – don't, don't, *don't* let me be afraid,' she whispered; then stood, and repeated the responses in clear and precise tones, her eyes fixed on the long stone figure of the Crusader against the wall in front of her.

He was in chain armour; the mesh of mail surrounded his face like the coif of a nun, and a high crown-like helmet came low down on his brows. His feet rested against a small lion, which Jane as a child had always thought was his favourite dog that had followed him to the Holy Wars. His huge mailed hand grasped the pommel of his sword, drawn an inch or two from its scabbard. Jane gazed at him as though she would draw into herself all the watchful stern repose of the sleeping giant. Behind the words of the responses, other words repeated themselves in her mind:

> The knight is dust,
> His good sword rust;
> His soul is with the saints, we trust.

'But he is *here*,' she told herself, 'you can't really be afraid with him here.'

There came the sudden silence before the hymn, and she wondered what nonsense she had been talking to herself. She knew the words of the service too well, that

was what it was; how could she ever attend to them?

They settled down for the sermon, a safe twenty minutes at least, in the Rector's remote and dreamlike voice. Jane's mind raced off at a tangent, almost painfully agile, yet confined always somewhere between the walls of the church.

'You shouldn't think of other things in church,' was a maxim that had been often repeated to her. In spite of it she thought of more other things in those two Sunday services than in the whole week between.

'What a lot of Other Things other people must have thought of too in this church,' she said to herself; the thought shifted and changed a little; 'there are lots of Other Things in this church; there are too many Other Things in this church.' Oh, she *mustn't* say things like that to herself or she would begin to be afraid again – she was not afraid yet – of course, she was not afraid, there was nothing to be afraid of, and if there were, the Crusader was before her, his hand on his sword, ready to draw it at need. And what need could there be? Her mother was beside her whose profile she could see without looking at it, *she* would never be disturbed, and by nothing.

But at that moment Mrs Lacey shivered, and glanced behind her at the little door by which Jane had entered. Jane passed her fur to her, but Mrs Lacey shook her head. Presently she looked round again, and kept her head turned for fully a minute. Jane watched her mother until the familiar home-trimmed hat turned again to the pulpit; she wondered then if her mother would indeed never be disturbed, and by nothing.

She looked up at the crooked angel in the tiny window of medieval glass. His red halo was askew; his oblique face had been a friend since her childhood. A little flatnosed face in the carving round the pillar grinned back at her and all but winked.

'How old are you?' asked Jane.

'Six hundred years odd,' he replied.

'Then you should know better than to wink in church, let alone always grinning.'

But he only sang to a ballad tune:

> 'Oh, if you'd seen as much as I,
> It's often you would wink.'

'In the name of the Father and the Son and the Holy Ghost—'

Already! *Now* they would soon be outside again, out of the church for a whole safe week. But they would have to go through that door first.

She waited anxiously till her father went up to the altar to give the blessing. After she was confirmed, she, too, would have to go up to the altar. She would have to go. Now her father was going. He took so long to get there, he seemed so much smaller and darker as he turned his back on the congregation; it was really impossible sometimes to see that he had on a white surplice at all. What was he going to do up there at the altar, what was that gleaming pointed thing in his hand? *Who* was that little dark man going up to the altar? Her fingers closed tight on her prayer book as the figure turned round.

'You idiot, of course it's father! There, you can see it's father.'

She stared at the benevolent nut-cracker face, distinct enough now to her for all the obscurity of the chancel. How much taller he seemed now he had turned round. And of course his surplice was white – quite white. What *had* she been seeing?

'May the peace of God which passeth all understanding—'

She wished she could kneel under the spell of those words for ever.

'Oh, yes,' said the little flat-nosed face as she rose from her knees, 'but you'd find it dull, you know.' He was grinning atrociously.

The two Rectory girls filed out after their mother, who carefully fastened the last button on her glove before she opened the door on which hung the skins of men that had been flayed alive. As she did so, she turned round and looked behind her, but went out without stopping. Jane almost ran after her, and caught her arm. Mrs Lacey was already taking off her gloves.

'Were you looking round for Tom Elroy, mother?' asked Alice.

'No, dear, not specially. I thought Tom or someone had come up to our door, but the church does echo so. I think there must be a draught from that door, but it's funny, I only feel it just at the end of the evening service.'

'You oughtn't to sit at the end of the pew then, and with your rheumatism. Janey, you always come in last. Why don't *you* sit at the end?'

'I won't!' snapped Jane.

'Whatever's the matter, Jane?' asked her mother.

'Why should I sit at the end of the pew? Why can't we move out of that pew altogether? I only wish we would.'

Nobody paid any attention to this final piece of blasphemy, for they had reached the lighted hall of the Rectory by this time and were rapidly dispersing. Jane hung her coat and hat on the stand in the hall and went into the pantry to collect the cold meat and cheese. The maids were always out on Sunday evening. Alice was already making toast over the dining-room fire; she looked up as the Rector entered, and remarked severely : 'You shouldn't quote Latin in your sermons, father. Nobody in the church understands it.'

'Nobody understands my sermons,' said Mr Lacey, 'for nobody listens to them. So I may as well give myself the occasional pleasure of a Latin quotation, since only a dutiful daughter is likely to notice the lapse of manners. Alice, my dear, did I give out in church that next Friday is the last Confirmation class?'

'Friday!' cried Jane, in the doorway with the cheese.

'Next Friday the last class? Then the Confirmation's next week.'

'Of course it is, and high time, too,' said Alice, 'seeing that you were sixteen last summer. Only servant girls get confirmed *after* sixteen.'

That settled it then. In a spirit of gloomy resignation Jane engulfed herself in an orange.

There were bright stars above the church tower when she went to bed. She kept her head turned away as she drew the curtains, so that she should not see the gargoyles stretching their necks towards her window.

Friday evening found Jane at the last Confirmation class in the vestry with her father and three farmers' daughters, who talked in a curious mixture of broad Somerset and high school education and knew the catechism a great deal better than Jane.

After they had left, she followed closely at her father's elbow into the church to remove hymn books and other vestiges of the choir practice that had taken place just before the class. The lamp he carried made a little patch of light wherever they moved; the outlying walls of darkness shifted, but pressed hard upon it from different quarters. The Rector was looking for his Plotinus, which he was certain he had put down somewhere in the church. He fumbled all over the Rectory pew while Jane tried on vain pretexts to drag him away.

'I have looked in that corner – thoroughly,' she said.

The Rector sighed.

> 'What shall I say
> Since Truth is dead?'

he inquired. 'So far from looking in that corner, Jane, you kept your head turned resolutely away from it.'

'Did I? I suppose I was looking at the list of Rectors. What a long one it is, and all dead but you, father.'

He at once forgot Plotinus and left the Rectory pew to pore with proud pleasure over the names that began with one Johannes de Martigny and ended with his own.

'A remarkably persistent list. Only two real gaps – in the Civil Wars and in the fourteenth century. That was at the time of the Black Death, when there was no rector of this parish for many years. You see, Jane? – 1349, and then there's no name till 1361 – Giraldus atte Welle. Do you remember when you were a little girl, very proud of knowing how to read, how you read through all the names to me, but refused to say that one? You said, "It's a dreadful name," and when I pressed you, you began to cry.'

'How silly! There's nothing dreadful in Giraldus atte Welle,' began Jane, but as she spoke she looked round her. She caught the Rector's arm. 'Father, there isn't anyone in the church besides us, is there?'

'My dear child, of course not. What's the matter? You're not nervous, are you?'

'No, not really. But we can find the Plotinus much easier by daylight. Oh – and father – don't let's go out by the little door. Let's pretend we're the General Congregation and go out properly by the big door.'

She pulled him down the aisle, talking all the way until they were both in his study. 'Father doesn't *know*,' she said to herself – 'he knows less than mother. It's funny, when he would understand so much more.'

But he understood that she was troubled. He asked: 'Don't you want to get confirmed, Jane?' and then: 'You mustn't be if you don't want it.'

Jane grew frightened. There would be a great fuss if she backed out of it now after the very last class. Besides, there was the Crusader. Vague ideas of the initiation rites of knight and crusader crossed her mind in connection with the rite of Confirmation. He had spent a night's vigil in a church, perhaps in this very church. One could never fear anything else after that. If only she didn't have to go right up to the altar at the Communion Service. But she would not think of that; she told the Rector that it was quite all right really, and at this

moment they reached the hall door and met Mrs Lacey
hurrying towards them with a letter from Hugh, now at
Oxford, who was coming home for the vacation on Wednesday.

'He asks if he may bring an undergraduate friend for
the first few days – a Mr York who is interested in old
churches and Hugh thinks he would like to see ours. He
must be clever – it is such a pity Elizabeth is away – she
is the only one who could talk to him; of course, he will
enjoy talking with you, father dear, but men seem to
expect girls too to be clever now. And just as Janey's
Confirmation is coming on – she isn't taking it seriously
enough as it is.'

'*Mother!* Don't you want us to play dumb crambo like
the last time Hugh brought friends down?'

'Nonsense,' said the Rector hastily. 'Dumb crambo re-
quires so much attention that it should promote serious-
ness in all things. I am very glad the young man is coming, my love, and I will try my hardest to talk as cleverly
as Elizabeth.'

He went upstairs with his wife, and said in a low
voice: 'I think Jane is worrying rather too much about
her Confirmation as it is. She seems quite jumpy sometimes.'

'Oh – *jumpy*, yes,' said Mrs Lacey, as though she refused to consider jumpiness the right qualification for
Confirmation. The question of the curtains in the spare
room, however, proved more immediately absorbing.

Hugh, who preferred people to talk shop, introduced his
friend's hobby the first evening at dinner. 'He goes grub-
bing over churches with a pencil and a bit of paper and
finds things scratched on the walls and takes rubbings of
them and you call them *graffiti*. Now, then, father, any
offers from our particular property?'

The Rector did not know of any specimens in his
church. He asked what sort of things were scratched on
the walls.

'Oh, anything,' said York, 'texts, scraps of dog Latin, aphorisms – once I found the beginning of a love song. When a monk, or anyone who was doing a job in the church, got bored, he'd begin to scratch words on the wall just as one does on a seat or log or anything today. Only we nearly always write our names and they hardly ever did.'

He showed some of the rubbings he had taken. Often, he explained, you couldn't see anything but a few vague scratches, and then in the rubbing they came out much clearer. 'The bottom of a pillar is a good place to look,' he said, 'and corners – anywhere where they're not likely to be too plainly seen.'

'There are some marks on the wall near our pew,' said Jane. 'Low down, nearly on the ground.'

He looked at her, pleased, and distinguishing her consciously for the first time from her rather sharp-voiced sister. He saw a gawky girl whose grave, beautiful eyes were marred by deep hollows under them, as though she did not sleep enough. And Jane looked back with satisfaction at a pleasantly ugly, wide, good-humoured face.

She showed him the marks next morning, both squatting on their heels beside the wall. Hugh had strolled in with them, declaring that they were certain to find nothing better than the names of the present choir boys, and had retired to the organ loft for an improvisation. York spread a piece of paper over the marks and rubbed his pencil all over it and asked polite questions about the church. Was it as haunted as it should be?

Jane, concerned for the honour of their church, replied that the villagers had sometimes seen lights in the windows at midnight; but York contemptuously dismissed that. 'You'd hear as much of any old church.' He pulled out an electric torch and switched it on to the wall.

'It's been cut in much more deeply at the top,' he remarked; 'I can read it even on the wall.' He spelt out slowly: ' "*Nemo potest duobus dominis servire*." That's a text from the Vulgate. It means: "No man can serve two masters." '

'And did the same man write the rest underneath, too?'

'No, I should think that was written much later, about the end of the fourteenth century. Hartley will tell me exactly. He's a friend of mine in the British Museum, and I send him the rubbings and he finds out all about them.'

He examined the sentence on the paper by his torch, while Hugh's 'improvisation' sent horrible cacophanies reeling through the church.

'Latin again, and jolly bad – monkish Latin, you know. Can't make out that word. Oh!'

'Well?'

'It's in answer to the text above, I think. I say, this is the best find I've ever had. Look here, the first fellow wrote, "No man can serve two masters," and then, about a century after, number two squats down and writes – well, as far as I can make it out, it's like this: "Show service therefore to the good, but cleave unto the evil." Remarkable sentiment for a priest to leave in his church, for I'd imagine only the priest would be educated enough to write it. Now why did he say that, I wonder?'

'Because evil is more interesting than good,' murmured Jane.

'Hmph. You agree with him then? What kind of evil?'

'I don't know. It's just – don't you know how words and sentences stick in your head sometimes? It's as though I were always hearing it.'

'Do you think you'll hear it tomorrow?' asked York maliciously. He had been told that tomorrow was the day of her Confirmation. She tried to jump up, but as she was cramped from squatting so long on her heels she only sat down instead, and they both burst out laughing.

'I'm sorry,' said York, 'I didn't mean to be offensive. But I'd like to know what's bothering you.'

'What do you mean?'

'Oh, you know. But never mind. I dare say you can't

say.' This at once caused an unusual flow of speech from Jane.

'Why should evil be interesting?' she gasped. 'It isn't in real life – when servants steal the spoons and the villagers quarrel with their neighbours. Mrs Elroy came round to father in a fearful stew the other day because old Mrs Croft had made a maukin of her.'

'A what?'

'An image – you know – out of clay, and she was sticking pins in it, and Mrs Elroy declared she knew every time a pin had gone in because she felt a stab right through her body.'

'What did your father say?'

'He said it was sciatica, but she wouldn't believe it, and he had to go round to Mrs Croft and talk about Christmas peace and good will, but she only leered and yammered at him in the awful way she does, and then Alice said that Christmas blessings only came to those who live at peace with their neighbours, and Mrs Croft knew that blessings meant puddings, so she took the pins out, and let the maukin be, and Mrs Elroy hasn't felt any more stabs.'

'Mrs Croft is a proper witch then?'

York stood up, looking rather curiously at her shining eyes.

'Cloud Martin has always been a terrible bad parish for witches,' said Jane proudly.

'You find *that* form of evil interesting,' he said.

Jane was puzzled and abashed by his tone. She peered at the wall again and thought she could make out another mark underneath the others. York quickly took a rubbing and, examining the paper, found it to be one word only, and probably of the same date as the last sentence, which had caused so much discussion about evil.

' "Ma – ma," ah, I have it. "*Maneo* – I remain," that's all.'

' "*I remain?*" Who remains?'

'Why, the same "I" who advises us to cleave to evil.

Remembering, perhaps, though it hadn't been said then, that the evil that men do lives after them.'

She looked at him with startled eyes. He thought she was a nice child but took things too seriously.

Hugh's attempts at jazz on the organ had faded away. As Jane and York left the church by the little door, they met him coming out through the vestry.

'Lots of luck,' said York, handing him the paper. 'Did you turn on the verger or anyone to look as well?'

'No – why? Aren't the family enough for you?'

'Rather. I was only wondering what that little man was doing by the door as we went out. You must have seen him, too,' he said, turning to Jane, 'he was quite close to us.'

But as she stared at him, he wished he had not spoken.

'Must have been the organist,' said Hugh, who was looking back at the church tower. 'Do you like gargoyles, York? There's a rather pretty one up there of a devil eating a child – see it?'

On the Sunday morning after the Confirmation, the day of her first Communion, Jane rose early, dressed by candle-light, met her mother and sister in the hall, and followed them through the raw, uncertain darkness of the garden and churchyard. The chancel windows were lighted up; the gargoyles on the church tower could just be seen, their distorted shapes a deeper black against the dark sky.

Jane slipped past her mother at the end of the pew. Except for the lights in the chancel, and the one small lamp that hung over the middle aisle, the church was dark and one could not see who was there. Mr Lacey was already in the chancel and the service began. Jane had been to this service before, but never when the morning was dark like this. Perhaps that was what made it so different. For it *was* different.

Her father was doing such odd things up there at the altar. Why was he pacing backwards and forwards so

often, and waving his hands in that funny way? And
what *was* he saying? She couldn't make out the words –
she must have completely lost the place. She tried to find
it in her prayer book, but the words to which she was
listening gave her no clue; she could not recognise them
at all, and presently she realised that not only were the
words unknown to her, but so was the language in which
they were spoken. Alice's rebuke came back to her:
'You shouldn't quote Latin in your sermons, father.' But
this wasn't a sermon, it was the Communion Service.
Only in the Roman Catholic Church they would have the
Communion Service in Latin, and then it would be the
Mass. Was father holding Mass? He would be turned out
of the Church for being Roman. It was bewildering, it
was dreadful. But her mother didn't seem to notice anything.

Did she notice that there were other people up there at
the altar?

There was a brief pause. People came out of the darkness behind her, and went up to the chancel. Mrs Lacey
slipped out of the pew and joined them. Jane sat back
and let her sister go past her.

'You are coming, Janey?' whispered Alice as she
passed.

Jane nodded, but she sat still. She had let her mother
and sister leave her; she stared at the two rows of dark
figures standing in the chancel behind the row of those
who knelt; she could not see her mother and sister among
them; she could see no one whom she knew.

She dared not look again at the figures by the altar;
she kept her head bowed. The last time she had looked
there had been two others standing by her father – that
is, if that little dark figure had indeed been her father. If
she looked now, would she see him there? Her head bent
lower and sank into her hands. Instead of the one low
voice murmuring the words of the Sacrament, a muffled
chant of many voices came from the chancel.

She heard the scuffle of feet, but no steps came past her

down into the church again. What were they doing up there? At last she had to look, and she saw that the two rows were standing facing each other across the chancel, instead of each behind the other. She tried to distinguish their faces, to recognise even one that she knew. Presently she became aware that why she could not do this was because they had no faces. The figures all wore dark cloaks with hoods and there were blank white spaces under the hoods.

'It is possible,' she said to herself, 'that those are masks.' She formed the words in her mind deliberately and with precision as though to distract her attention; for she felt in danger of screaming aloud with terror, and whatever happened she must not draw down on her the attention of those waiting figures. She knew now that they were waiting for her to go up to the altar.

She might slip out by the little door and escape, if only she dared to move. She stood up and saw the Crusader lying before her, armed, on guard, his sword half-drawn from its scabbard. Her breath was choking her. 'Crusader, Crusader, rise and help me,' she prayed very fast in her mind. But the Crusader stayed motionless. She must go out by herself. With a blind, rushing movement, she threw herself on to the little door, dragged it open, and got outside.

Mrs Lacey and Alice thought that Jane, wishing for solitude, must have returned from the Communion table to some other pew. Only Mr Lacey knew that she had not come up to the Communion table at all; and it troubled him still more when she did not appear at breakfast. Alice thought she had gone for a walk; Mrs Lacey said in her vague, late Victorian way that she thought it only natural Jane should wish to be alone for a little.

'I should say it was decidedly more natural that she should wish for sausages and coffee after being up for an hour on a raw December morning,' said her husband with unusual asperity.

It was York who found her half an hour later walking very fast through the fields. He took her hands, which felt frozen, and as he looked into her face he said, 'Look here, you know, this won't do. What are you so frightened of?' And then broke off his questions, told her not to bother to try to speak but to come back to breakfast, and half-pulled her with him through the thick, slimy mud, back to the Rectory. Suddenly she began to tell him that the Early Service that morning had all been different – the people, their clothes, even the language, it was all quite different.

He thought over what she stammered out, and wondered if she could somehow have had the power to go back in time and see and hear the Latin Mass as it used to be in that church.

'The old Latin Mass wasn't a horrible thing, was it?'

'Jane! Your father's daughter needn't ask that.'

'No. I see. Then it wasn't the Mass I saw this morning – it was—' She spoke very low so that he could hardly catch the words. 'There was something horrible going on up there by the altar – and they were waiting – waiting for me.'

Her hand trembled under his arm. He thrust it down into his pocket on the pretext of warming it. It seemed to him monstrous that this nice, straightforward little schoolgirl whom he liked best of the family, should be hag-ridden like this.

That evening he wrote a long letter to his antiquarian friend, Hartley, enclosing the pencil rubbings he had taken of the words scratched on the wall by the Rectory pew.

On Monday he was leaving them, to go and look at other churches in Somerset. He looked hard at Jane as he said goodbye. She seemed to have completely forgotten whatever it was that had so distressed her the day before, and at breakfast had been the jolliest of the party. But when she felt York's eyes upon her, the laughter died out of hers; she said, but not as though she had intended to say it: 'You will come back for Wednesday.'

'Why, what happens on Wednesday?'

'It is full moon then.'

'That's not this Wednesday then, it must be Wednesday week. Why do you want me to come back then?'

She could give no answer to that. She turned self-conscious and began an out-of-date jazz song about 'Wednesday week way down in old Bengal!'

It was plain she did not know why she had said it. But he promised himself that he would come back by then, and asked Mrs Lacey if he might look them up again on his way home.

In the intervening ten days he was able to piece together some surprising information which seemed to throw a light on the inscriptions he had found at Cloud Martin.

In the reports of certain trials for sorcery in the year 1474, one Giraldus atte Welle, priest of the parish of Cloud Martin in Somerset, confessed under torture to having held the Black Mass in his church at midnight on the very altar where he administered the Blessed Sacrament on Sundays. This was generally done on Wednesday or Thursday, the chief days of the Witches' Sabbath when they happened to fall on the night of the full moon. The priest would then enter the church by the little side door, and from the darkness in the body of the church those villagers who had followed his example and sworn themselves to Satan, would come up and join him, one by one, hooded and masked, that none might recognise the other. He was charged with having secretly decoyed young children in order to kill them on the altar as a sacrifice to Satan, and he was finally charged with attempting to murder a young virgin for that purpose.

All the accused made free confessions towards the end of their trial, especially in so far as they implicated other people. All however were agreed on a certain strange incident. That just as the priest was about to cut the throat of the girl on the altar, the tomb of the Crusader opened, and the knight who had lain there for two centuries arose and came upon them with drawn sword, so that they scattered and fled through the church, leaving the girl unharmed on the altar.

With these reports from Hartley in his pocket, York travelled back on the Wednesday week by slow cross-country trains that managed to miss their connections and land him at Little Borridge, the station for Cloud Martin, at a quarter-past ten. The village cab had broken down, there was no other car to be had at that hour, it was a six-mile walk up to the Rectory, there was a station hotel where it would be far more reasonable to spend the night, and finish his journey next morning. Yet York refused to consider this alternative; all through the maddening and uncertain journey, he had kept saying to himself, 'I shall be late,' though he did not know for what. He had promised Jane he would be back this Wednesday, and back he must be. He left his luggage at the station and walked up. It was the night of the full moon, but the sky was so covered with cloud as to be almost dark. Once or twice he missed his way in following the elaborate instructions of the station-master, and had to retrace his steps a little. It was hard on twelve o'clock when at last he saw the square tower of Cloud Martin church, a solid blackness against the flying clouds.

He walked up to the little gate into the churchyard. There was a faint light from the chancel windows, and he thought he heard voices chanting. He paused to listen, and then he was certain of it, for he could hear the silence when they stopped. It might have been a minute or five minutes later, that he heard the most terrible shriek he had ever imagined, though faint, coming as it did from the closed church; and knew it for Jane's voice. He ran up to the little door and heard that scream again and again. As he broke through the door he heard it cry: 'Crusader! Crusader!' The church was in utter darkness, there was no light in the chancel, he had to fumble in his pockets for his electric torch. The screams had stopped and the whole place was silent. He flashed his torch right and left, and saw a figure lying huddled against the altar. He knew that it was Jane; in an instant he had reached her. Her eyes were open, looking at him, but they did not know him, and she did not seem to understand him when he spoke. In a strange, rough accent of broad Somerset that he could scarcely distinguish she said, 'It was my body on the altar.'

Linda

Joan Mahé

I'm an old woman now – I was born over seventy years ago in a village called Bramley, the very place in which it all happened. We Romany tribes move about nearly all the year round and once the vans are pitched, any place is home. But for us older folk, Bramley is different. We used to stay there several weeks each year, always in the early autumn, and we came to know it better than other places. Living a nomad existence, I've seen and heard many strange things, but of all of them, I'll never forget what happened when I was fortune-telling at Bramley Fair one early September not so many years ago.

It was fairly late and I was thinking about taking in my painted sign and closing down for the night, when I noticed him. He stood staring at my notice but not making any move towards the door. I could tell by the cut of his suit that he was gentry, though I thought it a bit strange that he wasn't wearing an overcoat, for there was quite a chill in the air. He went on staring as if he was looking without seeing. I went down my wooden steps from the van towards him but he was too preoccupied to notice – he just stood there with his shoulders drooping and his long thin arms hanging loosely by his sides. Then I saw the doll. He was holding a large rag doll by an arm and it trailed pathetically on the ground beside him.

'There's still time, young sir,' I said. And this broke his reverie. He turned and looked at me and I saw that his hair was grey, not blond as I had at first thought.

I went up the steps and stood in the doorway of my van and he followed me without saying a word. When the curtain was drawn, we sat one on each side of my table and I saw that he had placed the rag doll between us. You can tell a lot from a person's face, and it was my business to notice, but there was too much anxiety in this man's eyes for me to give him my usual patter. I simply held out my arm and he placed one of his long slender hands in my roughened one. What did he want from me? Feeling uneasy, I asked him, 'Do you want me to tell your fortune, sir?'

At that, he shifted nervously in his chair. Then, pulling himself together and clearing his throat, he said, 'I came to the fair this evening because I needed to be in a crowd – people in fairs lose themselves in having a good time. I came thinking I might be able to do that too. It seemed to work for a little while – I even won a prize at one of the stalls and then I was handed this,' he poked the soft padded figure with his finger, 'and immediately it reminded me of the other doll – the one I had come here to forget.'

'Tell me about the doll you wanted to forget,' I interrupted.

'You'll think me ridiculous,' he began. 'It's only a doll in a dream. I say *only*, but I am haunted and obsessed by it. The doll lies there on the broken table in that terrible upstairs room.'

'Start at the beginning,' I suggested quietly, pulling my shawl around my shoulders for warmth.

'That's just it. The beginning was years and years ago. I had that same dream then when I was only seven. Night after night I had it, and now, after all those years, it's come back – the same in every detail. It's uncanny.'

'You don't want me to tell your fortune. It's the present, not the future, that's worrying you. What do you think I can do to help you?' I asked, trying to break the silence.

For the first time he looked at me and really seemed to

see me. He leaned forward and said with urgency, 'I saw the zodiac signs outside your van – they caught my attention. I thought you might be able to interpret . . . I'm sorry, I ought to have known . . .'

'Maybe I can, maybe I can't,' I said sharply. 'But if you don't tell me about it, you'll never know which.'

My simple tactic succeeded. Pushing the doll to one side, he clasped his hands together on the table in front of him and began :

'My name is Jason Mansfield and my father and mother bought a house in Bramley called "Hightrees" about a month after my seventh birthday.'

When he said 'Hightrees', it seemed as if it ought to mean something to me. I had known that name. No image of the house came to my mind, but the name meant something. I was sure it did. Hightrees . . . Hightrees . . . I repeated the name in my mind and a sense of sadness came over me.

As Jason Mansfield went on with his tale, I tried to recall what I had once known about that house.

'The dreams began as soon as we moved into the house, and now they've come back. Each time it's the same. I see myself walking at night along a gravelled drive to a large house. It's in darkness, but I'm impelled by some force to enter the house although I'm terrified. With only the moonlight through the windows to light my way I walk through a cupboard and climb a steep, narrow flight of steps.'

'Through a cupboard?' I questioned him, for he had stopped his tale again, as if he were contemplating what lay beyond the cupboard.

'That's what's so strange – I always go through the cupboard and there are the stairs and at the top a room. In the room are all the toys – always the same toys, the same disorder and the same cobwebs and dust over everything.'

'Tell me all you can remember about the room,' I urged

him, leaning forward and touching the doll. What had *I* known of that house, that room?

'It's not easy to distinguish anything because there's only moonlight to see by. But one by one, I'm able to pick out a doll's house, a skipping rope, a wooden hoop and a top, and then my eyes are drawn to the big rag doll lolling all awry on a sagging, broken table. It's the doll that drives me out of the room. I turn and rush out and then I fall. The falling seems to go on and on and I wake in terror.'

While my visitor was recounting his dream, I found myself gripping the rag doll that lay on the table between us. The soft body was like another I had touched. I pulled it towards me.

'When I was seven and first had this dream,' Jason was telling me, 'I screamed for my mother and wouldn't let her leave me alone. She comforted me, but I couldn't sleep. She told me I would forget it in the morning, but it remained so real that I wouldn't leave her for a minute all day. The next night, she stayed with me until I was asleep. But as soon as she left me to go to her own bed, she heard my screams. I was going through the same nightmare, and every detail was as it had been on the first night. And once again she had to stay with me and miss her own sleep because I was too terrified to close my eyes. When this happened four nights in succession and we were both beginning to be ill from lack of sleep, the doctor advised my mother to let me go to stay with my grandmother for a while.'

'And did the dreams stop then?' I asked, running my fingers over the large flat face of the doll.

'Immediately. As it happened, my father was sent abroad by his firm just two months later, and we never came back to live in Hightrees so I never slept in the house again. Not, at least, until last night. You see, my parents didn't sell the house. They rented it out, and I inherited it several years ago. I came back to spend last night there to prove to myself that the nightmares, which I had never forgotten, belonged to my childhood. I didn't reason about this – I felt impelled to do it.'

Without warning, Jason Mansfield got up from his chair and moved towards the door. His face showed that the nightmare was still with him. He had decided that I would not be able to help him. I could sense his disappointment. As his hand reached out to draw back the curtain, I held out the rag doll which he had left on the table, and this simple gesture brought the memories flooding back.

Suddenly I was a young girl again, and I was being forced to hand back a doll that I longed for to Linda, its owner. Her tear-stained face came back to me clearly. She often used to come and play with me near the caravan, and she always brought her doll. From the first I had coveted it and each time she came I wanted it more and more. Then one day, when she was not looking, I took it and hid it. She cried and cried for it, but I did not tell her where it was. But my mother came, and she knew what I had done and made me give it back. I remembered the soft wool of its plaited hair as Linda snatched it from me, and I remembered how she had gone away promising to come again the next day.

She never came again. My mother told me that she had died. She was trying to hide her doll on a ledge at the top of her house, and fell down a flight of stairs.

And now, as I handed another rag doll to this stranger, I was able to tell him, 'The doll in your dreams belonged to a girl of eight called Linda. She lived at Hightrees.'

He swung round and came back to the table. Studying my face to see if I were telling the truth, he said, 'Then I shall never be free of the nightmare as long as I stay there.'

Feeling that I had, after all, been able to do something for this dejected man and that he might now reward me with the expected silver pieces, I went on, 'You must return to Hightrees now, Mr Mansfield. It is only there that you will find the answer.'

But his hand did not go to his pocket. He had something else to ask of me, and something that I did not welcome.

'Come with me,' he said. 'Come back with me to High-trees and help me to find the answer.' His voice was so urgent and so desperate that, without any thought of reward now, I found myself pulling my shawl up over my head and going with him.

We did not talk on the way. It was moonlight and I remember noticing that the church clock showed half-past nine as we skirted the village green. The stone pillars marking the entrance to the drive to Jason Mansfield's house were a good fifteen minutes' walk further on. I had never walked up that long gravelled drive before, and I still remember the noise of our feet as we neared the dark house that evening. He had a torch with him and shone it on the ground so that we avoided puddles. It was the moonlight that showed me the shape of the tall house with its three storeys and its gables.

And it was the moonlight, softened by the grime on the windows, that lighted our way as we went into the house and began to climb the stairs. The torch helped us to find the way up. 'I want to look round with you up-stairs first of all,' my companion said. 'It was already late when I arrived last night, and I slept downstairs. I haven't even taken off the dust covers from the furniture upstairs yet.'

There were three bedrooms, and we went into each one in turn. Beds, chairs and tables were piled up every-where, and we stumbled about in the half-darkness, tap-ping walls and looking into cupboards.

'I should have waited until the electricity was con-nected,' Jason Mansfield said apologetically after a while. 'It really is unreasonable of me to have brought you here this evening.' He sat down on a chair covered by a sheet. 'I didn't want to relive that nightmare tonight. I hoped you might be able to help me to free myself from it.'

Standing there in the house where Linda had lived, I

had a sense of fear and foreboding. What was hidden? Where was it hidden?

'How do you get to the attic floor?' I asked him.

'What attic floor,' he answered.

'I saw windows in the gables as we came up the drive.'

Jason Mansfield got up and went into the corridor. He pointed to a room we had already been in. 'That was my room when I was a boy, he said; then he pushed open the door of another room we had been through, 'and that was my parents' bedroom. We've just come out of the guest room and, apart from the bathroom, that's all the rooms there are up here.'

Shining the torch ahead of him, he walked past the bathroom and opened a door. I was just behind him and I saw it was a shallow linen cupboard.

'There's nowhere else,' he said, closing the door, unless,' and he opened it again, 'it could possibly be hollow at the back here.' With the end of his torch, he began to tap. And immediately, we both knew that there was space at the back of the thin boarding which formed the rear of the closet.

Sheets, pillowcases, blankets, tablecloths and napkins were thrown out into the corridor. In five minutes Mr Mansfield had emptied every shelf. Then one by one he knocked out the thin shelves with his fist. He worked impatiently, almost feverishly. Picking up one of the planks that had formed a shelf, he rammed the back-boarding till it cracked. 'Stand back,' he warned me, as he swung the plank against the boarding. It went through. He rammed it again and again, and tore out the splintered wood with his hands. Once he had made a hole, he kicked hard and enlarged it. He shone his torch through and peered in to see what lay behind.

'You were right,' he cried. 'That's the way up to the attic floor.' He kicked and kicked until he had to lean against the wall and rest. 'It's almost big enough for us to go through,' he panted. 'These stairs were already closed off when I came here as a boy, I'm sure of that.'

Then he wrenched away the remaining pieces of wood, and I saw a steep, narrow flight of stairs reaching up into the darkness.

'Hold on to my jacket,' he told me. 'I'll lead the way with the torch.' I did as he asked, but I did not want to go up to the third floor.

At the top of the stairs was a windowless passage with two doors. The first door opened easily. It revealed an empty room. We looked down on the garden from the small window in the gable. The walls with their yellowed, peeling wallpaper held no secrets. Jason Mansfield moved immediately along the corridor, shining the torch ahead of him. He turned the handle of the other door. This one did not move. He tried again. It was stuck fast.

The only light was that from the torch. I touched the door through which no one had passed for so many years, and my sense of foreboding grew.

'Leave it, Mr Mansfield,' I warned him. 'Leave that room undisturbed.'

But already he had thrust the torch into my hands and was heaving his whole weight against the door.

Abruptly the door gave way and we stood there on the threshold of a small room, lit by the moonlight falling through a grimy window. But this room was not empty. A chill of apprehension passed through me, and I drew my shawl closely around my shoulders. I saw from Mr Mansfield's drawn face that he was awed by what the open door revealed. Thick dust lay everywhere, but under it, scattered all over the floor, were a child's toys. He snatched back the torch and shone it first on a doll's house and then in turn on a skipping rope, a wooden hoop and a top, until it came to rest on a lop-sided table on which lay sprawling a large rag doll.

As I stared at the doll my fingers remembered the softness of its stuffed body and the texture of the calico of its large flat face. It was Linda's doll. The doll I had longed for as a child. The doll she had cried for when I took it from her. And these were all Linda's toys. No one

had seen them for over sixty years. I did not want to enter the room. I wanted to leave that place where we were intruders. 'Don't go in, sir,' I pleaded. But even as I spoke, I was pushed aside by small hostile hands. Mr Mansfield had not moved. Someone had passed between us. Someone had come out of the attic room. The touch told me that it was Linda, and that she had known me. She had abandoned her doll after all this time. Light steps pattered away from us along the corridor towards the stairs. My companion called out, 'Come back!' and rushed along the dark corridor following the footsteps. He had taken the torch. I stood alone in the darkness.

I could see nothing, but I heard the cracking of old dry wood and knew the banister had given way. Scuffled steps and a heavy thudding sound confirmed my fears. Mr Mansfield had plunged down the steep stairs. He cried out and I felt my way along the corridor, keeping a hand on the wall on my left so that I stayed away from the broken banister. All was silent by the time I reached the top of the stairs and pushed open the door of the other attic room to allow a wan shaft of light from the moon to come through.

Now it grieves me that I ever went with Jason Mansfield to Hightrees. Often in the evening when I go out to take in my painted sign from outside the caravan, I wish with all my heart that I had gone out for it earlier that September evening. Then I would have been closed up before he came by. If I had, his nightmare might never have become a reality. He would have gone away from Hightrees without ever discovering the hidden room. Jason Mansfield might still be alive.

Billy Bates' Story

Geoffrey Palmer and Noel Lloyd

My name is William Joseph Bates, though everyone calls me Billy Bates. I'm nearly thirteen – which is a better way of saying that I'm twelve and a half. I'm supposed to be good at writing stories, but that isn't why I'm writing *this* one. Something happened to me that I don't understand and I thought that writing it all down might explain things. Whether it will or not, I shan't know till I've come to the end.

This funny experience really began at school, which is a strange place for a ghost story to begin. You see, there was this special essay we had to write for a competition. One of the school governors had offered a one-pound book token for the best story called 'An Exciting Adventure', and I won it for my age-group. I was presented with the book token in front of the whole school, which I quite enjoyed, even though I did have to bash Phil Masters in the playground afterwards for squinting at me as I was going up to the platform and making me laugh right in the Head's face.

But now I wish I hadn't won that prize. If I hadn't I would have gone straight home to tea and afterwards met some of my pals in the park for a game of football, and then I shouldn't have been writing this. As it was, I went home on my own, the lads having decided to give me time to get over feeling big-headed at my success, though it really hadn't affected me at all.

I almost forgot to tell you that my prize essay was a so-called ghost story. On the main road near the flats where I live there's an old derelict house. This was the house which had sparked off my story for the competition. I described it as a crooks' hideout and told how the gang and I had discovered this and then scared the crooks out of their wits by pretending to be ghosts. There wasn't much to it but it must have been more exciting than the other stories to win the prize.

As I walked home on my own I had to pass this house. The crumbling walls were covered with tattered creeper, and the garden was full of tin cans, dirty mattresses and broken boxes, partly hidden by a jungle of tall weeds. I looked round to make sure that no one was watching me, then gave a little bow. 'Thanks very much, house,' I said. ''Tis due to you that I was victorious.' I must have sounded like one of the Three Musketeers.

At that moment I caught sight of Phil Masters turning a corner into the road. I wondered if he'd seen me acting the fool, or if he wanted to return the bashing I'd given him, so I decided to play safe. I nipped smartly through the broken fence and entered the house through the broken-down door in the basement.

When I was inside I wasn't exactly scared, even though I didn't feel like laughing. It was pretty weird. The windows were boarded over and it was very dark. Most of the floorboards were rotten and it was a tricky job to avoid falling down one of the many holes. There was a smell like old cupboards, and a creaking noise that might have been caused by me treading on the broken boards – or by rats; a nasty thought when you hadn't got anything to throw at them.

I should have gone straight back to the safety of the outside world, but I was feeling pleased with the old house for helping me to win the book token, and I suddenly realised that I had never really explored it thoroughly. So, treading carefully, I made my way out of the basement and up the rickety stairs to the ground floor. I found myself in a big squarish hall but I couldn't make out many details because very little light came through the boarded-up windows. From the hall a door led into what was, I supposed, the front room. I pushed it open and went in. The door swung to behind me, closing with a little bang. The room was empty except for some rubbish in one corner, great pieces of wallpaper hanging from the walls and a huge fireplace which looked as though it might fall down at any moment.

Then, for no reason that I could think of, I went all hot and cold. My throat tightened and my heart started to pump away like mad. There's nothing to be afraid of, I told myself, hoping that I was telling myself the truth and, just to prove it, I began to whistle. The next moment I would have been out of that room like a scalded cat if the floor had been safe, for my whistling was interrupted by a voice. 'Hush, boy,' it said, 'I can't abide that tiresome noise.'

It wasn't an angry or threatening voice, but my hair was suddenly standing on end, and I must have looked pretty scared with my mouth open and my eyes popping out.

'There's no need to be frightened, child,' the voice went on.

Child! I may be only thirteen – nearly – but I'm tall for my age, and 'child' made me feel as though I were back in a sailor suit. 'I'm *not* frightened,' I lied, and my voice sounded like a transistor radio when the battery is running out. 'I just didn't see you, that's all.' I turned round and still didn't see anyone, and a cold shiver attacked me from stem to stern.

'No,' said the voice, almost in my ear, 'not many people do – but here I am.'

I tried to say 'Where?' but it was not easy to talk with my teeth chattering. In any case, there wasn't any need. She was there, right in front of me – a little old woman not much taller than me, wearing a dark dress down to her ankles. There was just enough light for me to see her wispy white hair and pale wrinkled face, and I stopped trembling because it was a *kind* face, though anxious. I didn't know what to say next, but she kept the conversation going.

'I am so pleased that you have come,' she said, just as if she had been expecting me. 'It is not often I can get through and when I do manage it, there is never anyone here.'

'Get through where?' I asked, thinking that she meant on the telephone.

'Oh, just through – but never mind that. You wouldn't understand, child.'

Here we go again, I thought. 'I'm *not* a child,' I retorted, and then it was her turn to get flustered.

'Of course you're not – you're a big boy, I can see that now. So big and clever that I know you will do something for me.'

'I will if I can,' I said, 'but who are you and what are you doing here?'

'My name is Mrs Cottrell,' she said after a pause, 'and this is my house.'

'But surely you don't live here,' I said, in a matter-of-fact voice.

She hesitated. 'For many years I—' she began, then changed the subject. 'If you are going to help me, you must do so at once – there is no time to lose.'

'What is it?' I asked quickly, because it had just occurred to me that if this *was* her house she might think of asking me what *I* was doing there.

'I want you to take something to the authorities for me – the police, the vicar, the doctor – it does not matter which – so that Terence may be helped before it is too late.'

'OK,' I said, then, in case she didn't like slang, I added, 'Very well. What do you want me to take?'

'My jewels, boy! They said that Terence had stolen them after he had frightened me to death, but he did no such thing! They also accused him of manslaughter, but fortunately he was acquitted.'

I gave a little laugh just to show that I had a sense of

humour and knew that she couldn't have been man-slaughtered when she was standing there before my eyes. *She* didn't laugh, though, so I changed mine into a cough.

'Terence would never steal my jewels,' the old lady went on sternly, 'and they could find no proof that he had. But the stigma of thief was on him, and within a short time he went out of his mind.'

'You mean he went mad and was innocent all the time?' I asked, trying to sort out all this rigmarole in my mind.

'Exactly. For a long time I have tried to establish his innocence but nobody has stayed here long enough to give me the help that you have kindly offered.'

I puffed out my chest, feeling pretty smug. Then I had a worrying thought. 'But why haven't you gone to the police, Mrs Cottrell?'

'I cannot go beyond these four walls,' she said abruptly. I waited to hear why, but she didn't seem inclined to tell me. 'Come, boy, I will show you where the jewels are hidden, then you can take the information to whomever you choose.'

She made for the door with a sort of skater's glide. I started to follow her, and then suddenly my whole world turned upside down. The door was closed – and she had passed right through it!

I'm not clear about the next few minutes. I know my head was spinning like a roulette wheel, and my heart was trying to force its way through my throat. I must have tugged the door open and stumbled down the stairs into the basement and then out into the garden. In the open air my legs gave way and I collapsed into a clump of rose-bay willow herb in a dead faint.

I don't know how long I lay there and when I came to I wasn't clear about what had happened, but felt very frightened. I staggered through the gate, still groggy, and straight into the arms of Mr Meredith, who lives next door but one to me in the flats.

'Steady on, Billy,' he said. 'What's the matter with

you? You're white as a sheet – have you seen a ghost or something?'

Then it all came back to me. 'Yes, I have,' I blurted out and promptly fainted again, almost pulling Mr Meredith to the ground with me.

The next thing I remember was my mum coming into the bedroom with a bowl of soup. 'You did give us a fright, love,' she said as she plumped the pillow for me to sit up. 'Drink this and you'll soon feel better.'

I insisted that there was nothing wrong with me, but *she* insisted that I had caught a chill through some complaint she always called 'outgrowing your strength'. Mind you, the best way to pacify a worried mother is not to say, as I did, 'I haven't got a chill – I've seen a ghost.' All that did was to send her rushing downstairs for Dad. I tried to tell them everything, but it was no use. 'Take it easy, son, you'll feel better in the morning,' was Dad's reaction, and they went away, shaking their heads and clucking about sending for a doctor.

I had two big worries myself. The first was why I had been stupid enough to be frightened of little Mrs Cottrell, ghost or no ghost, when it was obvious that she wouldn't have hurt a fly. The other was how to tell the police about the jewels if I didn't know where they were. I called myself all sorts of names for getting panicky at the wrong moment. After all, why *should* ghosts open doors if they don't need to? Then there was poor old Terence. How could I help him – whoever he was – without more information? And Mrs Cottrell had said it was urgent.... I spent the next half-hour making plans.

In the morning I hurried down to breakfast and flashed my biggest smile at Mum and Dad. I didn't give them a chance to tut-tut about my so-called chill. I left them in no doubt that I was fit enough to run the 1500 metres before eating a single cornflake. What convinced them that I was brimming over with good health was my offer to dry up before going to school. What's more, I did it! After I had put the last plate away I called good-bye to Mum and set off for school – or, to be more accurate, for the derelict house.

I felt more than a bit silly stumbling about the old house calling 'Mrs Cottrell – where are you?' But she must have decided that I was no use to her after all, for she didn't appear. I went to the back of the house and had a look round to see if I could locate any possible hiding-places for the jewels, but I might have saved my time. The rooms were in almost total darkness and there could have been a score of places. Reluctantly I decided I had better go to school.

The day was an awful drag, but I got through it somehow. After school I went back to the house. Still no sign of Mrs Cottrell. So I went to the police station.

The police were all right but they treated the whole thing as a joke and told me to lay off cheese last thing at night and to remember that they were busy men. They also suggested that it would be better if I kept away from empty houses unless I wanted to get into trouble.

The vicar was more understanding and listened patiently without making any jokes. He said something about exercising the ghost, but I told him that Mrs Cottrell was pretty old and didn't need much exercise. Then he explained that he'd said 'exorcising', and that it was a kind of religious way of getting rid of ghosts. Anyway, we had a look at the parish registers for many years back and there wasn't a single Cottrell mentioned. That could mean, the vicar said, that she had probably been a Methodist or something. So I said good-bye to him and thank you, and went home none the wiser.

After tea I went to the library, and there I found somebody with some sense. It was Mr Collins, the Reference Librarian, and if I'd been the Lord Mayor himself I couldn't have been better treated. I asked him how I could find out about a Mrs Cottrell of 101 Netherton Road, and he went to work just as if a starting-gun had gone off in his ear. In a couple of minutes he produced the electoral registers of people entitled to vote going back to the Domesday Book by the look of them and left me to plough through them while he went off to attend to other people, though whenever he had a spare moment he would come back and give me a hand.

I began to get a bit fed-up after a time. It was a dreary job, not made any better by having to keep dead quiet because of all the people sitting around with their heads buried in books. It was rather like trying to do your homework in church.

Then suddenly the silence was broken by a loud, high-pitched cry, and everybody looked up and frowned – and Mr Collins went as red as a tomato. It was he who had made the noise, you see. He coughed, straightened his tie, and whispered hoarsely, 'Diligence rewarded at last, old son.'

He pointed to a list of names on the sheet he was holding. There were dozens of names and numbers on it, but one of them almost jumped off the page and hit me. '101, Cottrell, Louisa Maude'.

'You see!' I said. 'There *was* a Mrs Cottrell! But what does this mean?'

'It means,' said Mr Collins, 'that your Mrs Cottrell was living at 101 Netherton Road in 1935, but not—' He looked up another list and went on, 'Not in 1936.'

'So she must have died in 1935,' I said, catching on quickly, 'or early in 1936.'

'Or else she moved out of the district.'

'No, she didn't move. I – I know that.' Mr Collins didn't ask me why I was so sure, thank goodness, because I didn't feel like telling him the story in whispers. 'Is there any way of finding out whether she did die about this time?' I asked.

'Wait here,' Mr Collins said, as though I'd got up to go, and hurried away himself. In a couple of minutes he had returned with two enormous bound books which he put on the table in front of me. 'Copies of the local paper for 1935 and 1936,' he murmured. 'I should try the later one if I were you.' Then he dashed away to answer the telephone.

I didn't much like the idea of going through all those newspapers. It would take hours and the library was due to close in forty-five minutes. But I opened the 1936 volume at random, somewhere near the beginning. Looking back, what happened seemed too good to be true and a bit mad, but at the time it didn't surprise me very much. I believe now that Mrs Cottrell was helping me, because the very first item I saw was a headline: 'Adopted son cleared of manslaughter charge.' It was followed by: 'Terence Cottrell, adopted son of Mrs Louisa Cottrell, a widow, of 101 Netherton Road, was acquitted yesterday . . .'

But there's no need to give you the rest of it. To cut a long story short, this is what had happened. Mrs Cottrell had lived alone in the house, apart from a woman who came in daily to do the cleaning. Terence, whom she and her husband had adopted when he was a baby, worked in an office at Barnet and didn't live at home. He gambled a lot and had got into debt. He daren't ask Mrs Cottrell for money because she was opposed to gambling in any shape or form and wouldn't even buy raffle tickets at the Church Fête, and he had planned to sneak into the house when she was asleep and steal some of her jewellery. He actually broke into the house to make it look like an ordinary burglary, but Mrs Cottrell heard a noise and waited for the intruder with a poker. According to Terence, when she saw who the 'burglar' was she must have had a heart attack, for she fell and hit her head on the marble fireplace. He panicked, left her lying there and ran out of the house – straight into the arms of a passing policeman. The doctor who was called confirmed that Mrs Cottrell had had a heart attack. There was no proof that Terence had actually stolen anything, so he got off, and that was about all.

I thanked Mr Collins and went home, trying to find the answers to all sorts of questions. Why had the house been empty all these years? If Terence had inherited it, why hadn't he sold it? Why hadn't he found the jewels afterwards if his story at the trial had been true? Had he really gone mad, as Mrs Cottrell had said? Was he alive or dead? If alive, he must be about sixty-six or -seven now. Most important of all, where was he now?

It was hard work trying to be my usual cheerful self when I got home, but I had to try, otherwise it would have meant soup in bed again. Fortunately, Mum and Dad didn't suspect a thing.

I had been in bed about a couple of hours, tossing and turning all over the place, and at last faced up to the fact that I wasn't going to get to sleep. I knew that I had to go to the old house, and the sooner the better. *She* might be there, or if not, I might find a clue to some of the problems that were worrying me.

I slipped out of bed and dressed by the light of the moon. It must have been nearly midnight when I crept past my parents' room, tip-toed downstairs and let myself out of the front door. When I reached the old house and slipped through into the garden I felt a sudden stab of fear and wished like anything that I hadn't come. The front of the house looked like a hideous face, the two upper windows its sightless eyes, and the wooden slats of the lower ones were like mis-shapen teeth in a grinning mouth. I think I would have slunk away if there had not been a scuttering sound behind me. I ran for the basement door before I realised that it was only a cat, probably more scared of me than I was of it.

I took a deep breath and went in. I wondered what would happen if I disturbed a sleeping tramp, or fell and broke an ankle and had to spend the night with the mice and rats . . . Then I remembered how Mrs Cottrell had trusted me – how she had been sure that I would help her – and some of my courage came back. She would see that I didn't come to any harm – so I went straight to the front room. There was no tramp there – that was one problem out of the way.

'Mrs Cottrell,' I called softly, 'are you here?' The only answer was my own voice bouncing back from the dead wood. I called again and again, but nothing happened. Then I said, 'I want to help Terence. I've found out what happened in 1936, but I don't know where he is. Won't you help me, Mrs Cottrell?'

I was just about to give up and go when there was something that I can't describe – a change in the feel of the room. It was as though a breeze had blown through it very lightly without there having been an actual breeze. At the same time my scalp began to prickle. Then I heard a voice. It was very faint and seemed to be struggling against something. 'I can't come through,' it said.

'Where are you?' I turned round and round, hoping to see the old lady.

'It's no use,' the voice said, even more faintly.

I spoke loudly, as you do when you're trying to attract the attention of someone who is walking away. 'Where is Terence?'

From Mrs Cottrell came two words. They sounded like 'Benfield Totting', but they were so muffled that I wasn't sure whether I had heard them properly.

'Please say that again,' I said, but this time there was no reply. For a minute or two I waited, straining my ears into the silence, but something told me that it was useless and there was nothing to do but give up and go home.

'Benfield Totting, Benfield Totting,' I kept on saying to myself on the way back, and I must have gone to sleep with the words on my lips.

The next night I went to the library again. I thought Mr Collins would groan when he saw me but in fact he greeted me like his prodigal son. 'Ah,' he said, then gave his little cough. 'I'm glad you've come. I've found out something about your Mrs Cottrell. There was a piece in another issue of the local paper about her will. She left everything – house and contents, and her jewels – to her adopted son. It seems, though, that after the trial

Terence Cottrell had a breakdown and never actually lived in the house.'

'I wondered about that,' I said, trying to make my voice sound as grown-up as possible. 'I suppose it didn't say in the paper where he did go?'

'As a matter of fact, it did. He went to Burnfield's Clinic at Tottenham.'

You've read about people hitting the roof – I didn't exactly do that but it was a near thing. 'Benfield Totting!' I shouted. 'Benfield Totting – that's it – that's what she was trying to say!'

About a hundred and twenty people said 'Shush!' and Mr Collins grabbed me and propelled me into the passage outside. 'My dear boy,' he said, breathing hard, 'you must *never* do that again.'

'I'm sorry,' I said, and I was, because I wouldn't have done anything to annoy Mr Collins after what he had done for us – Mrs Cottrell and me, that is. 'But what is this Burnfield's thing at Tottenham?'

'It's a hospital for the – er – mentally sick. I fear that if Terence Cottrell went there, he must have been very ill.'

'Would they let me see him?' I asked.

'I couldn't say – it would depend on how ill he is. Are you a relative?'

'No, it's just that I've promised his mother that I would try to help him.'

'His mother – you mean Mrs Cottrell?'

'That's right,' I answered, lost in thought.

'But – but she died in 1936 . . .'

'That's right,' I said again, smiled, thanked him, and hurried off, just in case he decided that *I* was due for a spell in Burnfield's Clinic.

I had enough information now to convince anyone that my story was worth looking into. But somehow I knew that no one would listen. Mum and Dad would put everything down to growing pains, the police would be too busy catching present-day criminals to bother about

clearing someone wrongly accused over thirty years ago.
If I went to the Clinic they'd be sure to turn me away. I
thought I would try the vicar again ...

He was just as friendly as he had been before. He gave
me a cup of tea and a biscuit and I told him every single
thing that had happened. 'All I want to know, sir,' I said,
'is whether there is a Terence Cottrell at Burnfield's, and
I've come to you because a vicar can usually get in anywhere.'

'I'm flattered,' he said, smiling. Then he began to puff
at a foul old pipe. 'As it happens, I do go to Burnfield's
occasionally, to visit one of my parishioners. I think I
am well enough known there to be able to find out what
you want to know. Wait here while I telephone.'

When he returned he said very thoughtfully, 'It is
quite extraordinary.'

'Do you mean he *is* there?' I asked, jumping to my
feet.

'*Was* there, Billy. I'm afraid that Terence Cottrell died
about half past twelve this morning.'

I don't care who knows this but I sat down again and
burst into tears. Who was I crying for? I don't know –
perhaps it was for myself because the whole story had
suddenly collapsed about my ears; or for Mrs Cottrell
who would never get her wish for Terence to be cleared;
or for Terence who had never known how she felt about
him. Later on I realised why Mrs Cottrell's voice had
faded away. It must have been about half past twelve
when I had said. 'Where is Terence?' – and at that
moment she had met him again after more than thirty
years ...

And that was the end of the story as I wrote it a year
ago. I put it away, and the details had begun to grow a
bit dim in my mind, though I never forgot I had seen the
old lady's ghost. Then, a few days ago, a long stretch of
Netherton Road was knocked down to make way for a
new block of flats, and Number 101 was one of the first

houses to go. For the first time since 1936 it hit the head-lines again. 'Workman finds treasure in derelict house,' the local paper said.

I don't know what happened to the treasure and, since Terence is dead, I don't care. I daren't think what might have happened if Mrs Cottrell had been able to show me where it was hidden, but I'm pretty sure that no one would have believed that I'd been guided by a ghost. So I've decided to add this postscript to my story. I've sent a copy to the police, and one to Mr Collins at the library. Mum and Dad can read it too. After all this time they can hardly stop my pocket-money for sneaking out in the middle of the night. Perhaps they'll believe it – and per-haps they won't.

Remembering Lee

Eileen Bigland

From the time she was four years old Polly Golspie's small life revolved around David Logan, who was three years her senior. The children were brought – one might almost say thrown – together by Mrs Golspie's fierce snobbishness and Mrs Logan's laziness and, because they were both lonely, they stayed together.

Since Polly's father was chief engineer at Mr Logan's foundry, and since the little industrial town of Belkirk offered few opportunities to those consumed by social ambitions, Mrs Golspie naturally concentrated her attention on the owners of Loganlaw, the big square house on the hill. At the supper-table one May evening she reverted to her favourite subject.

'It's the wonderful view they must have over the Firth of Forth,' she sighed.

'Aye,' growled her husband, 'and gey soon the view's all they'll have left. Ye mind what Karl Marx said about they damned capitalists. . . .'

'James Golspie!' screeched his wife, 'don't ye dare mention that creature to me; he'll be our ruin yet. Here's you worked your way up at the foundry and all you can do is to bite the hand that fed you!'

James, a giant of a man with a shock of red hair, knew from long habit how to deflect his wife's train of thought. 'Simmer doon,' he said kindly. 'From all accounts they're in a fine pickle up at Loganlaw. The maids walked out this morning, all six of them.'

'Why?' demanded Mrs Golspie.

'I heard tell,' began James, then paused. You couldn't

tell a woman with Elspeth's clacking tongue that a house-maid had seen a ghost up by the old keep. 'Och, just women's nonsense,' he went on; 'they said it was lonely. Can you beat that, with a cinema near on their doorstep?'

Mrs Golspie spent the rest of the evening pressing her best frock. She was working out a plan.

Next morning she put on the frock and dressed a pro-testing Polly in a frilly blue muslin, a fawn coat with a little cape, and a blue straw bonnet. 'It prickles,' said Polly, tilting the bonnet over one ear, 'and the buttons on the cape catch my hair.'

Mrs Golspie eyed her daughter coldly. It never ceased to surprise her that a child who looked like a wee fairy could be so stubborn. She crammed the bonnet down over the small pointed face and gave a final twist to the red-gold curls. 'Hold your wheesht, and into the push-chair you get.'

Polly stamped her foot. 'I'm four,' she announced. 'I *walk*.'

'Listen to me,' said her mother desperately, 'if you get in your chair and bide quiet while I talk to the lady we're going to see, I'll give you a whole bag of sweeties to your very self.'

Polly's eyes grew round. It was her first experience of bribery and she found it enjoyable. 'I'll be a mouse,' she promised, climbing into the hated chair.

They went along the main street, up the hill at the end of the town, and turned in through a pair of grand gates leading to a wide, tree-lined drive. 'There now,' said Mrs Golspie as they rounded a corner, 'is yon – I mean that – not beautiful?'

Young as she was Polly appreciated that first sight of Loganlaw with the sun shining on copper-beech trees, on a velvety green lawn, on bright herbaceous borders, on the many long windows of what was surely the biggest grey stone house in the world. On one side of the house an orchard foamed with blossom; on the other a carpet of bluebells surrounded a tumbledown old tower. Polly pointed to it. 'What's that?'

'It's the keep.' Then her mother's voice changed to what father called her 'swell accent' as a small boy on a bicycle charged towards them followed by a lady who seemed to be still wearing her nightgown. 'Good morning, Mrs Logan. Don't tell me that's your baby son? My, how he's grown!'

'Of course he has,' said the lady crossly, 'and he's driving me quite mad. Have you come from the registry?'

Mrs Golspie bridled. 'Oh, no, but Mr Golspie – my husband – being chief engineer at Logan's I heard about your domestic troubles and wondered if I could – er – help?'

'Heaven be praised!' said Mrs Logan. 'It's too ghastly, the boiler seems possessed, and the frig is leaking, and I'm absolutely no use in a kitchen – Oh, *do* come in!'

Mrs Golspie gave a little cough. 'Er – and the dear children?'

'Oh, they'll be all right. David, take little what's-her-name round the garden.'

David walked up to the push-chair and watched Polly fumbling with its straps. 'Butterfingers,' he said rudely, and added, 'I loathe girls.'

Polly glared at him so ferociously that he took a step backward. 'I hate boys, and I'm not what's-her-name, I'm Polly Golspie.'

'What a temper,' said David, but he bent to undo the straps.

When Polly had climbed down the two stood and regarded each other solemnly. David saw a tiny girl with very bright blue eyes; Polly saw a thin boy with a dark, proud face. Suddenly they both grinned.

'Maybe you're not so bad after all,' he remarked. 'Bet you can't shin up that tree,' and he nodded towards the nearest beech.

Polly shinned – to the ruination of her best garments. During the next two hours she played, in turn, the parts of a member of the bandar-log, Flora Macdonald taking the Bonny Prince to Skye, a maiden captured by a cannibal king, and a white man being burnt at the stake by an Indian brave.

'You'll do,' said David laconically, as they sprawled exhausted on the grass.

Polly beamed at him. From that moment she was his adoring slave. For the next four months the children were inseparable. When the Logans had servants – which was not very often – they played in the Loganlaw garden or, if wet, in the house. Otherwise they rampaged through Polly's small home while her mother looked on with an indulgent smile. Normally houseproud, she surveyed the wreckage of her front parlour with equanimity – was she not 'in with the gentry'? – and when Mrs Logan presented her with the negligée Polly had thought was a nightgown, and went on a visit to her native London leaving David in her 'dear Elspeth's' care, Mrs Golspie's cup of bliss brimmed over.

'That sweet she was,' she told her husband. 'Poor thing, she was just pining for a glimpse of her own folks, so I just said, "Och, David's no' a pennyworth of trouble." '

'She's a bad yin,' said James Golspie, 'and it's no' right for the master's son to be stravaiging round with the likes of us. Any road,' and he glowered at the windowpane David had smashed with a cricket-ball that afternoon, 'he'll hae to mind his manners while he's here.'

For all his revolutionary talk James had a queer, crabbed loyalty to the Logan family, whom he regarded in his heart as a breed apart – after all, his father and grandfather had worked for them – and when John Logan called him into his office the following morning his first thought was, 'It'll be about the laddie. Elspeth should have minded her place.'

It was about David, but in a wholly unexpected way. Logan was a cold, taciturn man, but today he seemed almost friendly. In his abrupt manner he thanked James for the kindness shown to David by him and his wife.

'The boy's been running wild,' he went on, 'and I'm having him start lessons with old Dr Fleming, the minister. Later he will go to a Scottish public school. Meanwhile, as his mother plans to be away a great deal in future, I should be grateful if you and Mrs Golspie could have him to board with you. There must, of course, be some financial arrangement.' He gave a short sigh and looked straight at James.

And without hesitation James agreed to the remarkable proposition. If ever he had seen despair in a man's eyes he saw it in Logan's. Without being told, he knew that something had gone sadly wrong with the Logan marriage, knew too that the tall, spare figure opposite him had love for only one human being, his son. As they finished their short discussion and he turned to go, Logan said: 'She's a bonny child, your Polly. She'll be good for David.'

Strangely enough he was right. For all her fairy-like appearance and her slavish devotion to David, there was a sturdiness in her character lacking in his.

The next three years were enchanted for both of them. The fact that Polly went to the elementary school at five while David continued his studies with Dr Fleming did not worry them, for there were the evenings, weekends, holidays to spend together. The rough moorland behind the town was a favourite playground, and when they tired of it they clambered along the rocky shore of the Firth seeking limpets, sea-anemones, cowrie shells. As they grew older they played more in and around Loganlaw – but there was one place that Polly was never anxious to visit, and that was the old keep.

David could not understand her aversion to it. He and his father were very proud of the keep, much prouder than of the big house which only dated back to 1800, for their forebears had lived for centuries there, and even now the old tower was carefully preserved. 'Father says we can play in the upstairs room,' he told Polly; 'there's only a lot of old chests with papers in them. We could have grand games pretending to be Montrose's men holding out against the enemy.'

'I'm not going in there,' said Polly flatly, and even when David jeered at her for being a 'cowardy custard' she refused to budge. She didn't know why but the thought of entering the keep sent shivers down her spine.

David was ten and Polly seven when Mrs Logan came home for the last time. Her stays at Loganlaw had been growing less and less frequent and hitherto she had paid little attention to her son, but on the afternoon after her arrival Polly heard her light, high voice calling David. 'Your mother's calling you,' she said.

It was a very hot day and David was making himself yet hotter by building a fire outside the wigwam they had rigged up in the orchard. 'Och, let her call,' he panted, between puffs at the smouldering wood. Rewarded at last by a flicker of flame he sat back on his heels. 'She's an awful silly, anyway,' he added dispassionately.

'David!' the voice was nearer now. 'Oh, there you are – heavens, you look like a savage! Still playing with your little village friend?' Mrs Logan's laugh held a hint of cruelty. 'I want to speak to you – I know, let's go to the keep.'

Polly sat very still, her hands clenched tightly in her lap. Presently she began to rock her small body to and fro. 'By the pricking of my thumbs, something wicked this way comes'; then she shook her head. It was *she* who was wicked, saying such things about Mrs Logan, but somehow the colour had gone out of the day. Very busily she began to puff at the fire. David would be pleased if she got it really alight.

But twilight was falling and the fire a heap of ash before David returned, wildly excited. 'I say, Polly, whatever do you think's happened? Mother's leaving Father, and she's going to marry an Italian and live in a castle near Rome, and I'm going with her. It sounds absolutely super – listen!' and he plunged into details.

Polly felt as if her heart had done a somersault inside

her chest. David was leaving her, going to live in some foreign place.

'Polly, you're not listening!'

David's laughing brown face was close to her own, but she couldn't see it properly and, oh, dear, she mustn't cry, David hated cry-babies. 'We're late,' she mumbled, scrambling to her feet. 'I'm going home.' She ran blindly through the orchard and as she reached the drive she cannoned into something that turned out to be Mr Logan.

'Is there a beastie after you?' he enquired kindly.

'Oh yes,' she wailed, and then she was sobbing in Mr Logan's arms and telling him all about it.

At last he patted her back. 'Don't worry, Polly, David's not going away. Now I'll drive you home, your mother will be worrying.'

'But – but David?'

'I'll see to him later,' said Mr Logan grimly.

Always afterwards Polly's memories of that dreadful summer were jumbled in her mind. There was a great to-do among the good folk of Belkirk who thought divorce was on a par with murder; and Mrs Logan went flouncing off to Italy; and David mooched around scowling and took to spending hours by himself in the upstairs room of the keep.

Then Lee came, and nothing was ever quite the same again.

Of course, Polly kept reminding herself, Lee wasn't a real person, he was just another of David's inventions. She first heard of him on a September day when David marched into the toyshop and came out with a box of plasticine. 'Now go into the draper's and get me some pins – sharp ones,' he said.

'Whatever for?' asked Polly.

David put his head on one side and half-closed his eyes. 'I'll show you when we reach the wigwam,' he said with an air of mystery. 'Lee told me how to make something.'

'Who's Lee?'

He glanced at her scornfully. 'A friend of mine. You don't know him.' He began to walk up the hill to Logan-law so quickly that Polly had to run to keep up with him. 'You mean a pretend friend?' she panted, 'you don't know any boy called Lee.'

David stopped. 'I do. I do!' he said; 'don't you dare say I don't know Lee!'

It was a horrible day altogether. When they reached the wigwam David made a little figure out of plasticine and then stuck pins all over it. 'There!' he kept saying as he jabbed the pins in, 'that'll settle you!' and the queer part was that David didn't look like himself at all while he was sticking the pins in. His face was sharper, thinner, his upper lip lifted in a snarl like Dr Fleming's old collie dog.

'What are you making?' asked Polly in a trembling voice.

'You're too silly to know,' David mocked her, 'only Lee and I know. Now light a fire.'

When the fire was going he took a long stick and poked the little figure carefully into the middle of it, then crouched beside the flames muttering a lot of long words Polly couldn't catch. 'That'll teach him,' he said at last, and raked the now sadly shrivelled figure from the fire. When it had cooled off he wrapped it in a grubby hand-kerchief and rose to his feet. 'Come on,' he said tersely.

'What are you going to do with it?'

But David shook his head and capered on ahead of her. 'Lee said I wasn't to tell you. He doesn't like you.'

The next day, however, Mrs Golspie kept David in bed as he had a feverish cold. 'I doubt he's sickening for something,' Mrs Golspie said to Polly, 'but it's too late to keep the pair of you apart, so away up and sit beside the lad. It's a mercy you don't go back to school till next week.'

David seemed to be dozing when she crept into his room, but presently he spoke: 'Did you hear how father was this morning?'

Polly blinked. 'But Mr Logan isn't ill, I saw him driving down to the foundry about nine o'clock.'

To her consternation David sat bolt upright in bed. 'I don't believe it,' he cried; 'he's sick, he's dying!' Again his lip lifted in a snarl. 'We witched him, Lee and I.'

'The boy's wandering,' said Mrs Golspie from the door-way. 'Lie you down, David, and I'll put a wet cloth round your head.'

For ten days David ran a high temperature. 'I can't make it out,' said the worried doctor, 'his chest is clear and he has no definite symptoms. He hasn't had any shock of any kind, has he? Who's this Lee he keeps babbling about?'

But neither Mr Logan nor the Golspies had ever heard of a boy called Lee – 'but maybe Polly knows,' they said.

Polly heard them talking on the landing and as they walked downstairs she slid into David's room. 'David,' she whispered urgently, 'they're asking about Lee.'

He peered at her over the bedclothes, and it was a funny thing but his eyes had a red glint in them. 'Don't you tell,' he croaked, 'don't dare tell he lives in the keep.'

'No,' breathed Polly. 'Is he – is he a *kelpie*?'

David gave the ghost of a laugh. 'No, he's – oh, never mind. I'm going to sleep now.'

Polly tiptoed out and sat on the top step of the stairs. She ought to have known Lee lived in the keep. That was why she'd never wanted to go into it. . . .

'Polly!' called her mother.

She walked slowly downstairs and into the parlour. The grown-ups looked very solemn. They asked her if she knew anyone called Lee.

By nature an honest child she had never told a direct falsehood, but she had to now for David's sake. 'He's a boy we met up on the moors,' she said in a clear, small voice.

'What sort of a boy?' asked Mr Logan sharply.

Polly swallowed hard. 'A nice boy, but kind of raggedy. I think he was a tinker.'

She felt sure her face was scarlet, but nobody noticed because they were all talking at once about tinkers and what a bad lot they were.

After that the moors were put out of bounds. David mended slowly and even when he was better he seemed to prefer pottering about Belkirk to visiting Loganlaw. By Christmas he had apparently forgotten Lee. Only Polly knew he was still in the keep. She couldn't explain this knowledge, even to herself, but it was there in the back of her mind, and she began to think of Lee as a wild animal, always lurking in the background waiting for a chance to pounce. The thing to do, of course, was to prevent David from going near the keep, but with the coming of spring that became impossible.

Once again the keep drew David like a magnet, and each time he emerged from a visit to the upstairs room Polly knew that Lee had pounced. Now, however, he didn't make David ill, he just made him what Polly called bad. When Lee had pounced David did nasty things he would never have dreamed of doing in the ordinary way. Once, when he and Polly were alone in the Loganlaw dining-room, he threw the pepper-pots and salt-cellars into the fire and crowed with delight when the silver began to melt. Then there was the day he took a suit from his father's wardrobe and slashed it into strips with a sharp knife, and the time he rigged up a booby-trap in the shed for the old gardener so that the poor man broke his wrist.

Those were only a few of the happenings during the next two years; yet David was normally such a bright, kindly lad that nobody except Polly suspected he was behind them. Bewildered and frightened, she still had an intense loyalty towards her playmate so she kept quiet even when Mr Logan blamed the local police for allowing some gang of hooligans to keep on raiding Loganlaw, and when the man and wife he had hired to keep house left with loud protests about 'bogey-men'.

As she watched David she grew dimly aware that there

was a rhythm about his outbursts and that they only occurred when the moon was at the full. She did not know why this should be so, but she bent all her small energies on trying to prevent him visiting the keep on the dates she studied closely in the calendar and by the time she was ten and David thirteen she thought happily that her efforts were succeeding.

She was wrong.

Years before David had been entered for Fettes. Now, on a warm June evening, his father told him he would go there the following September. Immediately David begged for another year at home. 'No, no,' said Mr Logan. 'Dr Fleming is most insistent that you start this autumn.'

David raged to Polly. 'What does that stupid old man know? If it wasn't for his nonsense I could get round Father. I wonder . . .' He paused, and in apprehension Polly watched his face change. The features became thinner, sharper, the upper lip began to curl. 'David!' she said desperately, 'there's a fair over at Leven tomorrow, let's go.'

'I don't want to,' he answered flatly, and drifted off in the direction of the keep.

He still lodged with the Golspies, and two afternoons later Polly met him coming out of the bathroom with a small key in his hand. 'That's father's,' she said quickly.

'Nosey Parker!' replied David rudely, and ran helter-skelter down the stairs.

Terror rose in Polly. In his spare time Mr Golspie conducted all kinds of scientific experiments in a hut at the bottom of the garden, and as Mrs Golspie was mortally afraid lest the children poison themselves with the various solutions and crystals he used, these were kept locked in a cupboard in the bathroom. Surely David hadn't stolen something from it? And if he had, what did he propose to do with it?

She hurried after him, but he had vanished. 'He's away to Dr Fleming's for his Latin lesson,' said her mother. 'Sit ye down and shell these peas.'

Polly's fear lessened as she performed the familiar task, and when David returned full of good spirits the last of her unease vanished. Listening to him laughing and joking with her parents it was impossible to believe he had any dark thought in his mind.

But next morning Dr Fleming's fat maid Mary panted up the path with the news that the old gentleman had been taken suddenly and terrifyingly ill in the night. 'The doctor canna' make it oot. . . . Awfu' sickness, and such pain . . . a' these questions aboot what's he eaten, and me cooked for him thirty year. . . .' These snatches of talk floated through the open kitchen door. Polly glanced towards David. He was sitting with his head cocked to one side, and a funny little smile played round his mouth. 'David, you didn't?' she whispered, but he looked at and through her and the expression in his eyes told the answer she dreaded – Lee had pounced again.

Dr Fleming did not die, but he was very ill indeed. Somehow – it never transpired exactly how – he had accidentally swallowed cyanide of potassium. But still Polly kept silent. Whatever David had done she had to protect him. Besides, he was going away from Belkirk, away from the keep, away from Lee. *Away from Lee* – surely that was all that mattered?

'How whey-faced you are,' Mrs Golspie kept repeating through the first winter David was gone, 'it's Parrish's Food for you.'

So Polly obediently took the medicine and slowly, very slowly, the dead weight at her heart lifted. Mr Logan and David spent both Christmas and Easter holidays staying with relations in Edinburgh, and the next summer they went fishing up in Sutherlandshire. Without David Polly felt only half alive, yet she was fiercely glad about his continued absence. It kept him away from Lee; moreover, she felt that he wanted to be away, to forget Lee. Anxiously she scanned his frequent, careless letters. He liked Fettes . . . he had made lots of friends . . . the Games master was a splendid chap and said he'd make a jolly good forward in a year or two. . . . Never once did he mention the keep.

The next year was 1939 and not until 1944 did David come home to Loganlaw. Polly was fifteen then, and showing signs of great beauty, but although they had been apart for so long she and David fell into their old relationship without effort. In the autumn David would be called up, but for this one snatched summer the two went back to the ploys of childhood, roaming the moors together, guddling trout in the hill streams, looking for cowries on the shore – and never once did David visit the keep.

Then one August night Mr Logan, worn out with the strain of running the foundry in wartime, died in his sleep. After his funeral Polly and David wandered through the rooms of Loganlaw, sad at heart. 'He loved you so much,' said Polly, as they stood by the dead man's desk in his study. David reached out and took her hand. 'I know.' Then his voice broke, 'Oh, Polly, and I tried to kill him once, do you remember? I did awful things – other things – I tried to poison Dr Fleming. God, I was mad, mad . . .!'

'It wasn't you,' said Polly sturdily, 'it was Lee.'

A shudder ran through David, and he squeezed her hand so tight she gave a cry of pain. 'Keep me away from Lee, Polly. Stay with me, never let me go!'

In that instant Polly became a woman. 'Never', she said, cradling David's head in her arms, 'never, I promise.'

David was overseas for four long years. Discharged from the army he went up to Cambridge, and it was not until 1952 that he came back to Loganlaw, a tall, bronzed young man but essentially the same David she had played with so long ago. 'And you're the same too,' he said, rumpling Polly's red-gold hair, 'a funny, canny wee thing. Twenty-three now, aren't you? Oh, Polly, Polly, you're the only one I ever wanted all the time I was away. I can't live without you – when are you going to come and live with me at Loganlaw?'

'Whenever you want,' she said.

But Mrs Golspie had other ideas. Polly must have a trousseau, there must be a grand wedding, she wanted at least three months in which to make preparations. And because David and Polly were completely absorbed in each other they let her have her way. 'And during the day when I'm at the foundry,' said David, 'you can do your worst with Loganlaw, the place has been let go to ruin the past eight years.'

Every morning Polly made her way up the hill, and a week before their wedding she had the house looking like a new pin. 'I've only to hang the drawing-room curtains,' she told David. 'Come and fetch me when you finish about six o'clock.'

All day she sang as she worked and she was making herself some tea when a knock came at the back door. Opening it she found Douglas, a simple-minded old man who had done odd jobs about the garden for Mr Logan. Was there anything he could do? he asked.

Polly set him to tidying up the garage and later took him a cup of tea. 'Ye've made the place fair bonny,' he said, 'except for yon,' and he jerked a thumb towards the keep; 'there'll be no happiness at Loganlaw till they pu' it down, stane by stane. It's aye been wisht since yon Jasper Lee hid there.'

Polly jumped. 'Who?' she demanded.

Old Douglas chuckled. 'They think I'm daft, but I'm the only one that remembers. It happened when I was a laddie. I dinna' mind where Jasper Lee came from, but he was a killer – aye, he strangled a man back oot on the moors, and he strangled the polisman they sent to catch him. He hid in the keep, but he couldna get oot, ye see, for the polis were stravaiging all round knowing he was some place.'

Polly shook his arm urgently. 'But what happened to him?'

'Och, they found him there months later. He'd died o' starvation.' With the inconsequentiality of the very old, Douglas began reminiscing about other ancient happenings near Belkirk, but Polly was out of the kitchen and speeding across the grass to the keep. In a minute or two she stood on the threshold of that upstairs room she had feared since childhood. There was naught in the room save two old oak chests and a rickety chair. The air smelt musty and though the sun beat in through the narrow, deep-set window Polly felt suddenly very cold. Then out of the emptiness something, she didn't know what, moved towards her and a thing like a dead hand touched her cheek. With a wild scream she turned and stumbled down the stairway, groped her way out of the door and fell headlong on the grass.

The next thing she knew David was on his knees beside her. 'For pity's sake, Polly, whatever is wrong? You must have fainted, my poor wee bird.'

She looked up at him. 'Oh, David, do you remember Lee?'

He drew in his breath sharply. 'My God, that *you* should remind me of him!' He took his arms from her and got to his feet. 'He's there still,' he said in a husky voice. 'He wants me, I know he wants me!'

When Polly fully recovered her wits he was gone and a full moon was rising over the hill. Somehow she dragged herself back to the house and into the hall where the telephone stood on a table. But as she lifted the receiver she remembered a man had called that afternoon to say it would not be in working order till tomorrow. Unable to make her legs carry her further she sank into a chair. 'David,' she whimpered, 'David, come back!'

A cloud passed across the moon and the house was very dark and still. Then there came the sound of footsteps and the electric light snapped on. David stood there, his hand on the switch. His face was white and haggard, and his mouth was parted in that awful familiar snarl. 'Lee said you'd send me back to him,' he said. 'Lee hates

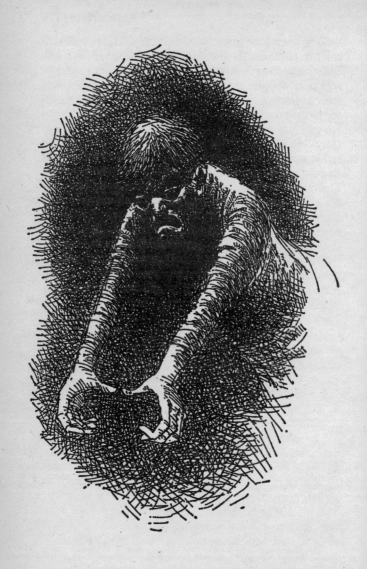

you, he wants me to kill you.' Suddenly he threw out his arms in front of him and began to walk towards her, and Polly's cry died in her throat as cruel fingers tightened round it. But just as the pressure grew unbearable David gave a choking cough and released his grip before slumping to the ground.

On a fine October morning Polly sat beside David's bed in his room at Loganlaw. The fever which had possessed him for many weeks had gone, but he was still strangely ill. Presently Polly rose and crossed to the long window. Four men were demolishing the keep, and even as she watched she saw them bend down to remove the last big stones. At a sound from the bed she swung round. David had propped himself on one elbow. 'Goodbye, poor Lee,' he muttered, 'you'll never come back any more.' Then he sank back on his pillows, his face tranquil. Polly gazed down at him as he fell into a deep, natural sleep. 'Never any more,' she repeated slowly, 'never any more.'

Jack-in-the-Box

Ray Bradbury

He looked through the cold morning windows with the
Jack-in-the-Box in his hands, prying the rusted lid. But no
matter how he struggled, the Jack would not jump to the
light with a cry, or slap its velvet mittens on the air, or
bob in a dozen directions with a wild and painted smile.
Crushed under the lid, in its jail, it stayed crammed tight
coil on coil. With your ear to the box, you felt pressure
beneath, the fear and panic of the trapped toy. It was like
holding someone's heart in your hand. Edwin could not
tell if the box pulsed or if his own blood beat against the
lid.

He threw the box down and looked to the window.
Outside the window the trees surrounded the house
which surrounded Edwin. He could not see beyond the
trees. If he tried to find another World beyond them, the
trees wove themselves thick with the wind, to still his
curiosity, to stop his eyes.

'Edwin!' Behind him, Mother's waiting, nervous breath
as she drank her breakfast coffee. 'Stop staring. Come
eat.'

'No,' he whispered.

'What?' A stiffened rustle. She must have turned.
'Which is more important, breakfast or that window?'

'The window . . .' he whispered and sent his gaze running the paths and trails he had tried for thirteen years.
Was it true that the trees flowed on ten thousand miles
to nothingness? He could not say. His sight returned
defeated, to the lawn, the steps, his hands trembling on
the pane.

He turned to eat his tasteless apricots, alone with his mother in the vast and echoing breakfast room. Five thousand mornings at this table, this window, and no movement beyond the trees.

The two of them ate silently.

She was the pale woman that no one but the birds saw in old country houses in fourth-floor cupola windows, each morning at six, each afternoon at four, each evening at nine, and also passing by one minute after midnight, there she would be, in her tower, silent and white, high and alone and quiet. It was like passing a deserted greenhouse in which one last wild white blossom lifted its head to the moonlight.

And her child, Edwin, was the thistle that one breath of wind might unpod in a season of thistles. His hair was silken and his eyes were of a constant blue and feverish temperature. He had a haunted look, as if he slept poorly. He might fly apart like a packet of ladyfinger firecrackers if a certain door slammed.

His mother began to talk, slowly and with great caution, then more rapidly, and then angrily, and then almost spitting at him.

'Why must you disobey every morning? I don't like your staring from the window, do you hear? What do you want? Do you want to see them?' she cried, her fingers twitching. She was blazingly lovely, like an angry white flower. 'Do you want to see the Beasts that run down paths and crush people like strawberries?'

Yes, he thought, I'd like to see the Beasts, horrible as they are.

'Do you want to go out there?' she cried, 'like your Father did before you were born, and be killed as he was killed, struck down by one of those Terrors on the road, would you like that!'

'No...'

'Isn't it enough they murdered your Father? Why should you even think of those Beasts!' She motioned toward the forest. 'Well, if you really want to die that much, go ahead!'

She quieted, but her fingers kept opening and closing on the tablecloth. 'Edwin, Edwin, your Father built every part of this World, it was beautiful for him, it should be for you. There's nothing, nothing, beyond those trees but death; I won't have you near it! This *is* the World. There's no other worth bothering with.'

He nodded miserably.

'Smile now, and finish your toast,' she said.

He ate slowly, with the window reflected in secret on his silver spoon.

'Mom . . . ?' He couldn't say it. 'What's . . . dying? You talk about it. Is it a feeling?'

'To those who must live on after someone else, a bad feeling, yes.' She stood up suddenly. 'You're late for school! Run!'

He kissed her as he grabbed his books. 'Bye!'

'Say hello to teacher!'

He fled from her like a bullet from gun. Up endless staircases, through passages, halls, past windows that poured down dark gallery panels like white waterfalls. Up, up through the layer-cake Worlds with the thick frostings of Oriental rug between, and bright candles on top.

From the highest stair he gazed down through four intervals of Universe.

Lowlands of kitchen, dining room, parlour. Two Middle Countries of music, games, pictures, and locked, forbidden rooms. And here – he whirled – the Highlands of picnics, adventure, and learning. Here he roamed, idled, or sat singing lonely child songs on the winding journey to school.

This, then, was the Universe. Father (or God, as Mother often called him) had raised its mountains of wallpapered plaster long ago. This was Father-God's creation, in which stars blazed at the flick of a switch. And the sun was Mother, and Mother was the sun, about which all the

Worlds swung, turning. And Edwin, a small dark meteor, spun up around through the dark carpets and shimmering tapestries of space. You saw him rise to vanish on vast comet staircases, on hikes and explorations.

Sometimes he and Mother picnicked in the Highlands, spread cool snow linens on red-tuffed, Persian lawns, on crimson meadows in a rarefied plateau at the summit of the Worlds where flaking portraits of sallow strangers looked meanly down on their eating and their revels. They drew water from silver taps in hidden tiled niches, smashed the tumblers on hearthstones, shrieking. Played hide-and-seek in enchanted Upper Countries, in unknown, wild, and hidden lands, where she found him rolled like a mummy in a velvet window drape or under sheeted furniture like a rare plant protected from some wind. Once, lost, he wandered for hours in insane foothills of dust and echoes, where the hooks and hangers in closets were hung only with night. But she found him and carried him weeping down through the levelling Universe to the Parlour where dust motes, exact and familiar, fell in showers of sparks on the sunlit air.

He ran up a stair.

Here he knocked a thousand thousand doors, all locked and forbidden. Here Picasso ladies and Dali gentlemen screamed silently from canvas asylums, their gold eyes burning when he dawdled.

'Those Things live *out there*,' his mother had said, pointing to the Dali-Picasso families.

Now running quickly past, he stuck out his tongue at them.

He stopped running.

One of the forbidden doors stood open.

Sunlight slanted warm through it, exciting him.

Beyond the door, a spiral stair screwed around up in sun and silence.

He stood, gasping. Year after year he had tried the doors that were always found locked. What would happen now if he shoved this one full open and climbed the stair? Was some Monster hiding at the top?

'Hello!'

His voice leapt up around the spiralled sunlight. 'Hello
. . .' whispered a faint, far lazy echo, high, high, and
gone.

He moved through the door.

'Please, please, don't hurt me,' he whispered to the
high sunlit place.

He climbed, pausing with each step to wait for his
punishment, eyes shut like a penitent. Faster now, he
leapt around and around and up until his knees ached
and his breath fountained in and out and his head banged
like a bell and at last he reached the terrible summit of
the climb and stood in an open sun-drenched tower.

The sun struck his eyes a blow. Never, never so much
sun! He stumbled to the iron rail.

'It's there!' His mouth opened from one direction to
another. 'It's there!' He ran in a circle. 'There!'

He stood above the sombre tree barrier. For the first
time he stood high over the windy chestnuts and elms
and as far as he could see was green grass, green trees,
and white ribbons on which beetles ran, and the other
half of the world was blue and endless, with the sun
lost and dropping away in an incredible deep blue room
so vast he felt himself fall with it, screamed, and clutched
the tower ledge, and beyond the trees, beyond the white
ribbons where the beetles ran he saw things like fingers
sticking up, but he saw no Dali-Picasso terrors, he saw
only some small red-and-white-and-blue handkerchiefs
fluttering high on great white poles.

He was suddenly sick; he was sick again.

Turning, he almost fell flat down the stairs.

He slammed the forbidden door, fell against it.

'You'll go blind.' He crushed his hands to his eyes. 'You
shouldn't have seen, you shouldn't, you shouldn't!'

He fell to his knees, he lay on the floor twisted tight,
covered up. He need wait but a moment – the blindness
would come.

Five minutes later he stood at an ordinary Highlands window, looking out at his own familiar Garden World.

He saw once more the elms and hickory trees and the stone wall, and that forest which he had taken to be an endless wall itself, beyond which lay nothing but nightmare nothingness, mist, rain, and eternal night. Now it was certain, the Universe did not end with the forest. There were other worlds than those contained in Highland or Lowland.

He tried the forbidden door again. Locked.

Had he really gone up? Had he really discovered those half-green, half-blue vastnesses? Had God seen him? Edwin trembled. God. God, who smoked mysterious black pipes and wielded magical walking sticks. God who might be watching even now!

Edwin murmured, touching his cold face.

'I can still see. Thank you, thank you. I can *still* see!'

At nine-thirty, half an hour late, he rapped on the school door.

'Good morning, Teacher!'

The door swung open. Teacher waited in her tall grey, thick-clothed monk's robe, the cowl hiding her face. She wore her usual silver spectacles. Her grey-gloved hands beckoned.

'You're late.'

Beyond her the land of books burned in bright colours from the hearth. There were walls bricked with encyclopedias, and a fireplace in which you could stand without bumping your head. A log blazed fiercely.

The door closed, and there was a warm quiet. Here was the desk, where God had once sat, he'd walked this carpet, stuffing his pipe with rich tobacco, and scowled out that vast, stained-glass window. The room smelled of God, rubbed wood, tobacco, leather, and silver coins. Here, Teacher's voice sang like a solemn harp, telling of God, the old days, and the World when it had shaken with God's determination, trembled at his wit, when the

World was abuilding under God's hand, a blueprint, a cry, and timber rising. God's fingerprints still lay like half-melted snowflakes on a dozen sharpened pencils in a locked glass display. They must never be touched lest they melt away forever.

Here, here in the Highlands, to the soft sound of Teacher's voice running on, Edwin learned what was expected of him and his body. He was to grow into a Presence, he must fit the odours and the trumpet voice of God. He must some day stand tall and burning with pale fire at this high window to shout dust off the beams of the Worlds; he must be God Himself! Nothing must prevent it. Not the sky or the trees or the Things beyond the trees.

Teacher moved like a vapour in the room.

'Why are you late, Edwin?'

'I don't know.'

'I'll ask you again. Edwin why are you late?'

'One – one of the forbidden doors was open. . . .'

He heard the hiss of Teacher's breath. He saw her slowly slide back and sink into the large hand-carved chair, swallowed by darkness, her glasses flashing light before they vanished. He felt her looking out at him from shadow and her voice was numbed and so like a voice he heard at night, his own voice crying just before he woke from some nightmare. 'Which door? Where?' she said. 'Oh, it must be locked!'

'The door by the Dali-Picasso people,' he said, in panic. He and Teacher had always been friends. Was that finished now? Had he spoiled things? 'I climbed the stair. I had to, I had to! I'm sorry, I'm sorry. Please, don't tell Mother!'

Teacher sat lost in the hollow chair, in the hollow cowl. Her glasses made faint firefly glitters in the well where she moved alone. 'And what did you *see* up there?' she murmured. . .

'A big blue room!'

'Did you?'

'And a green one, and ribbons with bugs running on them, but I didn't, I didn't stay long, I swear, I swear!'

'Green room, ribbons, yes ribbons, and the little bugs running along them, yes,' she said, and her voice made him sad.

He reached out for her hand, but it fell away to her lap and groped back, in darkness, to her breast. 'I came right down, I locked the door, I won't go look again, ever!' he cried.

Her voice was so faint he could hardly hear what she said. 'But now you've seen, and you'll want to see more, and you'll always be curious now.' The cowl moved slowly back and forth. Its deepness turned toward him, questioning. 'Did you—*like* what you saw?'

'I was scared. It was big.'

'Big, yes, too big. Large, large, so large, Edwin. Not like *our* world. Big, large, uncertain. Oh, why did you do this! You knew it was wrong!'

The fire bloomed and withered on the hearth while she waited for his answer and finally when he could not answer she said, as if her lips were barely moving, 'Is it your Mother?'

'I don't know!'

'Is she nervous, is she mean, does she snap at you, does she hold too tight, do you want time alone, is that it, is that it, is that it?'

'Yes, yes!' he sobbed, wildly.

'Is that why you ran off, she demands all your time, all your thoughts?' Lost and sad, her voice. 'Tell me . . .'

His hands had gone sticky with tears. 'Yes!' He bit his fingers and the backs of his hands. 'Yes!' It was wrong to admit such things, but he didn't have to say them now, she said them, she said them, and all he must do is agree, shake his head, bite his knuckles, cry out between sobs.

Teacher was a million years old.

'We learn,' she said, wearily. Rousing from her chair, she moved with a slow swaying of grey robes to the desk where her gloved hand searched a long time to find pen and paper. 'We learn, Oh God, but slowly, and with pain, we learn. We think we do right, but all the time, all the time, we kill the Plan. . . .' She hissed her breath, jerked her head up suddenly. The cowl looked completely empty, shivering.

She wrote words on the paper.

'Give this to your mother. It tells her you must have two full hours every afternoon to yourself, to prowl where you wish. Anywhere. Except *out there*. Are you listening, child?'

'Yes.' He dried his face. 'But—'

'Go on.'

'Did Mother lie to me about *out there*, and the Beasts?'

'Look at me,' she said. 'I've been your friend, I've never beaten you, as your mother sometimes must. We're both here to help you understand and grow so you won't be destroyed as God was.'

She arose, and in rising, turned the cowl such a way that colour from the hearth washed over her face. Swiftly, the firelight erased her many wrinkles.

Edwin gasped. His heart gave a jolting thump. 'The fire!'

Teacher froze.

'The fire!' Edwin looked at the fire and back to her face. The cowl jerked away from his gaze, the face vanished in the deep well, gone. 'Your face,' said Edwin numbly. 'You look like Mother!'

She moved swiftly to the books, seized one down. She talked to the shelves in her high, singing, monotonous voice. 'Women look alike, you know that! Forget it! Here, here!' And she brought him the book. 'Read the first chapter! Read the diary!'

Edwin took the book but did not feel its weight in his hands. The fire rumbled and sucked itself brilliantly up the flue as he began to read and as he read Teacher sank back down and settled and quieted and the more he read the more the grey cowl nodded and became serene, the hidden face like a clapper gone solemn in its bell.

Firelight ignited the gold animal lettering of the shelved books as he read and he spoke the words but was really thinking of these books from which pages had been razored, and clipped, certain lines erased, certain pictures torn, the leather jaws of some books glued tight, others like mad dogs, muzzled in hard bronze straps to keep him away. All this he thought while his lips moved through the fire-quiet:

'In the Beginning was God. Who created the Universe and the Worlds within the Universe, the Continents within the Worlds and the Lands within the Continents, and shaped from His mind and hand His loving wife and a child who in time would be God Himself . . .'

Teacher nodded slowly. The fire fell softly away to slumbering coals. Edwin read on.

Down the banister, breathless, he slid into the Parlour. 'Mom, Mom!'

She lay in a plump maroon chair, breathless, as if she, too, had run a great way.

'Mom, Mom, you're soaking wet!'

'Am I?' she said, as if it was his fault she'd been rushing about. 'So I am, so I am.' She took a deep breath and sighed. Then she took his hands and kissed each one. She looked at him steadily, her eyes dilating. 'Well now, listen here, I've a surprise! Do you know what's coming tomorrow? You can't guess! Your birthday!'

'But it's only been ten months!'

'Tomorrow it is! Do us wonders, I say. And anything I *say* is so is *really* so, my dear.'

She laughed.

'And we open another secret room?' He was dazed.

'The fourteenth room, yes! Fifteenth room next year, sixteenth, seventeenth, and so on and on till your twenty-first birthday, Edwin! Then, oh, then we'll open up the triple-locked doors to the most important room and you'll be Man of the House, Father, God, Ruler of the Universe!'

'Hey,' he said. And, 'Hey!' He tossed his books straight up in the air. They exploded like a great burst of doves, whistling. He laughed. She laughed. Their laughter flew and fell with the books. He ran to scream down the banister again.

At the bottom of the stairs, she waited, arms wide, to catch him.

Edwin lay on his moonlit bed and his fingers pried at the Jack-in-the-Box, but the lid stayed shut; he turned it in his hands, blindly, but did not look down at it. To-morrow, his birthday – but why? Was he *that* good? No. Why then, should the birthday come so soon? Well, simply because things had got, what word could you use? Nervous? Yes, things had begun to shimmer by day as well as by night. He saw the white tremor, the moon-light sifting down and down of an invisible snow in his mother's face. It would take yet another of his birthdays to quiet her again.

'My birthdays,' he said to the ceiling, 'will come quicker from now on. I know, I know. Mom laughs so loud, so much, and her eyes are funny....'

Would Teacher be invited to the party? No. Mother and Teacher had never met. 'Why not?' 'Because,' said Mom. 'Don't you *want* to meet Mom, Teacher?' 'Some day,' said Teacher, faintly, blowing off like cobwebs in the hall. 'Some ... day....'

And where did Teacher go at night? Did she drift through all those secret mountain countries high up near the moon where the chandeliers were skinned blind with dust, or did she wander out beyond the trees that lay beyond the trees that lay beyond the trees? No, hardly that!

He twisted the toy in his sweating hands. Last year, when things began to tremble and quiver, hadn't Mother advanced his birthday several months, too? Yes, oh, yes, yes.

Think of something else. God. God building cold

midnight cellar, sun-baked attic, and all miracles between. Think of the hour of his death, crushed by some monstrous beetle beyond the wall. Oh, how the worlds must have rocked with His passing!

Edwin moved the Jack-in-the-Box to his face, whispered against the lid. 'Hello! Hello! Hello, hello . . .'

No answer save the sprung-tight coiled-in tension there. I'll get you out, thought Edwin. Just wait, just wait. It may hurt, but there's only one way. Here, here . . .

And he moved from bed to window and leaned far out, looking down to the marbled walk in the moonlight. He raised the box high, felt the sweat trickle from his armpit, felt his fingers clench, felt his arm jerk. He flung the box out, shouting. The box tumbled in the cold air, down. It took a long time to strike the marble pavement.

Edwin bent still further over, gasping.

'Well?' he cried. 'Well?' and again, 'You there!' and 'You!'

The echoes faded. The box lay in the forest shadows. He could not see if the crash had broken it wide. He could not see if the Jack had risen, smiling, from its hideous jail or if it bobbed upon the wind now this way, that, this way, that, its silver bells jingling softly. He listened. He stood by the window for an hour staring, listening, and at last went back to bed.

Morning. Bright voices moved near and far in and out the Kitchen World and Edwin opened his eyes. Whose voices, now whose could they be? Some of God's workmen? The Dali people? But Mother hated them; no. The voices faded in a humming roar. Silence. And from a great distance, a running, running grew louder and still louder until the door burst open.

'Happy Birthday!'

They danced, they ate frosted cookies, they bit lemon ices, they drank pink wines, and there stood his name on a snow-powdered cake as Mother chorded the piano into an avalanche of sound and opened her mouth to sing, then whirled to seize him away to more strawberries, more wines, more laughter that shook chandeliers into trembling rain. Then, a silver key flourished, they raced to unlock the fourteenth forbidden door.

'Ready! Hold on!'

The door whispered into the wall.

'Oh,' said Edwin.

For, disappointingly enough, this fourteenth room was nothing at all but a dusty dull-brown closet. It promised nothing as had the rooms given him on other anniversaries! His sixth birthday present, now, had been the schoolroom in the Highlands. On his seventh birthday he had opened the playroom in the Lowlands. Eighth, the music room; Ninth, the miraculous hell-fired kitchen! Tenth was the room where phonographs hissed in a continuous exhalation of ghosts singing on a gentle wind. Eleventh was the vast green diamond room of the Garden with a carpet that had to be cut instead of swept!

'Oh, don't be disappointed; move!' Mother, laughing, pushed him in the closet. 'Wait till you see how magical! Shut the door!'

She thrust a red button flush with the wall.

Edwin shrieked. 'No!'

For the room was quivering, working, like a mouth that held them in iron jaws; the room moved, the wall slid away below.

'Oh, hush now, darling,' she said. The door drifted down through the floor, and a long insanely vacant wall slithered by like an endlessly rustling snake to bring another door and another door with it that did not stop but travelled on while Edwin screamed and clutched his mother's waist. The room whined and cleared its throat somewhere; the trembling ceased, the room stood still. Edwin stared at a strange new door and heard his mother say go on, open it, there, now, there. And the new door gaped upon still further mystery. Edwin blinked.

'The Highlands! This is the Highlands! How did we

get here? Where's the Parlour, mom, where's the Parlour?'

She fetched him out through the door. 'We jumped straight up, and we flew. Once a week, you'll fly to school instead of running the long way around!'

He still could not move, but only stood looking at the mystery of Land exchanged for Land, of Country replaced by higher and further Country.

'Oh, Mother, Mother . . .' he said.

It was a sweet long time in the deep grass of the garden where they idled most deliciously, sipped huge cupfuls of apple cider with their elbows on crimson silk cushions, their shoes kicked off, their toes bedded in sour dandelions, sweet clover. Mother jumped twice when she heard Monsters roar beyond the forest. Edwin kissed her cheek. 'It's all right,' he said, 'I'll protect you.'

'I know you will,' she said, but she turned to gaze at the pattern of trees, as if any moment the chaos out there might smash the forest with a blow and stamp its Titan's foot down and grind them to dust.

Late in the long blue afternoon, they saw a chromium bird thing fly through a bright rift in the trees, high and roaring. They ran for the Parlour, heads bent as before a green storm of lightning and rain, feeling the sound pour blinding showers to drench them.

Crackle, crackle – the birthday burnt away to cellophane nothingness. At sunset, in the dim soft Parlour Country, Mother inhaled champagne with her tiny seedling nostrils and her pale summer-rose mouth, then, drowsy wild, herded Edwin off to his room and shut him in.

He undressed in slow-pantomimed wonder, thinking, this year, next year, and which room two years, three years, from today? What about the Beasts, the Monsters? And being mashed and God killed? What was killed? What was Death? Was Death a feeling? Did God enjoy it so much he never came back? Was Death a journey then?

In the hall, on her way downstairs, Mother dropped a champagne bottle. Edwin heard and was cold, for the thought that jumped through his head was, that's how Mother'd sound. If she fell, if she broke, you'd find a million fragments in the morning. Bright crystal and clear wine on the parquet flooring, that's all you'd see at dawn.

Morning was the smell of vines and grapes and moss in his room, a smell of shadowed coolness. Downstairs, breakfast was in all probability, at this instant, manifesting itself in a fingersnap on the wintry tables.

Edwin got up to wash and dress and wait, feeling fine. Now things would be fresh and new for at least a month. Today, like all days, there'd be breakfast, school, lunch, songs in the music room, an hour or two at the electrical games, then – tea in the Outlands, on the luminous grass. Then up to school again for a late hour or so, where he and Teacher might prowl the censored library together and he'd puzzle with words and thoughts about that world *out there* that had been censored from his eyes.

He had forgotten Teacher's note. Now, he must give it to Mother.

He opened the door. The hall was empty. Down through the deeps of the Worlds, a soft mist floated, through a silence which no footsteps broke; the hills were quiet; the silver fonts did not pulse in the first sunlight, and the banister, coiling up from the mists was a prehistoric monster peering into his room. He pulled away from this creature, looking to find Mother, like a white boat, drifted by the dawn tides and vapours below.

She was not there. He hurried down through the hushed lands, calling, 'Mother!'

He found her in the Parlour, collapsed on the floor in her shiny green-gold party dress, a champagne goblet in one hand, the carpet littered with broken glass.

She was obviously asleep, so he sat at the magical breakfast table. He blinked at the empty white cloth and the gleaming plates. There was no food. All his life wondrous foods had awaited him here. But not today.

'Mother, wake up!' He ran to her. 'Shall I go to school? Where's the food? Wake up!'

He ran up the stairs.

The Highlands were cold and shadowed, and the white glass suns no longer glowed from the ceilings in this day of sullen fog. Down dark corridors, through dim continents of silence, Edwin rushed. He rapped and rapped at the school door. It drifted in, whining, by itself.

The school lay empty and dark. No fire roared on the hearth to toss shadows on the beamed ceiling. There was not a crackle or a whisper.

'Teacher?'

He poised in the centre of the flat, cold room.

'Teacher!' he screamed.

He slashed the drapes aside; a faint shaft of sunlight fell through the stained glass.

Edwin gestured. He commanded the fire to explode like a popcorn kernel on the hearth. He commanded it to bloom to life! He shut his eyes, to give Teacher time to appear. He opened his eyes and was stupefied at what he saw on her desk.

Neatly folded was the grey cowl and robe, atop which gleamed her silver spectacles, and one grey glove. He touched them. One grey glove was gone. A piece of greasy cosmetic chalk lay on the robe. Testing it, he made dark lines on his hands.

He drew back, staring at Teacher's empty robe, the glasses, the greasy chalk. His hand touched a knob of a door which had always been locked. The door swung slowly wide. He looked into a small brown closet.

'Teacher!'

He ran in, the door crashed shut, he pressed a red button. The room sank down, and with it sank a slow mortal coldness. The World was silent, quiet, and cool. Teacher gone and Mother – sleeping. Down fell the room, with him in its iron jaws.

Machinery clashed. A door slid open. Edwin ran out.

The Parlour!

Behind was not a door, but a tall oak panel from which he had emerged.

Mother lay uncaring, asleep. Folded under her, barely showing as he rolled her over, was one of Teacher's soft grey gloves.

He stood near her, holding the incredible glove, for a long time. Finally, he began to whimper.

He fled back up to the Highlands. The hearth was cold, the room empty. He waited. Teacher did not come. He ran down again to the solemn Lowlands, commanded the table to fill with steaming dishes! Nothing happened. He sat by his mother, talking and pleading with her and touching her, and her hands were cold.

The clock ticked and the light changed in the sky and still she did not move, and he was hungry and the silent dust dropped down on the air through all the Worlds. He thought of Teacher and knew that if she was in none of the hills and mountains above, then there was only one place she could be. She had wandered, by error, into the Outlands, lost until someone found her. And so he must go out, call after her, bring her back to wake Mother, or she would lie here forever with the dust falling in the great darkened spaces.

Through the kitchen, out back, he found late afternoon sun and the Beasts hooting faintly beyond the rim of the World. He clung to the garden wall, not daring to let go, and in the shadows, at a distance, saw the shattered box he had flung from the window. Freckles of sunlight quivered on the broken lid and touched tremblingly over and over the face of the Jack jumped out and sprawled with its arms overhead in an eternal gesture of freedom. The doll smiled and did not smile, smiled and did not smile, as the sun winked on the mouth, and Edwin stood, hypnotized, above and beyond it. The doll opened its arms toward the path that led off between the secret trees, the forbidden path smeared with oily droppings of the Beasts. But the path lay silent and the sun warmed Edwin and he heard the wind blow softly in the trees. At last, he let go of the garden wall.

'Teacher?'

He edged along the path a few feet.

'Teacher!'

His shoes slipped on the animal droppings and he stared far down the motionless tunnel, blindly. The path moved under, the trees moved over him.

'Teacher!'

He walked slowly but steadily. He turned. Behind him lay his World and its very new silence. It was diminished, it was small! How strange to see it less than it had been. It had always and forever seemed so large. He felt his heart stop. He stepped back. But then, afraid of that silence in the World, he turned to face the forest path ahead.

Everything before him was new. Odours filled his nostrils, colours, odd shapes, incredible sizes filled his eyes.

If I run beyond the trees I'll die, he thought, for that's what Mother said. You'll die, you'll die.

But what's dying? Another room? A blue room, a green room, far larger than all the rooms that ever were! But where's the key? There, far ahead, a great half-open iron door, a wrought-iron gate. Beyond a room as large as the sky, all coloured green with trees and grass! Oh, Mother, Teacher . . .

He rushed, stumbled, fell, got up, ran again, his numb legs under him were left behind as he fell down and down the side of a hill, the path gone, wailing, crying, and then not wailing or crying any more, but making new sounds. He reached the great rusted, screaming iron gate, leapt through; the Universe dwindled behind, he did not look back at his old Worlds, but ran as they withered and vanished.

The policeman stood at the kerb, looking down the street.

'These kids. I'll never be able to figure them.'

'How's that?' asked the pedestrian.

The policeman thought it over and frowned. 'Couple seconds ago a little kid ran by. He was laughing and crying, crying and laughing, both. He was jumping up and down and touching things. Things like lampposts, the telephone poles, fire hydrants, dogs, people. Things like sidewalks, fences, gates, cars, plateglass windows, barber poles. Hell, he even grabbed hold and looked at me, and looked at the sky, you should have seen the tears, and all the time he kept yelling and yelling something funny.'

'What did he yell?' asked the pedestrian.

'He kept yelling, "I'm dead, I'm dead, I'm glad I'm dead, I'm dead, I'm dead, I'm glad I'm dead, I'm dead, I'm dead, it's *good* to be dead!"' The policeman scratched his chin slowly. 'One of them new kid games, I guess.'

The Canterville Ghost

A hylo-idealistic romance

Oscar Wilde

When Mr Hiram B. Otis, the American Minister, bought Canterville Chase, every one told him he was doing a very foolish thing, as there was no doubt at all that the place was haunted. Indeed, Lord Canterville himself, who was a man of the most punctilious honour, had felt it his duty to mention the fact to Mr Otis, when they came to discuss terms.

'We have not cared to live in the place ourselves,' said Lord Canterville, 'since my grand-aunt, the Dowager Duchess of Bolton, was frightened into a fit, from which she never really recovered, by two skeleton hands being placed on her shoulders as she was dressing for dinner, and I feel bound to tell you, Mr Otis, that the ghost has been seen by several living members of my family, as well as by the rector of the parish, the Rev. Augustus Dampier, who is a fellow of King's College, Cambridge. After the unfortunate accident to the Duchess, none of our younger servants would stay with us, and Lady Canterville often got very little sleep at night, in consequence of the mysterious noises that came from the corridor and the library.'

'My Lord,' answered the Minister, 'I will take the furniture and the ghost at a valuation. I come from a modern country, where we have everything that money can buy; and with all our spry young fellows painting the Old World red, and carrying off your best actresses and prima-donnas, I reckon that if there were such a thing as a ghost in Europe, we'd have it at home in a very short time in one of our public museums, or on the road as a show.'

'I fear that the ghost exists,' said Lord Canterville, smiling, 'though it may have resisted the overtures of your enterprising impresarios. It has been well known for three centuries, since 1584 in fact, and always makes its appearance before the death of any member of our family.'

'Well, so does the family doctor for that matter, Lord Canterville. But there is no such thing, sir, as a ghost, and I guess the laws of nature are not going to be suspended for the British aristocracy.'

'You are certainly very natural in America,' answered Lord Canterville, who did not quite understand Mr Otis's last observation, 'and if you don't mind a ghost in the house, it is all right. Only you must remember I warned you.'

A few weeks after this, the purchase was completed, and at the close of the season the Minister and his family went down to Canterville Chase. Mrs Otis, who, as Miss Lucretia R. Tappan, of West 53rd Street, had been a celebrated New York belle, was now a very handsome middle-aged woman, with fine eyes, and a superb profile. Many American ladies on leaving their native land adopt an appearance of chronic ill-health, under the impression that it is a form of European refinement, but Mrs Otis had never fallen into this error. She had a magnificent constitution, and a really wonderful amount of animal spirits. Indeed, in many respects, she was quite English, and was an excellent example of the fact that we have really everything in common with America nowadays, except, of course, language. Her eldest son, christened Washington by his parents in a moment of patriotism, which he never ceased to regret, was a fair-haired, rather good-looking young man, who had qualified himself for American diplomacy by leading the German at the Newport Casino for three successive seasons, and even in London was well known as an excellent dancer. Gardenias and the peerage were his only weaknesses. Otherwise he was extremely sensible. Miss Virginia E. Otis was a little girl of fifteen, lithe and lovely as a fawn, and with a fine freedom in her large blue eyes. She was a wonderful amazon, and had once raced old Lord Bilton on her pony twice round the park, winning by a length and a half, just in front of Achilles statue, to the huge delight of the young Duke of Cheshire, who proposed for her on the spot, and was sent back to Eton that very night by his guardians in floods of tears. After Virginia came the twins, who were usually called 'The Stars and Stripes' as they were always getting swished. They were delightful boys, and with the exception of the worthy Minister the only true republicans of the family.

As Canterville Chase is seven miles from Ascot, the nearest railway station, Mr Otis had telegraphed for a waggonette to meet them, and they started on their drive in high spirits. It was a lovely July evening, and the air was delicate with the scent of the pinewoods. Now and then they heard a wood pigeon brooding over its own sweet voice, or saw, deep in the rustling fern, the burnished breast of the pheasant. Little squirrels peered at them from the beech-trees as they went by, and the rabbits scudded away through the brushwood and over the mossy knolls, with their white tails in the air. As they entered the avenue of Canterville Chase, however, the sky became suddenly overcast with clouds, a curious stillness seemed to hold the atmosphere, a great flight of rooks passed silently over their heads, and, before they reached the house, some big drops of rain had fallen.

Standing on the steps to receive them was an old woman, neatly dressed in black silk, with a white cap and apron. This was Mrs Umney, the housekeeper, whom Mrs Otis, at Lady Canterville's earnest request, had consented to keep on in her former position. She made them each a low curtsy as they alighted, and said in a quaint, old-fashioned manner, 'I bid you welcome to Canterville Chase.' Following her, they passed through the fine Tudor hall into the library, a long, low room, panelled in black oak, at the end of which was a large stained-glass window. Here they found tea laid out for them, and, after taking off their wraps, they sat down and began to look round, while Mrs Umney waited on them.

Suddenly Mrs Otis caught sight of a dull red stain on the floor just by the fireplace and, quite unconscious of what it really signified, said to Mrs Umney, 'I am afraid something has been spilt there.'

'Yes, madam,' replied the old housekeeper in a low voice, 'blood has been spilt on that spot.'

'How horrid,' cried Mrs Otis; 'I don't at all care for blood-stains in a sitting-room. It must be removed at once.'

The old woman smiled, and answered in the same low, mysterious voice, 'It is the blood of Lady Eleanore de Canterville, who was murdered on that very spot by her own husband, Sir Simon de Canterville, in 1575. Sir Simon survived her nine years, and disappeared suddenly under very mysterious circumstances. His body has never been discovered, but his guilty spirit still haunts the Chase. The blood-stain has been much admired by tourists and others, and cannot be removed.'

'That is all nonsense,' cried Washington Otis; 'Pinkerton's Champion Stain Remover and Paragon Detergent will clean it up in no time,' and before the terrified housekeeper could interfere he had fallen upon his knees, and was rapidly scouring the floor with a small stick of what looked like a black cosmetic. In a few moments no trace of the blood-stain could be seen.

'I knew Pinkerton would do it,' he exclaimed triumphantly, as he looked round at his admiring family; but no sooner had he said these words than a terrible flash of lightning lit up the sombre room, a fearful peal of thunder made them all start to their feet, and Mrs Umney fainted.

'What a monstrous climate!' said the American Minister calmly, as he lit a long cheroot. 'I guess the old country is so overpopulated that they have not enough decent weather for everybody. I have always been of opinion that emigration is the only thing for England.'

'My dear Hiram,' cried Mrs Otis, 'what can we do with a woman who faints?'

'Charge it to her like breakages,' answered the Minister; 'she won't faint after that'; and in a few moments Mrs Umney certainly came to. There was no doubt, however, that she was extremely upset, and she sternly warned Mr Otis to beware of some trouble coming to the house.

'I have seen things with my own eyes, sir,' she said, 'that would make any Christian's hair stand on end, and many and many a night I have not closed my eyes in sleep for the awful things that are done here.' Mr Otis, however, and his wife warmly assured the honest soul that they were not afraid of ghosts, and, after invoking the blessings of Providence on her new master and mistress, and making arrangements for an increase of salary, the old housekeeper tottered off to her own room.

The storm raged fiercely all that night, but nothing of particular note occurred. The next morning, however, when they came down to breakfast, they found the terrible stain of blood once again on the floor. 'I don't think it can be the fault of the Paragon Detergent,' said Washington, 'for I have tried it with everything. It must be the ghost.' He accordingly rubbed out the stain a second time, but the second morning it appeared again. The third morning also it was there, though the library had been locked up at night by Mr Otis himself, and the key carried upstairs. The whole family were now quite interested; Mr Otis began to suspect that he had been too dogmatic in his denial of the existence of ghosts, Mrs Otis expressed her intention of joining the Psychical Society, and Washington prepared a long letter to Messrs Myers and Podmore on the subject of the Permanence of Sanguineous Stains when connected with crime. That night all doubts about the objective existence of phantasmata were removed for ever.

The day had been warm and sunny; and, in the cool of the evening, the whole family went out for a drive. They did not return home till nine o'clock, when they had a light supper. The conversation in no way turned upon ghosts, so there were not even those primary conditions of receptive expectation which so often precede the presentation of psychical phenomena. The subjects discussed, as I have since learned from Mr Otis, were merely such as form the ordinary conversation of cultured Americans of the better class, such as the immense superiority of Miss Fanny Davenport over Sarah Bernhardt as an actress; the difficulty of obtaining green corn, buckwheat cakes, and hominy, even in the best English houses; the importance of Boston in the development of the world-soul; the advantages of the baggage check system in railway travelling; and the sweetness of the New York accent as compared to the London drawl. No mention at all was made of the supernatural, nor was Sir Simon de Canterville alluded to in any way. At eleven o'clock the family retired, and by half-past all the lights were out. Some time after, Mr Otis was awakened by a curious noise in the corridor, outside his room. It sounded like the clank of metal, and seemed to be coming nearer every moment. He got up at once, struck a match, and looked at the time. It was exactly one o'clock. He was quite calm, and felt his pulse, which was not at all feverish. The strange noise still continued, and with it he heard distinctly the sound of footsteps. He put on his slippers, took a small oblong phial out of his dressing-case, and opened the door. Right in front of him he saw, in the wan moonlight, an old man of terrible aspect. His eyes were as red as burning coals; long grey hair fell over his shoulders in matted coils; his garments, which were of antique cut, were soiled and ragged, and from his wrists and ankles hung heavy manacles and rusty gyves.

'My dear sir,' said Mr Otis, 'I really must insist on your oiling those chains, and have brought you for that purpose a small bottle of the Tammany Rising Sun

Lubricator. It is said to be completely efficacious upon one application, and there are several testimonials to that effect on the wrapper from some of our most eminent native divines. I shall leave it here for you by the bedroom candles, and will be happy to supply you with more should you require it.' With these words the United States Minister laid the bottle down on a marble table, and, closing his door, retired to rest.

For a moment the Canterville ghost stood quite motionless in natural indignation; then, dashing the bottle violently upon the polished floor, he fled down the corridor, uttering hollow groans, and emitting a ghastly green light. Just, however, as he reached the top of the great oak staircase, a door was flung open, two little white-robed figures appeared, and a large pillow whizzed past his head! There was evidently no time to be lost, so, hastily adopting the Fourth Dimension of Space as a means of escape, he vanished through the wainscoting, and the house became quite quiet.

On reaching a small secret chamber in the left wing, he leaned up against a moonbeam to recover his breath, and began to try and realise his position. Never, in a brilliant and uninterrupted career of three hundred years, had he been so grossly insulted. He thought of the Dowager Duchess, whom he had frightened into a fit as she stood before the glass in her lace and diamonds; of the four housemaids, who had gone off into hysterics when he merely grinned at them through the curtains of one of the spare bedrooms; of the rector of the parish, whose candle he had blown out as he was coming late one night from the library, and who had been under the care of Sir William Gull ever since, a perfect martyr to nervous disorders; and of old Madame de Tremouillac, who, having wakened up one morning early and seen a skeleton seated in an arm-chair by the fire reading her diary, had been confined to her bed for six weeks with an attack of brain fever, and, on her recovery, had become reconciled to the Church, and had broken off her connection with that notorious sceptic Monsieur de Voltaire. He remembered the terrible night when the wicked Lord Canterville was found choking in his dressing-room, with the knave of diamonds half-way down his throat, and confessed, just before he died, that he had cheated Charles James Fox out of £50,000 at Crockford's by means of that very card, and swore that the ghost had made him swallow it. All his great achievements came back to him again, from the butler who had shot himself in the pantry because he had seen a green hand tapping at the window pane, to the beautiful Lady Stutfield, who was always obliged to wear a black velvet band round her throat to hide the mark of five fingers burnt upon her white skin, and who drowned herself at last in the carp-pond at the end of the King's Walk. With the enthusiastic egotism of the true artist he went over his most celebrated performances, and smiled bitterly to himself as he recalled to mind his last appearance as 'Red Ruben, or the Strangled Babe', his *début* as 'Gaunt Gibeon, the Bloodsucker of Bexley Moor', and the *furore* he had excited one lovely June evening by merely playing nine-pins with his own bones upon the lawn-tennis ground. And after all this, some wretched modern Americans were to come and offer him the Rising Sun Lubricator, and throw pillows at his head! It was quite unbearable. Besides, no ghosts in history had ever been treated in this manner. Accordingly, he determined to have vengeance, and remained till daylight in an attitude of deep thought.

The next morning when the Otis family met at breakfast, they discussed the ghost at some length. The United States Minister was naturally a little annoyed to find that his present had not been accepted. 'I have no wish,' he said, 'to do the ghost any personal injury, and I must say that, considering the length of time he has been in the house, I don't think it is at all polite to throw pillows at him' – a very just remark, at which, I am sorry to say, the twins burst into shouts of laughter. 'Upon the other hand,' he continued, 'if he really declines to use the Rising Sun Lubricator, we shall have to take his chains from him. It would be quite impossible to sleep, with such a noise going on outside the bedrooms.'

For the rest of the week, however, they were undisturbed, the only thing that excited any attention being the continual renewal of the blood-stain on the library floor. This certainly was very strange, as the door was always locked at night by Mr Otis, and the windows kept closely barred. The chameleon-like colour, also, of the stain excited a good deal of comment. Some mornings it was a dull (almost Indian) red, then it would be vermilion, then a rich purple, and once when they came down for family prayers, according to the simple rites of the Free American Reformed Episcopalian Church, they found it a bright emerald-green. These kaleidoscopic changes naturally amused the party very much, and bets on the subject were freely made every evening. The only person who did not enter into the joke was little Virginia, who, for some unexplained reason, was always a good deal distressed at the sight of the blood-stain, and very nearly cried the morning it was emerald-green.

The second appearance of the ghost was on Sunday night. Shortly after they had gone to bed they were suddenly alarmed by a fearful crash in the hall. Rushing downstairs, they found that a large suit of old armour had become detached from its stand, and had fallen on the stone floor, while, seated in a high-backed chair, was the Canterville ghost, rubbing his knees with an expression of acute agony on his face. The twins, having brought their peashooters with them, at once discharged two pellets on him, with that accuracy of aim which can only be attained by long and careful practice on a writing-master, while the United States Minister covered him with his revolver, and called upon him, in accordance with Californian etiquette, to hold up his hands! The ghost started up with a wild shriek of rage, and swept through them like a mist, extinguishing Washington

Otis's candle as he passed, and so leaving them all in total darkness. On reaching the top of the staircase he recovered himself, and determined to give his celebrated peal of demoniac laughter. This he had on more than one occasion found extremely useful. It was said to have turned Lord Raker's wig grey in a single night, and had certainly made three of Lady Canterville's French governesses give warning before their month was up. He accordingly laughed his most horrible laugh, till the old vaulted roof rang and rang again, but hardly had the fearful echo died away when a door opened, and Mrs Otis came out in a light blue dressing-gown. 'I am afraid you are far from well,' she said, 'and have brought you a bottle of Dr Dobell's tincture. If it is indigestion, you will find it a most excellent remedy.' The ghost glared at her in fury, and began at once to make preparations for turning himself into a large black dog, an accomplishment for which he was justly renowned, and to which the family doctor always attributed the permanent idiocy of Lord Canterville's uncle, the Hon. Thomas Horton. The sound of approaching footsteps, however, made him hesitate in his fell purpose, so he contented himself with becoming faintly phosphorescent, and vanished with a deep church-yard groan, just as the twins had come up to him.

On reaching his room he entirely broke down, and became a prey to the most violent agitation. The vulgarity of the twins, and the gross materialism of Mrs Otis, were naturally extremely annoying, but what really distressed him most was, that he had been unable to wear the suit of mail. He had hoped that even modern Americans would be thrilled by the sight of a Spectre In Armour, if for no more sensible reason, at least out of respect for their national poet Longfellow, over whose graceful and attractive poetry he himself had whiled away many a weary hour when the Cantervilles were up in town. Besides, it was his own suit. He had worn it with success at the Kenilworth tournament, and had been highly complimented on it by no less a person than the Virgin Queen herself. Yet when he had put it on, he had been completely overpowered by the weight of the huge breastplate and steel casque, and had fallen heavily on the stone pavement, barking both his knees severely, and bruising the knuckles of his right hand.

For some days after this he was extremely ill, and hardly stirred out of his room at all, except to keep the blood-stain in proper repair. However, by taking great care of himself, he recovered, and resolved to make a third attempt to frighten the United States Minister and his family. He selected Friday, the 17th of August, for his appearance, and spent most of that day in looking over his wardrobe, ultimately deciding in favour of a large slouched hat with a red feather, a winding-sheet frilled at the wrists and neck, and a rusty dagger. Towards evening a violent storm of rain came on, and the wind was so high that all the windows and doors in the old house shook and rattled. In fact, it was just such weather as he loved. His plan of action was this. He was to make his way quietly to Washington Otis's room, gibber at him from the foot of the bed, and stab himself three times in the throat to the sound of slow music. He bore Washington a special grudge, being quite aware that it was he who was in the habit of removing the famous Canterville blood-stain, by means of Pinkerton's Paragon Detergent. Having reduced the reckless and foolhardy youth to a condition of abject terror, he was then to proceed to the room occupied by the United States Minister and his wife, and there to place a clammy hand on Mrs Otis's forehead, while he hissed into her trembling husband's ear the awful secrets of the charnel-house. With regard to little Virginia, he had not quite made up his mind. She had never insulted him in any way, and was pretty and gentle. A few hollow groans from the wardrobe, he thought, would be more than sufficient, or, if that failed to wake her, he might grabble at the counterpane with palsy-twitching fingers. As for the twins, he was quite determined to teach them a lesson. The first thing to be done was, of course, to sit upon their chests, so as to produce the stifling sensation of nightmare. Then, as their beds were quite close to each other, to stand between them in the form of a green, icy-cold corpse, till they became paralysed with fear, and finally, to throw off the winding-sheet, and crawl round the room, with white bleached bones and one rolling eyeball, in the character of 'Dumb Daniel, or the Suicide's Skeleton', a role in which he had on more than one occasion produced a great effect, and which he considered quite equal to his famous part of 'Martin the Maniac, or the Masked Mystery.'

At half-past ten he heard the family going to bed. For some time he was disturbed by wild shrieks of laughter from the twins, who, with the light-hearted gaiety of schoolboys, were evidently amusing themselves before they retired to rest, but at a quarter past eleven all was still, and, as midnight sounded, he sallied forth. The owl beat against the window panes, the raven croaked from the old yew-tree, and the wind wandered moaning round the house like a lost soul; but the Otis family slept unconscious of their doom, and high above the rain and storm he could hear the steady snoring of the Minister for the United States. He stepped stealthily out of the wainscoting, with an evil smile on his cruel, wrinkled mouth, and the moon hid her face in a cloud as he stole past the great oriel window, where his own arms and those of his murdered wife were blazoned in azure and gold. On and on he glided, like an evil shadow, the very darkness seeming to loathe him as he passed. Once he thought he heard something call, and stopped; but it was only the baying of a dog from the Red Farm, and he went on, muttering strange sixteenth-century curses, and ever and anon brandishing the rusty dagger in the midnight air. Finally he reached a corner of the passage that led to luckless Washington's room. For a moment he paused there, the wind blowing his long grey locks about his head, and twisting into grotesque and fantastic folds the nameless horror of the dead man's shroud. Then the clock struck the quarter, and he felt the time was come. He chuckled to himself, and turned the corner; but no sooner had he done so, than, with a piteous wail of terror, he fell back, and hid his blanched face in his long, bony hands. Right in front of him was standing a horrible spectre, motionless as a carven image, and monstrous as a madman's dream! Its head was bald and burnished; its face round, and fat, and white; and hideous laughter seemed to have writhed its features into an eternal grin. From the eyes streamed rays of scarlet light, the mouth was a wide well of fire, and a hideous garment, like to his own, swathed with its silent snows the Titan form. On its breast was a placard with strange writing in antique characters, some scroll of shame it seemed, some record of wild sins, some awful calendar of crime, and, with its right hand, it bore aloft a falchion of gleaming steel.

Never having seen a ghost before, he naturally was terribly frightened, and, after a second hasty glance at the awful phantom, he fled back to his room, tripping up in his long winding-sheet as he sped down the corridor, and finally dropping the rusty dagger into the Minister's jack-boots, where it was found in the morning by the butler. Once in the privacy of his own apartment, he flung himself down on a small pallet-bed, and hid his face under the clothes. After a time, however, the brave old Canterville spirit asserted itself, and he determined to go and speak to the other ghost as soon as it was daylight. Accordingly, just as the dawn was touching the hills with silver, he returned towards the spot where he had first laid eyes on the grisly phantom, feeling that, after all, two ghosts were better than one, and that, by the aid of his new friend, he might safely grapple with the twins. On reaching the spot, however, a terrible sight met his gaze. Something had evidently happened to the spectre, for the light had entirely faded from its hollow eyes, the gleaming falchion had fallen from its hand, and it was leaning up against the wall in a strained and uncomfortable attitude. He rushed forward and seized it in his arms, when, to his horror, the head slipped off and rolled on the floor, the body assumed a recumbent posture, and he found himself clasping a white dimity bed-curtain, with a sweeping-brush, a kitchen cleaver, and a hollow turnip lying at his feet! Unable to understand this curious transformation, he clutched the placard with feverish haste, and there, in the grey morning light, he read these fearful words :

YE OTIS GHOSTE
Ye Onlie True and Originale Spook.
Beware of Ye Imitationes.
All others are Counterfeite

The whole thing flashed across him. He had been tricked, foiled, and outwitted! The old Canterville look came into his eyes; he ground his toothless gums together; and, raising his withered hands high above his head, swore, according to the picturesque phraseology of the antique school, that when Chanticleer had sounded twice his merry horn, deeds of blood would be wrought, and Murder walk abroad with silent feet.

Hardly had he finished this awful oath when, from the red-tiled roof of a distant homestead, a cock crew. He laughed a long, low, bitter laugh, and waited. Hour after hour he waited, but the cock, for some strange reason, did not crow again. Finally, at half-past seven, the arrival of the housemaids made him give up his fearful vigil, and he stalked back to his room, thinking of his vain hope and baffled purpose. There he consulted several books of ancient chivalry, of which he was exceedingly fond, and found that, on every occasion on which his oath had been used, Chanticleer had always crowed a second time. 'Perdition seize the naughty fowl,' he muttered, 'I have seen the day when, with my stout spear, I would have run him through the gorge, and made him crow for me an't were in death!' He then retired to a comfortable lead coffin, and stayed there till evening.

The next day the ghost was very weak and tired. The terrible excitement of the last four weeks was beginning to have its effect. His nerves were completely shattered, and he started at the slightest noise. For five days he kept his room, and at last made up his mind to give up the point of the blood-stain on the library floor. If the Otis family did not want it, they clearly did not deserve it. They were evidently people on a low, material plane of existence, and quite incapable of appreciating the symbolic value of sensuous phenomena. The question of phantasmic apparitions, and the development of astral bodies, was of course quite a different matter, and really not under his control. It was his solemn duty to appear in the corridor once a week, and to gibber from the large oriel window on the first and third Wednesday in every month, and he did not see how he could honourably escape from his obligations. It is quite true that his life had been very evil, but, upon the other hand, he was most conscientious in all things connected with the supernatural. For the next three Saturdays, accordingly, he traversed the corridor as usual between midnight and three o'clock, taking every possible precaution against being either heard or seen. He removed his boots, trod as lightly as possible on the old worm-eaten boards, wore a large black velvet cloak, and was careful to use the Rising Sun Lubricator for oiling his chains. I am bound to acknowledge that it was with a good deal of difficulty that he brought himself to adopt this last mode of protection. However, one night, while the family were at dinner, he slipped into Mr Otis's bedroom and carried off the bottle. He felt a little humiliated at first, but afterwards was sensible enough to see that there was a great deal to be said for the invention, and, to a certain degree, it served his purpose. Still, in spite of everything, he was not left unmolested. Strings were continually being stretched across the corridor, over which he tripped in the dark, and on one occasion, while dressed for the part of 'Black Isaac, or the Huntsman of Hogley Woods', he met with a severe fall, through treading on a butter-slide, which the twins had constructed from the entrance of the Tapestry Chamber to the top of the oak staircase. This last insult so enraged him, that he resolved to make one final effort to assert his dignity and social position, and determined to visit the insolent young Etonians the next night in his celebrated character of 'Reckless Rupert, or the Headless Earl'.

He had not appeared in this disguise for more than seventy years; in fact, not since he had so frightened pretty Lady Barbara Modish by means of it, that she suddenly broke off her engagement with the present Lord Canterville's grandfather, and ran away to Gretna Green with handsome Jack Castleton, declaring that nothing in the world would induce her to marry into a family that allowed such a horrible phantom to walk up and down the terrace at twilight. Poor Jack was afterwards shot in a duel by Lord Canterville on Wandsworth Common, and Lady Barbara died of a broken heart at Tunbridge Wells before the year was out, so, in every way, it had been a great success. It was, however, an extremely difficult 'make-up', if I may use such a theatrical expression in connection with one of the greatest mysteries of the supernatural, or, to employ a more scientific term, the higher-natural world, and it took him fully three hours to make his preparations. At last everything was ready, and he was very pleased with his appearance. The big leather riding-boots that went with the dress were just a little too large for him, and he could only find one of the two horse-pistols, but, on the whole, he was quite satisfied, and at a quarter past one he glided out of the wainscoting and crept down the corridor. On reaching the room occupied by the twins, which I should mention was called the Blue Bed Chamber, on account of the colour of its hangings, he found the door just ajar. Wishing to make an effective entrance, he flung it wide open, when a heavy jug of water fell right down on him, wetting him to the skin, and just missing his left shoulder by a couple of inches. At the same moment he heard stifled shrieks of laughter proceeding from the four-post bed. The shock to his nervous system was so great that he fled back to his room as hard as he could go, and the next day he was laid up with a severe cold. The only thing that at all consoled him in the whole affair was the fact that he had not brought his head with him, for, had he done so, the consequences might have been very serious.

He now gave up all hope of ever frightening this rude American family, and contented himself, as a rule, with creeping about the passages in list slippers, with a thick red muffler round his throat for fear of draughts, and a small arquebuse, in case he should be attacked by the twins. The final blow he received occurred on the 19th of September. He had gone downstairs to the great entrance-hall, feeling sure that there, at any rate, he would be quite unmolested, and was amusing himself by making satirical remarks on the large Saroni photographs of the United States Minister and his wife, which had now taken the place of the Canterville family pictures. He was simply but neatly clad in a long shroud, spotted with churchyard mould, had tied up his jaw with a strip of yellow linen, and carried a small lantern and a sexton's spade. In fact, he was dressed for the character of 'Jonas the Graveless, or the Corpse-Snatcher of Chertsey Barn', one of his most remarkable impersonations, and one which the Cantervilles had every reason to remember, as it was the real origin of their quarrel with their neighbour, Lord Rufford. It was about a quarter past two o'clock in the morning, and, as far as he could ascertain, no one was stirring. As he was strolling towards the library, however, to see if there were any traces left of the blood-stain, suddenly there leaped out on him from a dark corner two figures, who waved their arms wildly above their heads, and shrieked out 'Boo!' in his ear.

Seized with a panic, which, under the circumstances, was only natural, he rushed for the staircase, but found Washington Otis waiting for him there with the big garden-syringe; and being thus hemmed in by his enemies on every side, and driven almost to bay, he vanished into the great iron stove, which, fortunately for him, was not lit, and had to make his way home through the flues and chimneys, arriving at his own room in a terrible state of dirt, disorder, and despair.

After this he was not seen again on any nocturnal expedition. The twins lay in wait for him on several occasions, and strewed the passages with nutshells every night to the great annoyance of their parents and the servants, but it was of no avail. It was quite evident that his feelings were so wounded that he would not appear. Mr Otis consequently resumed his great work on the history of the Democratic Party, on which he had been engaged for some years; Mrs Otis organised a wonderful clambake, which amazed the whole county; the boys took to lacrosse, euchre, poker, and other American national games; and Virginia rode about the lanes on her pony, accompanied by the young Duke of Cheshire, who had come to spend the last week of his holidays at Canterville Chase. It was generally assumed that the ghost had gone away, and, in fact, Mr Otis wrote a letter to that effect to Lord Canterville, who, in reply, expressed his great pleasure at the news, and sent his best congratulations to the Minister's worthy wife.

The Otises, however, were deceived, for the ghost was still in the house, and though now almost an invalid, was by no means ready to let matters rest, particularly as he heard that among the guests was the young Duke of Cheshire, whose grand-uncle, Lord Francis Stilton, had once bet a hundred guineas with Colonel Carbury that he would play dice with the Canterville ghost, and was found the next morning lying on the floor of the card-room in such a helpless paralytic state, that though he lived on to a great age, he was never able to say anything again but 'Double Sixes'. The story was well known at the time, though, of course, out of respect to the feelings of the two noble families, every attempt was made to hush it up; and a full account of all the circumstances connected with it will be found in the third volume of Lord Tattle's *Recollections of the Prince Regent and his Friends*. The ghost, then, was naturally very anxious to show that he had not lost his influence over the Stiltons, with whom, indeed, he was distantly connected, his own first cousin having been married *en secondes noces* to the Sieur de Bulkeley, from whom, as every one knows, the Dukes of Cheshire are lineally descended. Accordingly, he made arrangements for appearing to Virginia's little lover in his celebrated impersonation of 'The Vampire Monk, or, the Bloodless Benedictine', a performance so horrible that when old Lady Startup saw it, which she did on one fatal New Year's Eve, in the year 1764, she went off into the most piercing shrieks, which culminated in violent apoplexy, and died in three days, after disinheriting the Cantervilles, who were her nearest relations, and leaving all her money to her London apothecary. At the last moment, however, his terror of the twins prevented his leaving his room, and the little Duke slept in peace under the great feathered canopy in the Royal Bed-chamber, and dreamed of Virginia.

A few days after this, Virginia and her curly-haired cavalier went out riding on Brockley meadows, where she tore her habit so badly in getting through a hedge, that, on her return home, she made up her mind to go up by the back staircase so as not to be seen. As she was running past the Tapestry Chamber, the door of which happened to be open, she fancied she saw some one inside, and thinking it was her mother's maid, who sometimes used to bring her work there, looked in to ask her to mend her habit. To her immense surprise, however, it was the Canterville Ghost himself! He was sitting by the window, watching the ruined gold of the yellow trees fly through the air, and the red leaves dancing madly down the long avenue. His head was leaning on his hand, and his whole attitude was one of extreme depression. Indeed, so forlorn, and so much out of repair did he look, that little Virginia, whose first idea had been to run away and lock herself in her room, was filled with pity, and determined to try and comfort him. So light was her footfall, and so deep his melancholy, that he was not aware of her presence till she spoke to him.

'I am sorry for you,' she said, 'but my brothers are going back to Eton to-morrow, and then, if you behave yourself, no one will annoy you.'

'It is absurd asking me to behave myself,' he answered, looking round in astonishment at the pretty little girl who had ventured to address him, 'quite absurd. I must rattle my chains, and groan through keyholes, and walk about at night, if that is what you mean. It is my only reason for existing.'

'It is no reason at all for existing, and you know you have been very wicked. Mrs Umney told us, the first day we arrived here, that you had killed your wife.'

'Well, I quite admit it,' said the Ghost petulantly, 'but it was a purely family matter and concerned no one else.'

'It is very wrong to kill anyone,' said Virginia, who at times had a sweet Puritan gravity, caught from some old New England ancestor.

'Oh, I hate the cheap severity of abstract ethics! My wife was very plain, never had my ruffs properly starched, and knew nothing about cookery. Why, there was a buck I had shot in Hogley Woods, a magnificent pricket, and do you know how she had it sent up to table? However, it is no matter now, for it is all over, and I don't think it was very nice of her brothers to starve me to death, though I did kill her.'

'Starve you to death? Oh, Mr Ghost, I mean Sir Simon, are you hungry? I have a sandwich in my case. Would you like it?'

'No, thank you, I never eat anything now; but it is very kind of you, all the same, and you are much nicer than the rest of your horrid, rude, vulgar, dishonest family.'

'Stop!' cried Virginia, stamping her foot, 'it is you who are rude, and horrid, and vulgar; as for dishonesty, you know you stole the paints out of my box to try and furbish up that ridiculous blood-stain in the library. First you took all my reds, including the vermilion, and I couldn't do any more sunsets, then you took the emerald-green and the chrome-yellow, and finally I had nothing left but indigo and Chinese white, and could only do moonlight scenes, which are always depressing to look at, and not at all easy to paint. I never told on you, though I was very much annoyed, and it was most ridiculous, the whole thing; for who ever heard of emerald-green blood?'

'Well, really,' said the Ghost, rather meekly, 'what was I to do? It is a very difficult thing to get real blood nowadays, and, as your brother began it all with his Paragon Detergent, I certainly saw no reason why I should not have your paints. As for colour, that is always a matter of taste: the Cantervilles have blue blood, for instance, the very bluest in England; but I know you Americans don't care for things of this kind.'

'You know nothing about it, and the best thing you can do is to emigrate and improve your mind. My father will be only too happy to give you a free passage, and though there is a heavy duty on spirits of every kind, there will be no difficulty about the Custom House, as the officers are all Democrats. Once in New York, you are sure to be a great success. I know lots of people there who would give a hundred thousand dollars to have a grandfather, and much more than that to have a family Ghost.'

'I don't think I should like America.'

'I suppose because we have no ruins and no curiosities,' said Virginia satirically.

'No ruins! no curiosities!' answered the Ghost; 'you have your navy and your manners.'

'Good evening; I will go and ask papa to get the twins an extra week's holiday.'

'Please don't go, Miss Virginia,' he cried; 'I am so lonely and so unhappy, and I really don't know what to do. I want to go to sleep and I cannot.'

'That's quite absurd! You have merely to go to bed and blow out the candle. It is very difficult sometimes to keep awake, especially at church, but there is no difficulty at all about sleeping. Why, even babies know how to do that, and they are not very clever.'

'I have not slept for three hundred years,' he said sadly, and Virginia's beautiful blue eyes opened in wonder; 'for three hundred years I have not slept, and I am so tired.'

Virginia grew quite grave, and her little lips trembled like rose-leaves. She came towards him. and kneeling down at his side, looked up into his old withered face.

'Poor, poor Ghost,' she murmured: 'have you no place where you can sleep?'

'Far away beyond the pine-woods,' he answered, in a low dreamy voice, 'there is a little garden. There the grass grows long and deep, there are the great white stars of the hemlock flower, there the nightingale sings all night long. All night long he sings, and the cold, crystal moon looks down, and the yew-tree spreads out its giant arms over the sleepers.'

Virginia's eyes grew dim with tears, and she hid her face in her hands.

'You mean the Garden of Death,' she whispered.

'Yes, Death. Death must be so beautiful. To lie in the soft brown earth with the grasses waving above one's head, and listen to silence. To have no yesterday, and no to-morrow. To forget time, to forgive life, to be at peace. You can help me. You can open for me the portals of Death's house, for Love is always with you, and Love is stronger than Death is.'

Virginia trembled, a cold shudder ran through her, and for a few moments there was silence. She felt as if she was in a terrible dream.

Then the Ghost spoke again, and his voice sounded like the sighing of the wind.

'Have you ever read the old prophecy on the library window?'

'Oh, often,' cried the little girl, looking up; 'I know it quite well. It is painted in curious black letters, and it is difficult to read. There are only six lines:

> When a golden girl can win
> Prayer from out the lips of sin,
> When the barren almond bears,
> And a little child gives away its tears,
> Then shall all the house be still,
> And peace come to Canterville.

But I don't know what they mean.'

'They mean,' he said sadly, 'that you must weep for me for my sins, because I have no tears, and pray with me for my soul, because I have no faith, and then, if you have always been sweet, and good, and gentle, the Angel of Death will have mercy on me. You will see fearful shapes in darkness, and wicked voices will whisper in your ear, but they will not harm you, for against the purity of a little child the powers of Hell cannot prevail.'

Virginia made no answer, and the Ghost wrung his hands in wild despair as he looked down at her bowed golden head. Suddenly she stood up, very pale, and with a strange light in her eyes. 'I am not afraid,' she said firmly, 'and I will ask the Angel to have mercy on you.'

He rose from his seat with a faint cry of joy, and

taking her hand bent over it with old-fashioned grace and kissed it. His fingers were as cold as ice, and his lips burned like fire, but Virginia did not falter, as he led her across the dusky room. On the faded green tapestry were broidered little huntsmen. They blew their tasselled horns and with their tiny hands waved to her to go back. 'Go back! little Virginia,' they cried, 'go back!' but the Ghost clutched her hand more tightly, and she shut her eyes against them. Horrible animals with lizard tails, and goggle eyes, blinked at her from the carven chimney-piece, and murmured 'Beware! little Virginia, beware! we may never see you again,' but the Ghost glided on more swiftly, and Virginia did not listen. When they reached the end of the room he stopped, and muttered some words she could not understand. She opened her eyes, and saw the wall slowly fading away like a mist, and a great black cavern in front of her. A bitter cold wind swept round them, and she felt something pulling at her dress. 'Quick, quick,' cried the Ghost, 'or it will be too late,' and, in a moment, the wainscoting had closed behind them, and the Tapestry Chamber was empty.

About ten minutes later, the bell rang for tea, and, as Virginia did not come down, Mrs Otis sent up one of the footmen to tell her. After a little time he returned and said that he could not find Miss Virginia anywhere. As she was in the habit of going out to the garden every evening to get flowers for the dinner-table, Mrs Otis was not at all alarmed at first, but when six o'clock struck, and Virginia did not appear, she became really agitated, and sent the boys out to look for her, while she herself and Mr Otis searched every room in the house. At half-past six the boys came back and said that they could find no trace of their sister anywhere. They were all now in the greatest state of excitement, and did not know what to do, when Mr Otis suddenly remembered that, some few days before, he had given a band of gypsies permission to camp in the park. He accordingly at once set off for Blackfell Hollow, where he knew they were, accompanied by his eldest son and two of the farm-servants. The little Duke of Cheshire, who was perfectly frantic with anxiety, begged hard to be allowed to go too, but Mr Otis would not allow him, as he was afraid there might be a scuffle. On arriving at the spot, however, he found that the gypsies had gone, and it was evident that their departure had been rather sudden, as the fire was still burning, and some plates were lying on the grass. Having sent off Washington and the two men to scour the district, he ran home, and despatched telegrams to all the police inspectors in the country, telling them to look out for a little girl who had been kidnapped by tramps or gypsies. He then ordered his horse to be brought round, and, after insisting on his wife and the three boys sitting down to dinner, rode off down the Ascot Road with a groom. He had hardly, however, gone a couple of miles when he heard somebody galloping after him, and, looking round, saw the little Duke coming up on his pony, with his face very flushed and no hat. 'I'm awfully sorry, Mr Otis,' gasped out the boy, 'but I can't eat any dinner as long as Virginia is lost. Please, don't be angry with me; if you had let us be engaged last year, there would never have been all this trouble. You won't send me back, will you? I can't go! I won't go!'

The Minister could not help smiling at the handsome young scapegrace, and was a good deal touched at his devotion to Virginia, so leaning down from his horse, he patted him kindly on the shoulders, and said, 'Well, Cecil, if you won't go back I suppose you must come with me, but I must get you a hat at Ascot.'

'Oh, bother my hat! I want Virginia!' cried the little Duke, laughing, and they galloped on to the railway station. There Mr Otis inquired of the station-master if any one answering the description of Virginia had been seen on the platform, but could get no news of her. The station-master, however, wired up and down the line, and assured him that a strict watch would be kept for her, and, after having bought a hat for the little Duke from a linen-draper, who was just putting up his shutters, Mr Otis rode off to Bexley, a village about four miles away, which he was told was a well-known haunt of the gypsies, as there was a large common next to it. Here they roused up the rural policeman, but could get no information from him, and, after riding all over the common, they turned their horses' heads homewards, and reached the Chase about eleven o'clock, dead-tired and almost heart-broken. They found Washington and the twins waiting for them at the gate-house with lanterns, as the avenue was very dark. Not the slightest trace of Virginia had been discovered. The gypsies had been caught on Broxley meadows, but she was not with them, and they had explained their sudden departure by saying that they had mistaken the date of Chorton Fair, and had gone off in a hurry for fear they might be late. Indeed, they had been quite distressed at hearing of Virginia's disappearance, as they were very grateful to Mr Otis for having allowed them to camp in his park, and four of their number had stayed behind to help in the search. The carp-pond had been dragged, and the whole Chase thoroughly gone over, but without any result. It was evident that, for that night at any rate, Virginia was lost to them; and it was in a state of the deepest depression that Mr Otis and the boys walked up to the house, the groom following behind with the two horses and the pony. In the hall they found a group of frightened servants, and lying on a sofa in the library was poor Mrs Otis, almost out of her mind with terror and anxiety, and having her forehead bathed with eau-de-cologne by the old housekeeper. Mr Otis at once insisted on her having something to eat, and ordered up supper for the whole party. It was a melancholy meal, as hardly anyone spoke, and even the twins were awestruck and subdued, as they were very fond of their sister. When they had finished, Mr Otis, in spite of the entreaties of the little Duke, ordered them all to bed, saying that nothing more could be done that night, and that he would telegraph in the morning to Scotland Yard for some detectives to be sent down immediately. Just as they were passing out of the dining-room, midnight began to boom from the clock tower, and when the last stroke sounded they heard a crash and a sudden shrill cry; a dreadful peal of thunder shook the house, a strain of unearthly music floated through the air, a panel at the top of the staircase flew back with a loud noise, and out on the landing, looking very pale and white, with a little casket in her hand, stepped Virginia. In a moment they had all rushed up to her. Mrs Otis clasped her passionately in her arms, the Duke smothered her with violent kisses, and the twins executed a wild war-dance round the group.

'Good heavens! child, where have you been?' said Mr Otis, rather angrily, thinking that she had been playing some foolish trick on them. 'Cecil and I have been riding all over the country looking for you, and your mother has been frightened to death. You must never play these practical jokes any more.'

'Except on the Ghost! except on the Ghost!' shrieked the twins, as they capered about.

'My own darling, thank God you are found; you must never leave my side again,' murmured Mrs Otis, as she kissed the trembling child, and smoothed the tangled gold of her hair.

'Papa,' said Virginia quietly, 'I have been with the Ghost. He is dead, and you must come and see him. He had been very wicked, but he was really sorry for all that he had done, and he gave me this box of beautiful jewels before he died.'

The whole family gazed at her in mute amazement, but she was quite grave and serious; and, turning round, she led them through the opening in the waiscoting down a narrow secret corridor, Washington following with a lighted candle, which he had caught up from the table. Finally, they came to a great oak door, studded with rusty nails. When Virginia touched it, it swung back on

its heavy hinges, and they found themselves in a little
low room, with a vaulted ceiling, and one tiny grated
window. Imbedded in the wall was a huge iron ring, and
chained to it was a gaunt skeleton, that was stretched out
at full length on the stone floor, and seemed to be trying
to grasp with its long fleshless fingers an old-fashioned
trencher and ewer, that were placed just out of its reach.
The jug had evidently been once filled with water, as it
was covered inside with green mould. There was nothing
on the trencher but a pile of dust. Virginia knelt down
beside the skeleton, and, folding her little hands together,
began to pray silently, while the rest of the party looked
on in wonder at the terrible tragedy whose secret was
now disclosed to them.

'Hallo!' suddenly exclaimed one of the twins, who had
been looking out of the window to try and discover in
what wing of the house the room was situated. 'Hallo!
the old withered almond-tree has blossomed. I can see the
flowers quite plainly in the moonlight.'

'God has forgiven him,' said Virginia gravely, as she
rose to her feet, and a beautiful light seemed to illumine
her face.

'What an angel you are!' cried the young Duke, and
he put his arm round her neck and kissed her.

Four days after these curious incidents a funeral started
from Canterville Chase at about eleven o'clock at night.
The hearse was drawn by eight black horses, each of
which carried on its head a great tuft of nodding os-
trich-plumes, and the leaden coffin was covered by a
rich purple pall, on which was embroidered in gold the
Canterville coat-of-arms. By the side of the hearse and
the coaches walked the servants with lighted torches, and
the whole procession was wonderfully impressive. Lord
Canterville was the chief mourner, having come up specially from Wales to attend the funeral, and sat in the first
carriage along with little Virginia. Then came the United
States Minister and his wife, then Washington and the

three boys, and in the last carriage was Mrs Umney. It was generally felt that, as she had been frightened by the ghost for more than fifty years of her life, she had a right to see the last of him. A deep grave had been dug in the corner of the churchyard, just under the old yew-tree, and the service was read in the most impressive manner by the Rev. Augustus Dampier. When the ceremony was over, the servants, according to an old custom observed in the Canterville family, extinguished their torches, and, as the coffin was being lowered into the grave, Virginia stepped forward and laid on it a large cross made of white and pink almond-blossoms. As she did so, the moon came out from behind a cloud, and flooded with its silent silver the little churchyard, and from a distant copse a nightingale began to sing. She thought of the ghost's description of the Garden of Death, her eyes became dim with tears, and she hardly spoke a word during the drive home.

The next morning, before Lord Canterville went up to town, Mr Otis had an interview with him on the subject of the jewels the ghost had given to Virginia. They were perfectly magnificent, especially a certain ruby necklace with old Venetian setting, which was really a superb specimen of sixteenth century work, and their value was so great that Mr Otis felt considerable scruples about allowing his daughter to accept them.

'My Lord,' he said, 'I know that in this country, mortmain is held to apply to trinkets as well as to land, and it is quite clear to me that these jewels are, or should be, heirlooms in your family. I must beg you, accordingly, to take them to London with you, and to regard them simply as a portion of your property which has been restored to you under certain strange conditions. As for my daughter, she is merely a child and has as yet, I am glad to say, but little interest in such appurtenances of idle luxury. I am also informed by Mrs Otis, who, I may say, is no mean authority upon Art – having had the privilege of spending several winters in Boston when she was a girl – that these gems are of great monetary worth, and if offered for sale would fetch a tall price. Under these circumstances, Lord Canterville, I feel sure that you will recognise how impossible it would be for me to allow them to remain in the possession of any member of my family; and, indeed, all such vain gauds and toys, however suitable or necessary to the dignity of the British aristocracy, would be completely out of place among those who have been brought up on the severe, and I believe immortal, principles of republican simplicity. Perhaps I should mention that Virginia is very anxious that you should allow her to retain the box as a memento of your unfortunate but misguided ancestor. As it is extremely old, and consequently a good deal out of repair, you may perhaps think fit to comply with her request. For my own part, I confess I am a good deal surprised to find a child of mine expressing sympathy with mediævalism in any form, and can only account for it by the fact that Virginia was born in one of your London suburbs shortly after Mrs Otis had returned from a trip to Athens.'

Lord Canterville listened very gravely to the worthy Minister's speech, pulling his grey moustache now and then to hide an involuntary smile, and when Mr Otis had ended, he shook him cordially by the hand, and said, 'My dear sir, your charming little daughter rendered my unlucky ancestor, Sir Simon, a very important service, and I and my family are much indebted to her for her marvellous courage and pluck. The jewels are clearly hers, and, egad, I believe that if I were heartless enough to take them from her, the wicked old fellow would be out of his grave in a fortnight, leading me the devil of a life. As for their being heirlooms, nothing is an heirloom that is not so mentioned in a will or legal document, and the existence of these jewels has been quite unknown. I assure you I have no more claim on them than your butler, and when Miss Virginia grows up I daresay she will be pleased to have pretty things to wear. Besides, you forget, Mr Otis, that you took the furniture and the ghost at a valuation, and anything that belonged to the ghost passed at once into your possession, as, whatever activity Sir Simon may have shown in the corridor at night, in point of law he was really dead, and you acquired his property by purchase.'

Mr Otis was a good deal distressed at Lord Canterville's refusal, and begged him to reconsider his decision, but the good-natured peer was quite firm, and finally induced the Minister to allow his daughter to retain the present the ghost had given her, and when, in the spring of 1890, the young Duchess of Cheshire was presented at the Queen's first drawing-room on the occasion of her marriage, the jewels were the universal theme of admiration. For Virginia received the coronet, which is the reward of all good little American girls, and was married to her boy-lover as soon as he came of age. They were both so charming, and they loved each other so much, that every one was delighted at the match, except the old Marchioness of Dumbleton, who had tried to catch the Duke for one of her seven unmarried daughters, and had given no less than three expensive dinner-parties for that purpose, and, strange to say, Mr Otis himself. Mr Otis was extremely fond of the young Duke personally, but, theoretically, he objected to titles, and, to use his own words, 'was not without apprehension lest, amid the enervating influences of a pleasure-loving aristocracy, the true principles of republican simplicity should be forgotten.' His objections, however, were completely overruled, and I believe that when he walked up the aisle of St George's, Hanover Square, with his daughter leaning on his arm, there was not a prouder man in the whole length and breadth of England.

The Duke and Duchess, after the honeymoon was over, went down to Canterville Chase, and on the day after their arrival they walked over in the afternoon to the lonely churchyard by the pine-woods. There had been a great deal of difficulty at first about the inscription on Sir Simon's tombstone, but finally it had been decided to engrave on it simply the initials of the old gentleman's name, and the verse from the library window. The Duchess had brought with her some lovely roses, which she strewed upon the grave, and after they had stood by it for some time they strolled into the ruined chapel of the old abbey. There the Duchess sat down on a fallen pillar, while her husband lay at her feet smoking a cigarette and looking up at her beautiful eyes. Suddenly he threw his cigarette away, took hold of her hand, and said to her, 'Virginia, a wife should have no secrets from her husband.'

'Dear Cecil! I have no secrets from you.'

'Yes, you have,' he answered, smiling, 'you have never told me what happened to you when you were locked up with the ghost.'

'I have never told any one, Cecil,' said Virginia gravely.

'I know that, but you might tell me.'

'Please don't ask me, Cecil, I cannot tell you. Poor Sir Simon! I owe him a great deal. Yes, don't laugh, Cecil, I really do. He made me see what Life is, and what Death signifies, and why Love is stronger than both.'

The Duke rose and kissed his wife lovingly.

'You can have your secret as long as I have your heart,' he murmured.

'You have always had that, Cecil.'

'And you will tell our children some day, won't you?' Virginia blushed.

Acknowledgements

The publishers are grateful to the following for permission to reproduce copyright material :

Edward Arnold Ltd for 'The Haunted Doll's House' from *Collected Short Stories* by M. R. James. James Barrie for 'Remembering Lee' by Eileen Bigland from *The Third Ghost Book*; Brandt & Brandt, New York, for 'The House of the Nightmare' by Edward Lucas White from *Lukandoo and Other Stories*; J. M. Dent & Sons Ltd for 'A Pair of Hands' by Sir Arthur Quiller-Couch from *Old Fires and Profitable Ghosts*; Barbara Ireson for 'Linda'; The Literary Trustees of Walter de la Mare and the Society of Authors as their representative for 'Miss Jemima' by Walter de la Mare; A. D. Peters & Co. Ltd for 'The Emissary' from *The October Country* by Ray Bradbury, and 'The Earlier Service' from *Madame Fears the Dark* by Margaret Irwin; A. D. Peters & Co. Ltd and Harold Matson Co. Inc., New York, for 'Jack-in-the-Box' from *The Small Assassin* by Ray Bradbury (copyright 1947, 1974 by Ray Bradbury); Barbara Softly for 'The Devil's Cure'; Geoffrey Palmer and Noel Lloyd for 'Billy Bates' Story' from *The Obstinate Ghost and Other Tales*.

BARBARA IRESON

If you're an eager Beaver reader, perhaps you ought to try some more of our spooky Barbara Ireson titles. They are available in bookshops or they can be ordered directly from us. Just complete the form below and enclose the right amount of money and the books will be sent to you.

☐	CREEPY CREATURES	£1.25
☐	GHOSTLY AND GHASTLY	£1.50
☐	FANTASY TALES	£1.10
☐	GHOSTLY LAUGHTER	£1.25
☐	FEARFULLY FRIGHTENING	£1.25

And if you would like to hear more about Beaver Books in general, don't forget to write and ask for our Beaver Bulletin. Just send a stamped, self-addressed envelope to Beaver Books, 17-21 Conway Street, London W1P 6JD and we will send you our latest one.

If you would like to order books, please send this form with the money due to:

HAMLYN PAPERBACK CASH SALES, PO BOX 11, FALMOUTH, CORNWALL TR10 9EN.

Send a cheque or postal order, and don't forget to include postage at the following rates: UK: 55p for the first book, 22p for the second, 14p for each additional book; BFPO and Eire: 55p for the first book, 22p for the second, 14p for the next seven books and 8p per book thereafter. Overseas: £1.00 for first book and 25p for each additional book.

NAME..

ADDRESS...

....

Please print clearly